Here We Stand:
Divided

(Surviving the Evacuation)

Frank Tayell

Dedicated to Tom

Published by Frank Tayell
Copyright 2016
All rights reserved

All people, places, and (especially) events are fictional.

ISBN-13: 978-1534878921
ISBN-10: 1534878920

Other titles:

Strike A Match
1. Serious Crimes
2. Counterfeit Conspiracy

Work. Rest. Repeat.
A Post-Apocalyptic Detective Novel

Surviving The Evacuation
Zombies vs The Living Dead
Book 1: London
Book 2: Wasteland
Book 3: Family
Book 4: Unsafe Haven
Book 5: Reunion
Book 6: Harvest
Book 7: Home
Book 8: Anglesey
Book 9: Ireland
Book 10: The Last Candidate

Here We Stand 1: Infected
Here We Stand 2: Divided

For more information, visit:
http://blog.franktayell.com
www.facebook.com/TheEvacuation

Prologue - The Conspiracy So Far
February 27th, Clearfield County, Pennsylvania

"Zombie!" Helena yelled.

Tom's attention had been so fixed on the burning motel in the rearview mirror he'd failed to notice the creature on the track ahead. There wasn't time to brake. He stamped on the gas pedal instead. The truck accelerated and slammed into the zombie with a bone-crunching crack. The tattered creature was thrown forward. Its head smacked into the windshield. Its twisted face filled his vision. The mouth opened, revealing a row of broken, blackened teeth. The front right tire hit a pothole. The entire truck bounced, and the zombie was thrown clear. By the time Tom had regained control and was able to look behind, the zombie was pushing itself to its feet.

"Are they following?" Helena asked.

"Zombies can't run. It'll never catch us," Tom said. "At least, I hope they can't run." Not for the first time in the week since the impossibly living dead had begun attacking people in New York, he had to remind himself that just because he hadn't seen it happen didn't mean it couldn't.

"I meant Powell," Helena said.

Tom took an involuntary glance in the mirror. The zombie was lost to sight. All he could see were trees and a thick plume of dirty smoke rising from the blazing motel.

"I wish I knew," he said.

They'd been expecting rescue by agents of President Grant Maxwell. It was Powell, the cabal's hatchet man, who'd arrived at the motel. The conspirator had been driving slowly. The undead had followed, lured into his vehicle's wake by the sound of the engine. Hopefully, that truly malevolent act had led to Powell being ripped apart by the zombies he'd tried to use as a weapon.

The tires hit another rut. Tom's head slammed into the roof, and he took that as a sign to slow down.

"Wish we'd taken the other truck," he said. "The one you set fire to."

"Why?"

"It was a four-wheel drive. This one's ten years overdue for the scrapyard."

Helena finally turned to face the front. "I couldn't see anyone, and they couldn't get past that burning truck." It was more of a question than a statement, but Tom said nothing. "I'd like to think he's dead," Helena continued. "I'd like to think they're all dead, but... but he's real, isn't he?"

"Real? You saw Powell for yourself," Tom said.

"I mean it's *all* real," she said. "Everything you told me. I don't think I believed it up until now. I didn't *want* to believe it. I was sure you were making some of it up, or that your time on the run was making you exaggerate or something, but they really came for you."

Tom swerved to avoid a waterlogged puddle almost big enough to be called a pond. In the month between the inauguration and the outbreak, snow had fallen across the northeastern United States, but the media outlets' gleefully predicted ice storms hadn't appeared. In the week since the outbreak, as Tom and Helena had driven, hiked, and run from New York to Pennsylvania, the few flurries of snow had been washed away by frequent rain. Right now he would have preferred that the ground was frozen and ice-covered. It would have offered more traction than this swampy morass. He shifted down into first and hoped the track led somewhere. At the moment it only seemed to head deeper into the forest.

"There really is a cabal. A conspiracy," Helena said. "They really did try to take over the government. But why did they come all the way here?"

"Good question," he grunted, swerving again, this time barely missing a fallen log.

"I mean, with everything that's going on, why did they waste the effort and resources and... and I just got it!"

"What?"

"Powell was trying to kill us, all of us," she said. "Me, Lawrence, Noah, Amy. He didn't want any witnesses. You told that kid, Nate, that we were there with you. He must have been the one who told Powell."

"Not him," Tom said. "No, he's too innocent to be caught up in this. Too young. But he told someone, and they sent Powell." He leaned forward in the seat and peered at the sky. "Keep an eye out for a helicopter."

"What? Why?"

"Because it's possible that Max did send someone to rescue us, and that Powell just got there first."

She glanced out the window. "It's not likely, is it?"

"We can but hope."

She gave an irritated grunt in reply. "Powell wanted to kill all of us. That's why he lured the zombies after him. But why?"

"Like you said, he didn't want any witnesses," Tom said. He wanted to tell her to stop talking, but similar questions were going through his own mind.

"Yes, but why? You have to know something," she said. "That has to be it. Something important. Something that could stop the zombies. They took Dr Ayers, and now they want you. It has to be connected. Or maybe it's a clue as to who was behind the outbreak."

The ground leveled out as the track widened, and he was able to put the truck into second.

"They came for me," he said. "That's the fact that matters. Powell wanted me dead, but his boss wants me alive. If he's dead, they'll send someone else. If he's not, Powell will keep looking. I've met people like him, people who get so obsessed with a course of action that they can't be turned away from it."

"People like you?" Helena asked.

It was a perceptive comment. Tom had fled to America as a teenager. He'd spent nearly three decades plotting revenge on the man responsible for the death of his family. Vengeance had only been put aside when he'd discovered Projects Archangel and Prometheus. A transatlantic cabal, with agents in many world governments, had created a vaccine that would cure some of the most deadly diseases. They planned to use this wonder drug to blackmail every nation on the planet and thus bring about their vision of a new, global hegemony. Even now, Tom wasn't sure if part of their

4

plan was to unleash plagues that would make the anti-viral a necessity. He did know that they planned to destroy non-compliant countries with radioactive fire.

The cabal had rigged the presidential election so that it would be a contest between Farley and Senator Clancy Sterling, both members of the conspiracy. That was why Tom had persuaded Governor Grant Maxwell to throw his hat in the ring. Max had won, but on the day of the inauguration, and before Tom could tell the newly sworn-in president about the conspiracy, he was framed for murder. He had the footage of Powell shooting the journalist, Imogen Fenster, but he'd been unable to get that evidence to Max. Instead, Tom had searched for proof of the conspiracy that the world would believe. Before he could, there was the outbreak. He didn't know who was behind it. Russia or China were the most obvious suspects, but it could have been almost any nation. Someone had learned of Archangel and Prometheus, and dusted off some ancient Cold War weapon, unleashing the unbelievable nightmare of walking corpses on the world.

"The road's curving," Helena said.

"I know."

The plume of smoke was now to their left, rather than directly behind them. Tom leaned forward, trying to spot a deer trail, hunter's path, or anything that would get them away from the motel. The track narrowed again. The trees closed in. Branches slapped against the window. Pine needles smeared the zombie's red-brown gore across the windshield. One branch after another bent and snapped, but each was bigger than the last. It was only a matter of time before a more immovable bough brought the truck to a final halt, and not much time at that. Vivid memories of the grinding horror they'd seen when hiking during the past week made him hesitate in pressing down on the brake. He had no choice. He eased his foot onto the pedal just as the woodland came to an abrupt end. The truck bounced out into sunlight, though not onto a track, but onto a cleared area of land filled with felled trees and torn-out stumps.

"There's a road!" Helena waved her arm to the right, but Tom had to navigate around a fallen log before he dared look. The road was on the far side of a plowed field, and he couldn't see a track or trail leading to it. Wishing there was a gear lower than first, he aimed the truck at the distant road. Separating the farmland from the farmed forest was a three-wire fence. It snapped a sharp above middle-C as the battered vehicle smashed through it.

"Come on. Come on," Tom muttered as the truck bounced in and out of the plowed furrows. Dirt sprayed up, coating the windows, but the road grew nearer. Nearer. Near enough he could make out the dents on the bumper of a white sedan that sped past. The truck lurched as the front tires hit the edge of the field. It tilted as they found purchase on the firmer soil of the road. It stalled as the rear wheels finally bogged down. He revved the engine, stamped on the gas, tried to reverse, and then slammed his fist into the steering wheel. They were stuck.

"I never was any good at gambling," Helena said, as she opened the door.

"What?"

"Luck. Mine's always been terrible."

He opened the door and stepped outside. The front wheels were on the compacted, gravel-edged ribbon at the side of the road. The rear were stuck in a foot of mud.

"Nothing in the back," Helena said. "No planks. No shovel. No chance to dig our way out." She threw a glance at the dirty black plume hovering above the tree line, not nearly far enough away. "I guess we walk."

Tom looked about for an alternative, but there wasn't one. The motel was barely a mile away in a straight line, and that was how the zombies would walk. They were slow, but they would come.

"North or south?" Helena asked.

"In one direction, it must link up with the road that runs outside the motel," Tom said. "We don't want that one." That road would be full of the undead, but as to which direction that was, he couldn't tell. More out of optimistic reflex than expectation, he raised his hand as a red minivan sped past. It didn't slow.

"I guess we don't want to head toward what they're fleeing," Helena said.

Tom took out his revolver. At some point he'd remembered to reload, but he only had two loose rounds in his pocket. "How much ammo do you have for that 9mm?"

She ejected the magazine. "Three rounds." She opened the bag she'd brought with her from the motel. "And we've got a quart of water, and two boxes of crackers. Not quite a feast."

Tom buttoned up the borrowed jacket. Like the rest of the clothes he'd taken from the manager's apartment in the motel, it had a pervasive smell of damp. The sat-phone and tablet were a comforting weight, but utterly useless to their immediate needs. He couldn't think of anyone they could call, at least not anyone who could help them. He found himself staring up at the sky. The clouds weren't thick.

"We'll cross this road, and take to the woods," he said, though those trees looked more like a thin screen than proper woodland.

"Because you think the zombies will follow the cars on this road?" she asked.

"Partly that, but mostly because if the cabal had the ability to compromise the White House communications system, they're more than capable of arranging for a satellite to watch over Powell and his attack. We stand a better chance of losing them if we stay under cover." Paranoia had kept him alive during his time on the run; now he second-guessed himself. Would it lead to their deaths? They'd taken to the woods before, and all it had proved was that their only skill to surviving the harsh winter wilderness was the ability to put one foot in front of the other.

Helena sighed. "When there are no good choices left..." she said, but didn't finish the thought. "We'll go after that RV has gone past, yes?"

It was a twelve-wheel monstrosity, the kind where the 'V' stood for vanity. The dented aluminum sidings gleamed where frequent collisions had abraded the metal. As it drew nearer, it was the wire-mesh on the windows that caught his eye, and so it had almost driven past before he noticed the barbed wire around the edge of the roof.

"That's the way to survive the apocalypse," he said as it drove past. "Not in a mobile home but a mobile fortress."

"Until the fuel runs out," Helena said.

The vehicle did something completely unexpected. It stopped about fifty yards down the road. Then it reversed almost as swiftly as it had driven past. A hatch on the roof opened. A woman stuck her head out. From what Tom could see of her arms and shoulders, she was wearing military fatigues.

"You stuck or out of fuel?" she asked.

"Stuck," Helena said.

Suspicion reared its head. In a flash, Tom thought he understood how these people solved the problem of fuel. They stole it from people who were stranded by the side of the road. His hand went to his pocket, and the revolver concealed within.

The woman ducked out of sight. Tom readied himself. The front passenger door opened and another woman stepped out. She wore distinctly civilian garb, and was a decade older than the soldier, but there was an unmistakable familial resemblance.

"Can't spare any gas, and don't have any room for passengers," the civilian said, "but we can give you a tow."

"Thank you, that's all we need," Helena said.

The civilian looked inside the RV's cab. Whatever signal she was waiting for was given. She reached inside. Tom's hands tightened on the revolver. When the woman turned around, a tow-cable was in her hands.

The soldier reappeared through the hatch on the roof, this time climbing up. She held a rifle, though when she raised it, it was to use the scope to scan their surroundings.

"Tie her off," the civilian said, throwing one end of the rope to Tom. He had to let go of the pistol's grip to grab the rope. His suspicions didn't subside until, a few minutes later, the truck was pulled out of the ditch, and the woman was coiling the rope. "Try the engine," she said.

Helena did. The truck bounced forward a few feet. The civilian seemed to relax and, when the soldier didn't switch her aim and shoot both him and Helena, Tom finally allowed himself to do the same.

"Thank you," he said. "I... I wasn't expecting anyone to help."

"Well, that's what we've got to do now," the civilian said. "Help each other. You can't cross to the other side and leave it for someone else. Not now. Not any more. Where are you from?"

"Originally? New York," Helena said. "But most recently from over there." She gestured toward the pillar of smoke.

"Was that zombies?" the woman asked.

"At least a hundred of them," Helena said. "We thought we could make a stand there. That we could fortify the motel, make it a refuge for others. But a truck came in, and the zombies followed it."

"A refuge?" The woman gave a nod of approval. "That's the right idea, but I guess that was the wrong place to do it. We keep hearing of strongholds and sanctuaries, but it's always rumors. Always a place just over the next hill or at the end of the next road. Never seem to find it. Did you hear about Washington?"

"We saw the president's broadcast on television," Tom said. "But I don't know what happened after."

"We got it on the radio," the woman said. "Heard that zombies killed the president."

"From what we saw, he got away," Tom said.

"Good luck to him if he did," the woman said, "but everyone else is trying to do the same. The roads were empty this morning. For the last couple of hours, they've been filling up. Where were you heading?"

"South," Tom said. "To Maryland."

"I wouldn't. The radio said that Washington's gone, and everyone's leaving the city. Go north. Get as far as you can, and far away from people. We've got to help everyone we can, but we can't help everyone. There're tens of millions leaving the cities. That's tens of millions of zombies in waiting."

"Zombie!" the soldier called out. Her voice was calm, but clear. "Four hundred yards." She raised an arm, pointing toward a distant figure staggering out of the woods, about thirty degrees from the plume of smoke.

"You sure it's one of them?" the civilian called back.

The soldier peered through the scope. "I'm sure."

"Watch for the wind," the civilian said.

The soldier muttered something under her breath and took aim. The shot echoed across the landscape, and the distant zombie collapsed.

"Time to go," the civilian said. "Good luck to you."

"Thank you, again," Helena said. "We're—"

"Just repay the favor," the woman said hurrying back to the RV. "The government might be gone, but America isn't. Not yet."

Tom watched the woman get back into the RV, and then headed to the truck.

"That zombie didn't come from the motel," Helena said, climbing into the driver seat. "So, north or south?"

South was Washington. That had been his plan. To go to the capital and find Max. "The president won't be in D.C. anymore. He'll be in a bunker." If he was still alive.

"So, not south?" she asked.

Saying no would be tantamount to giving up. He wasn't ready to do that, not if the cabal hadn't. "For now, we go north," he said. "For now."

The truck roared. The engine sounded happier now the tires had a firmer surface to bite.

"And where do we go later?" Helena asked. "North is a big place."

He guessed what she was hinting at. "Maine is the obvious answer," he said. "To my cottage there. I have supplies, and a computer with all the evidence on it. That was my original plan. Well, no, my original plan was to get out of America, but then the outbreak hit. I wanted to find somewhere to hide out for a few days, somewhere safe enough I could go through all the files I've gathered, find out how the outbreak began, and maybe find a way of stopping it."

"Not much chance of that now," she said.

"No, but I might be able to find where the cabal are based." It was unlikely. He peered at the dash. "That settles it," he said. "Look at the fuel gauge. We've got half a tank left. Follow the RV. When the tank runs dry, we'll hope they stop and offer us a ride." It was only delaying a decision in which there were no good choices, but after the shock and violence of the morning, he welcomed a few minutes without the need for constant planning.

The RV was already far ahead. As the road dipped and curved, they occasionally lost sight of it. Helena pushed down on the gas. The speedometer edged upwards.

"It's getting away," Tom said.

"There's nothing I can do about it," Helena said. "Heap of junk, it's topping out at forty miles an hour."

The RV was making about sixty, and soon it was lost to the horizon.

"I guess we need a new plan," Helena said.

Going to Maine felt like a surrender. It was familiar, but that didn't mean it was secure.

"No helicopters," he finally said. "If we'd seen one, or even heard one, then I'd say we should find a military unit and try to make our way up the chain of command until we reached Max. But there's no helicopter. Someone at the White House intercepted that message and sent Powell to the motel."

"So we can't reach the president? You're accepting that?" she asked.

"I am."

He looked at the sky, this time imagining the satellites looking down on them. "I'm thinking like it was two weeks ago," he said. "I'm used to hiding in plain sight, among a population of millions, where you can bug and surveil, hack and bribe."

"Right. So what answers would you find on those files you have in Maine? How many years did you spend searching for the cabal? How many names did you discover? And even if you found the names, even found a confession, what would you do then? What court would you take it to?"

11

"Yeah. There's no justice, just us."

"Sad to think that might be true," she said, "but if so, then we need to find Farley, not the president. So where did he live?"

"Virginia and Washington," Tom said. "But maybe that's not where we have to search. Dr Ayers's home was only forty miles from the motel. Powell drove there, and to the motel. Wherever he came from has to be near. Find that, and we might find Farley. At the very least, we'd find a clue as to where he is." Probably.

"We'll be out of gas in an hour," she said. "And out of food and water by nightfall. We'll find some more, but if what that woman said she heard on the radio is true, and everyone is now fleeing the cities, then within a week we'll be fighting for survival. I want to stop Farley, but I don't want to kill someone over the last bottle of water. I say we have one shot at taking out the cabal. We have to be realistic. It won't change much. It won't turn back the clock, but it might mean that that whoever survives this year doesn't have to face something even worse in the next. One week, one shot. There's a turning coming up. We could head back toward the motel?"

"We won't find them driving randomly along the roads," Tom said. "Keep going."

"I was thinking we could search the BearCat they drove there," she said.

"Ah. No, keep going. There'll be too many zombies. It's too great a risk for the chance that they had a map that wasn't destroyed by the fire."

She was right, though. Realistically, there was just one chance at stopping Farley. But if they were being realistic, it was his chance, not hers. She was a schoolteacher. Farley had heavily armed mercenaries. Yes, Helena had proven she could hold her own in a fight with the undead, and had helped him escape the motel, but it would be a very different situation without surprise on their side. Particularly when they only had a handful of rounds for a pair of handguns. Of course, it was all academic unless they found the cabal's base.

An eighteen-wheeled rig barreled past. The driver gave a long blast from the horn. Tom was uncertain whether it was a greeting or a warning. He watched the rig as it disappeared along the road and found he was looking at the sky. It was far preferable to watching the land on either side of the road. There were figures lurching toward them. Not many, and never more than a couple were in sight at any one time, but they were there.

The clouds were thinning, but perhaps the cabal didn't have access to a helicopter. Or their pilot was dead. Or... and then it came to him.

He took out the sat-phone. "Back before the outbreak," he said, "I was going to drive from New York to an airstrip. I was going to fly to Canada, drive to the coast, and be picked up by a fishing trawler. Last I heard, the trawler was stuck in the middle of a flotilla of refugees out in the Atlantic, but you can't move an airfield. It's a couple of hundred miles from here, but that's closer than Maine." He dialed the number. It rang. And rang. Tom was about to hang up when it was answered.

"*Sí?*"

"Julio?"

"Who else? You're alive. Ha! I should have known it would take more than the end of the world to kill you."

"Are you still at home, at the airfield?" Tom asked.

"I am," Julio said. "We are."

"Do you have a plane?"

"I have many planes," Julio gave a weary sigh. "None are for hire. I know I made you a promise, but that was at a different time, when the world was a very different place. Even if I wanted, the military have taken over."

"The military?"

"The Air Force. They took over the airstrip, but people saw the planes. They came here. Hundreds of them. Now there are more than we have seats for. When the exodus begins, it will be the children who go, the rest will have to stay behind."

"The exodus? When are you leaving?" Tom asked.

"I do not know. Captain Jenson has lost contact with her command. Did you hear about the president? Washington has fallen. The captain has taken her fighter up to find a safe landing site within range of our planes. Until she finds somewhere, we stay here, unless the zombies make a flight into the unknown our only chance of survival."

"So you've no immediate plans to leave? What about gasoline, can you spare that?"

"I think so. We don't need it for the planes," Julio said.

"And weapons? Can you put some guns and ammo aside?"

"*Sí.* I will leave you some gasoline, and some weapons, but I can't promise anything else," Julio said. "I can't even promise that we will be here. The undead come. We kill them, but there are always more."

Military personnel, that was what Tom needed. A plane that could survey the area, find from where Powell had come, and then help him end the cabal for once and for all.

"We're on our way," Tom said, and hung up.

"He has an airfield?" Helena asked.

"It's a flight school," Tom said. "He was a commercial pilot for whom I got a new identity after he saw something that no one should ever have to see. He turned witness and needed a new life. It's a farm, really, with an airstrip behind it."

"And how far is it?"

"About a hundred miles, give or take."

She tapped the fuel gauge. "Eyes open for stopped cars. I guess we'll be syphoning fuel again."

She sounded relaxed now that they had a plan. Tom felt the same. He did have a plan. He'd get Helena onto a plane and enlist the help of the Air Force personnel to destroy the cabal.

"Tom, look!" Helena stabbed a finger at the grime-covered windshield. Half a mile ahead, the RV had come to a halt just beyond a car that had driven into a ditch. There was a figure on the RV's roof. In one hand was a rifle. Helena pumped the gas, trying to coax a few more miles per hour out of the truck's rattling engine.

"We have to stop," she said.

14

"I know."

Between the car and the RV were two shambling figures. He knew they were undead. There was just something about the uncoordinated motion of the arms and legs that was utterly inhuman. He took out the revolver and checked it was still loaded.

"It's not the soldier," Helena said. The figure on the roof of the RV wasn't wearing fatigues. She was holding the rifle one-handed. She fired and spun around, falling to her knees with the recoil. She was clearly injured, but what was of greatest concern to Tom was that she'd been aiming at the far side of the RV.

Even before Helena slammed on the brakes, Tom knew they were too late. He threw open the door and jumped out before the truck had come to a complete halt. He staggered three paces across the asphalt before he found his balance. He raised the revolver as the two necrotic heads turned toward him. One was the soldier who'd been in the RV. The other was a man he'd not seen before, though by his almost normal appearance, only marred by red blood dripping from his gaping maw, he'd been recently alive. Tom aimed. Fired. The man went down. He aimed at the soldier. She took a lurching step toward him. Her mouth opened, and a ragged gasp came out.

"She's dead." He glanced up at the top of the RV. The woman wasn't in sight. The soldier was getting nearer. "She's dead," he repeated, and fired. She fell, and he felt a surge of anger at such a pointless death.

"Hey! Hey," he called, and he realized that he didn't know the woman's name, nor that of the soldier, nor even whether the undead man had been the driver or a passenger in the RV. "Are you okay?" he yelled. There was no answer from the roof of the vehicle. He opened the revolver and replaced the two spent rounds with the last cartridges from his pocket. He glanced behind. Helena had the 9mm raised and was edging toward the rear of the RV. It had stopped parallel to the road, with the front near the verge. Tom inched toward the cab. He passed the stalled car. There was a motionless figure inside, and four corpses lying between it and the RV. All four were undead. Three had been shot. The fourth, an overweight man wearing enough plaid to decorate a barn, had a machete embedded in his skull.

The zombies must have been gathered around the car. The people in the RV had seen it. They'd stopped, but they'd been overwhelmed. Precisely how didn't matter right now. Tom remembered the shot that the woman on the roof had fired at the far side of the vehicle. The other zombies would have to be dealt with before they could check whether she was still alive. As he edged around the cab, he saw that he was correct. There *were* other zombies. Eight of them.

His first shot was rushed. It missed, but got the creatures' attention. They turned their vacant expressions toward him. He fired again. A zombie fell. He shifted aim, trying to ignore the expression, the clothes, the elaborate butterfly tattoo on its neck. He fired. He aimed, trying not to look in those vacant eyes as his bullet smashed straight through the left, blowing away the back of its head. He had to take a step back, and around the engine. They were getting closer. Their heads bobbed up and down. He fired, missed, and was reminded just how small a target a head was. He fired again. The bullet caught the creature a glancing blow, tearing off a chunk of its rotting scalp. It spun around, and its flailing arms spun the zombie behind it backward. Tom backed up another step and fired, knowing that the hammer would hit a spent round. *Click.* He ran back a few steps. Looked around. Saw the machete. He grabbed at it, but it was stuck fast. He stamped down on the dead zombie's face, pulling it clear with a wet, sucking crack.

There was a shot. Helena had fired. He couldn't see what she was aiming at, and when he looked for her, realized he couldn't see her, either. She fired again. And again, and now she was out of ammunition, and the zombies would be heading toward her. She backed away from the rear of the RV, toward the truck, the empty gun still raised. Tom ran along the side of the vehicle.

"No!" she yelled. "Watch out!"

He stopped just as a zombie staggered round the back of the vehicle. He swung low as the monstrous creature threw its pendulous arms at his face. The machete slammed into its knee, neatly slicing through tendon and muscle. He ripped the blade free, and as the zombie staggered forward, it fell, toppling almost on top of him. Holding his breath against the rank expulsion of infected air, he threw the creature to one side. Unable to support its own weight, it fell. The zombie's arms beat the ground as it tried to push itself onto a leg oozing gore from where it had been nearly sliced through.

Before there was time for revulsion to sweep over him, another creature staggered around the edge of the RV. More tattered than the rest, its face was smeared with mud. Tom raised the machete, but before he could strike, Helena ran forward. She held a metal bar above her head and swung it down on the creature's crown. Bone broke with a resounding crack that almost drowned out her feral scream. She swung again, and again, before he grabbed her arm and dragged her back.

"It's dead," he said. "Dead."

She sobbed. Not with fear, but with absolute rage.

"It's dead," Tom repeated. As if to give the lie to that statement, there was a guttural hiss from the zombie he'd crippled. He stalked over to the creature and hacked the machete down on its skull.

"Now they're both dead." He walked around the vehicle, machete raised, but there were no more moving zombies. Nor were there any signs of survivors.

"The woman," Helena said. "Hey! Can you hear me? Are you alive?" she called out. There was a moment of silence, then a faint knocking from inside the vehicle. Hope flared, but was almost immediately extinguished when the knocking grew erratic.

"She's turned," Helena whispered.

Tom walked over to the car. "The driver's dead," he said. "Long dead. At least a few days. There's an empty pill bottle on the seat next to her."

"The RV, Tom," Helena said. "We need to… to do something about the woman. We can't just leave her."

"I know. I know," Tom sighed. "I was looking for weapons." He looked at the machete. Gore covered its handle. He wiped his palm against his leg and thought about how many zombies he'd come in close proximity to. He remembered what Dr Ayers had written on the whiteboard in her home: *It's not a virus.* Did that mean that blood and brain matter weren't always infectious?

The knocking grew louder.

Or did it just mean that he'd been lucky? No matter how good a streak was, luck always ran out.

"We need weapons," he said, walking over to the RV's rear door. "And gasoline. Food, too. It's all inside."

The knocking came again.

"One minute they're friends, allies, our saviors," Helena said, coming over to help him pry the barbed wire away from the door. "The next, they're corpses that we have to rob."

"Yeah. Go up to the roof. Distract her," Tom said, "I'll open the door and... and do the rest."

She grabbed at the ladder and climbed up. She stamped on the roof, and then bellowed down through the hatch. "I wanted to thank you," she yelled. "An hour ago, you saved our lives. You said we should repay the favor, and this is the only way we can. I'm sorry. She's underneath me, Tom. I can see her."

Tom hammered the machete into the lock. The door popped open. He took a step back. He saw the woman, the same one who had come to their aid, illuminated under the open skylight. Her front was covered in blood. Her face was almost unrecognizable.

"Come on," he said softly. "It'll be over soon." And even as the undead woman took a step toward them, he realized how wrong the words were. He raised the machete. It *wouldn't* be over soon. Even if the zombies all suddenly collapsed, the memory of this would live on forever, tainting the past and coloring the future. She staggered toward him, her arms banging into the sides of the RV, knocking over items neatly stowed on shelves. She reached the door and toppled forward as she failed to manage the steps. The zombie landed face first on the cold ground. Tom brought the machete down, bringing a swift end to the zombie who'd been a person who'd done nothing but help strangers in need.

There were no other bodies in the vehicle. That was a relief. Tom had been dreading the discovery of children. Dead or undead, he wasn't sure which would be worse. They did find fuel.

"That's about sixty gallons," Helena said. "And enough food for a week."

Tom picked up the rifle. "Three and half magazines, and another seventy rounds of ammo for a 9mm." There was a spare pistol on the driver seat. There were also two boxes of shotgun shells, but no sign of the shotgun.

"We'll take enough gas to get us to the airfield," Helena said. "We'll leave the rest, most of the food, and the shotgun shells. We don't need it. Someone else might."

Tom didn't argue. It was a small offering, and utterly insufficient. He did take a small portable radio. They locked the RV, went back to the truck, and continued driving.

Chapter 1 - No Admittance
Clinton County, Pennsylvania

"And you….. in California… ago?" a stuttering voice on the radio asked.

Most of the reply was drowned out by the same static that distorted the question.

"Really? And what…?" the reporter asked. The signal was lost. Tom twisted the dial.

"The seven seals are broken," a man boomed. "The sky shall turn black. The…" Tom turned the dial, preferring static to another raving rant.

"It's opened. Not broken," Helena said. "I understand why people turn to religion when times are darkest, but if they are going to quote, and have to do it from that particular verse, they could at least get it right."

"All we know is that there are zombies in Washington." The signal was faint, but Tom recognized the voice of the woman they'd heard a few days before. "We don't know that the president's dead. We don't know that the country is lost. We don't…" Tom wasn't sure if they'd lost the signal, or if the woman had finally given up. Certainly, when she started speaking again, it was with a weariness that hadn't been there before. "I *do* know the zombies are in the streets outside. We lost Corporal Grenville and Private Browne an hour ago. No, lost isn't the right word. I know where they are. They're right outside the door. We won't leave. We can't. The parking lot has been overrun. I recognize some of the zombies. My neighbors. My friends. I… I wonder if they stayed because we continued to broadcast. I'll never know. The bank is on fire. The flames will spread. The town will burn. We will die, but that doesn't mean you have to. If…" The signal faded. Tom nudged the dial, but when the station came back, it was the sound of an old country western song about an eternally unrequited love.

He turned the radio off and the sat-phone on. "Not much battery," he said, waiting for the screen to load. Helena said nothing as she gripped and re-gripped the steering wheel.

"There," he said. "The satellite's over a desert. There's a road, a few buildings, not much else. Let's see if I can get a different satellite."

"Can you find something nearer?" she asked. "Maybe... maybe you could look for a town that's on fire."

"I can only see what the satellites are over. I could try to change the orbit by a few degrees, but even then it's still a guess as to what it's showing a picture of. There *is* fire and smoke in this one, but it's coastal. Baltimore, I think. I could be wrong. Hell, it might not even be America."

A lime-green sports car overtook them at what had to be at least a hundred miles an hour. The truck rocked in the car's slipstream. Helena gave a short growl, and then she sighed and stretched, as if forcing herself to forget the grim report they'd just heard on the radio.

"So," she said loudly, and seemed uncertain what to say next. "How did you... How did you get access to those satellites?"

Tom took one last look at the smoke-shrouded port before shutting the tablet down. "About fifteen years ago, a kid hacked into the DMV. Corrie Guinn is her name. I managed to get to her before the cops did and got the kid a place at college. You could think of it as a scholarship if you like."

"Could I think of it as a pre-emptive pay-off?" she asked. "You were basically hiring her, right?"

"That's why I was looking for someone with her skill set, but after I met her, not so much. She's very good, but not reliable. Not in the line of work I do. Too... erratic. There was a team at the university doing some government research that was beyond top-secret. Within a month of arriving, she'd managed to hack into NORAD, and installed a less than salubrious welcome message on all of their terminals. That's quite a feat, and she did it because she was bored. She's the kind of person who sees a firewall as a challenge, and a password as a puzzle to be cracked. I got her out of trouble again, this time by using the contacts I'd developed in various branches of government. I pointed out that someone this good was an asset to be cultivated. That she just needed to grow up a bit, learn some responsibility, and then she could be tasked with hacking China. To help prove my point, I told her to learn Mandarin. Instead, she learned

Russian, but it only took her a month to become fluent. She needed supervision, and it had to be somewhere she could use her skills. You know Lisa Kempton?"

"The billionaire?"

"Back then she was just a multi-millionaire who'd cashed in on the tech-bubble. She was always on the watch for capable women with a disruptively keen mind. I thought Corrie was a good fit. Here's the thing. I didn't do it out of the kindness of my heart."

"I could have guessed that."

"I felt sorry for her, sure," Tom said. "And had no intention of putting her in harm's way. Not directly at least. This was before I knew about the cabal. I was pursuing this British politician. I wanted him dead, but I wanted to destroy his reputation first. Lisa Kempton had made a very public donation to his election campaign. It made no sense. She was a tech CEO with interests in the U.S. and Asia, and he was a parochial Englishman with little interest in the world beyond Dover. I thought Corrie would get me access to the files that would explain why. She didn't. She self-destructed in what was, in retrospect, an entirely predictable fashion. Before she burned out, she did get me access to the satellites."

"Huh. So Kempton's part of the cabal?"

"I'd say she's a fellow traveler rather than a card-carrying member. She financed parts of the project that couldn't be run through the government. In return, her company was going to get the contract to produce the anti-viral. I would say that she saw the cabal as a tool toward her own ultimate power."

A minivan shot out of a side road, swerving in front of them. Helena tapped the brakes. The van was so overloaded that it struggled to do more than the truck's forty miles an hour top speed. Helena slowed again, letting a gap form between their two vehicles.

"What kind of things did Kempton finance?" she asked.

"There's the ordinary stuff, the donations to keep politicians from investigating precisely to where government funds were disappearing. Then there's the other stuff, like the abduction of test subjects."

"Oh. I can guess what happened to them." She glanced in the rearview mirror and pushed down on the gas. A big-rig was behind them, slowly gaining ground. Their truck stood no chance of overtaking the minivan.

"There's an intersection ahead. Which way?" she asked.

"Follow the minivan."

"You sure? The other road looks clearer."

"It'll take us in the wrong direction," he said.

They followed the minivan. The rig had settled in a hundred feet to their rear.

"Damn. Can't see much of the road behind, now. What happened to the programmer?" she asked.

"Corrie? She went to farm alpacas out west. After six months, she disappeared. Went completely off the grid. I got a few messages from her in the years since, but she'd go silent anytime I asked where she was or why she'd run. In hindsight, I guess she must have discovered the same thing I did."

Silence settled. Tom turned the tablet back on, waited for a signal, and began searching through his files to see if he had a record of any property Lisa Kempton had purchased in Pennsylvania. It was a long shot, but those were all they had left. The app flashed, alerting him to a new message from Bill Wright.

"Here's something. They're going to evacuate the cities."

"What? Who? How?"

"No, I mean in Britain," he said. "It's a message from Bill. They're implementing his evacuation plan. They're going to set up enclaves along the coast, move the population out of the cities to where they can be more easily fed. He wants to know… Oh."

"What?"

"Quigley's taken over. The foreign secretary," he added. "He's the PM now. I bet that was a coup." He wondered if he could find out. Other than Bill Wright, he had a few contacts in the British government.

"Is that bad?" Helena asked.

"Quigley being in charge? Yes. Very bad. He's a—"

"Zombie!"

Tom looked up. A ragged creature in a long skirt staggered out of the open door of a farmhouse. The minivan accelerated, but the zombie was stopped by a closed gate. Its arms waved at them as they drove past.

"She's probably safe, then," Helena said.

"Who?" Tom asked, looking in the mirror until the zombie was lost behind the bulk of the rig following them.

"The programmer. Corrie. If she knew what was coming, she's made preparations. She's safe?"

"Probably," he said.

"Good. I was going to be an actor."

"Oh?" Tom forced his brain to switch gears at this abrupt change in conversation. "This was the new life you were after? You were going to quit teaching and try acting?"

"No. Teaching was what I did after I stopped acting."

"In the theatre?" he asked.

"No. TV. I was going to be big. I suppose that's what all actors think. It's certainly what all those people I jockeyed with while waiting for an audition thought."

"Were you in anything I might have seen?" he asked.

"A few commercials, and some pilots that were never picked up. But my big break was that serial killer show, *Fifty-Two*. Do you remember it?"

"Sure. Fifty-two episodes over fifty-two weeks, with a different victim each week." He'd seen the end of a couple of episodes, though only when he'd turned the set on to catch the beginning of the news. Mostly, he remembered it from the ubiquitous advertising, and the frequent complaints that it was too violent for network television.

"I was the sorority girl killed in the bathtub," Helena said. "In the third episode? It would have been my big break, but they cut my lines, and decided they didn't need me for the autopsy scene the following week."

"Ah. That's why you went into teaching?"

"No. That was because of Jessica. Just being attached to that show was enough to get me into a pilot for a sitcom about two sisters trying to make it in the big city. The actress who was meant to play my sister dropped out. They needed someone for the pilot or it wouldn't get made. I suggested Jessica. They gave her a screen test, and the camera loved her, and she loved it. A little too much. The pilot didn't get picked up, but she got offered a few parts. Small ones, like mine, but she thought they were big. I guess we suffered from the same delusion, but where she thought she was going to be a star, I looked at her as if I was looking in the mirror. I knew it wasn't going to happen for either of us, so I quit. She didn't. She kept at it, and kept getting knocked back. She got enough small parts to keep the flame alive, but enough rejections that when that cult found her, she was easy to reel in. I should have looked out for her, but I didn't."

And Tom thought he now understood what had brought that memory to the forefront of her mind. "But you said she escaped," he said.

"Right, but whatever momentum she'd built up had gone. Her career was over. Our mother was dead, and she… We had a fight. A big one. Jessica didn't come to the funeral because her 'faith' wouldn't allow it. They don't believe in death, you see, just transformation and ascendency. That's what they call it, except it's just another part of the scam." She swore.

"I went down there, after I'd buried our mother. They let me speak to her. I yelled and screamed, and that was just what they wanted. I didn't realize that until after, when it was too late. They wanted her to know she had no one but her fellow believers, no family except them. So, yeah, she got out, but I didn't know about it until a click-bait article popped up on my newsfeed. It was one of those 'where are they now' things. Specifically, she was in a small town in Texas, but she'd already fled by the time I got there. I hired a detective to track her down, followed her to Toronto, and she left again. She could be anywhere in the world, and I won't ever see her again. I know that the last time I saw her was after I sought her out. She has to know that means I love her, that I made the effort of finding her. That's the only comfort I've got. I did everything I could to reconnect with the only family I have."

That comment hit too close to home.

"You ruined a lot of lives, Tom," she said. "You know that? The programmer. That kid in the White House, Nate. If he wasn't working for Powell, he's probably trapped in Washington. There are others, aren't there? There have to be. Dozens. Hundreds. All those people who could have been something, but aren't."

"I know," he said. "I came to terms with that a long time ago. My only comfort is that the cause has been proven just, even if my original motives weren't."

A compact came level with them. Its engine whined as it struggled to overtake. The roof was covered with half-a-dozen bulging suitcases, tied down with washing line. Helena stamped on the brake as it pulled in, just in front of them. She gave a short growl of irritation. "There's a kid in there," she said.

The child, perhaps seven years old, was wedged in the backseat between more luggage and a greyhound that was making a spirited attempt at burrowing through the rear windshield. There were eight cars between the compact and the point the road curved out of sight. Behind them, the rig blocked most of the view, but in his mind's eye Tom could imagine them as part of a long stream of traffic stretching far beyond the horizon.

"I don't know," she said. "I really don't, except those people in the RV had it right. We have to help one another, and that's we should have been doing all along. Not... not anything else. But that programmer, Corrie, she's probably safe, somewhere. Maybe that woman in the radio station will find a way to escape. And maybe Jessica kept running north, and she got work in some lumber camp so remote that even the zombies won't find her. Maybe."

"Maybe," he said. "That's more or less the hope I'm holding onto."

She sighed. "Thirty-five. We're definitely slowing down."

Tom knew it and knew what it meant. He glanced at the oncoming lane just as a convoy of cars overtook them. They each bore the logo of a rental company. "And everyone's heading the same way," he said.

"So where are they going? Thirty."

The compact ahead of them suddenly swerved to the left, off the road, and onto a track that Tom could barely see.

"Do we follow?" Helena asked, tapping on the brakes.

"No. No. Don't!" Tom said.

"You sure?"

"Don't!" They passed the track. He turned to watch the compact bounce along a path. A four-wheel drive that had been trailing the rig pulled off the road, following it. A third car joined the truck.

"We should have taken that track," Helena said.

"This truck isn't built for off-road, and that compact certainly isn't. It'll stall and block every vehicle behind. We're moving slow, but at least we're moving."

"I feel sorry for the kid in the back of that car. He'll be walking soon." She tapped the brake. "Twenty-five. So will we. I know we can't help everyone, but I can't help but think every face I see is only minutes from death."

The minivan, once again the vehicle immediately in front, accelerated. Helena stamped on the gas pedal hard enough that the dashboard shook. Tom thought he knew why the traffic was suddenly freeing up, and it became obvious within a few seconds. Impatience had finally broken whatever mental block was keeping some drivers to obey the law of the road. They drove across the median and sped down the opposite side of the road. Within a mile, as those cars reached whatever blockage lay ahead, vehicles on both sides of the road slowed, this time with an abrupt finality.

The red lights on the minivan flashed on as it came to a halt. Helena slammed on the brakes. The truck stopped. All was far from silent. A few horns blared, a few bumpers crunched, and a few voices were raised in anger at a driver who'd not stopped in time. Helena uncurled her fingers from the wheel and turned the engine off.

They were on a shallow incline. Ahead and to the left, the road curved around a meadow. Beyond was a water tower, and the rooftops of a small town. On the right lay managed woodland.

Three vehicles ahead, a four-wheel drive jolted forward, knocking down the fence delineating the field from the road. The truck behind it followed, its wheels churning up the dull winter grass. The minivan sped forward, managing ten yards before it got bogged down in the saturated soil. An impatient horn blared from the rig immediately behind. Tom turned in his seat, but the cab was too close for him to see the driver.

"We're walking, right?" Helena swiftly sorted through the food in the boxes, muttering, "Can't take this. Or this. How far to the airfield?"

"Seventy miles, give or take. Probably a bit less."

"We can walk that in three days, right? So water's more important than food. What about the fuel? Can't take that, I suppose. Seems a shame to leave it. Another two hours, and we'd have reached the airfield."

Two hours in a car, but three days on foot. They had more than enough supplies to sit here and wait that long, but what for? It was over an hour since they'd seen their last zombie, but that was just another way of saying that the nearest zombie was no more than a day's lurch away. No doubt there were more creatures, and far closer.

"Yep, we're walking." He got out of the truck.

The driver of the rig stuck his head out of the window.

"Move forward!" he bellowed. Ignoring him, Tom reached in and picked up the assault rifle. The driver's head retreated behind the illusory safety of his windshield.

There was no point moving the vehicle a meager few yards. The driver of the minivan was standing in the meadow by his vehicle, throwing covetous glances at the distant town, and hopeful ones at the people on the road. Perhaps the man was hoping for a push, or a tow. A few other trucks took to the meadow. Tom slung the rifle, checked his pockets for the sat-phone, tablet, and the 9mm he'd taken from RV. He picked up the machete. Helena passed him one of the bags and threw the other over her shoulder. She had her automatic pistol in her hand.

"Any chance we're coming back?" she asked. Before he could reply, she answered for him. "No. I guess not." She dropped the keys on the driver's seat and closed the door.

Walking along the median strip, she picked her way through the stalled vehicles. Tom followed, a few paces behind, watching the people. They weren't the only ones to leave their cars, nor the only ones armed. Most, however, looked better prepared than they were. There was a profusion of lurid fleece jackets, neatly strapped backpacks, and tightly laced boots. By contrast, his and Helena's mud-splattered clothes, though they were the best pick of a bad selection, looked like rags. The better prepared were drifting off into the woods. It was those dressed in denim and cotton who stayed on the road. Tom's attention was on the people staying in their vehicles. Usually it was a solitary driver, though sometimes with younger passengers. All exhibited the same shifting nervousness. Each passing refugee was further proof they would have to get out, but only emphasized that they were unlikely to find a better refuge than their vehicles.

More troubling were the cars with a solitary occupant in the backseat. It was possible that some had weighed the slim chance of rescue as greater than that of a journey through the wilderness, but some were clearly unconscious. He met the eyes of an older man huddled under a tartan rug. The man gave a short, shallow shake of his head. Tom moved on.

Two cars ahead, he saw a teenager in the backseat of a car. His eyelids fluttered. He couldn't be more than fourteen. Tom wanted to help. He wanted to do something, but there was nothing anyone could do. On the boy's leg was a bloody bandage, another on his hand.

"I'm sorry," he whispered, and walked on. There really was nothing he could do for the boy, the old man, or any of these refugees.

"Nothing," he said aloud. Guilt stung as sharp as the truth in that simple realization. In front, there were hundreds of people drifting toward the town. Behind them were even more. This had been the event he'd wanted to avoid when leaving Manhattan. They were on foot, seventy miles from an uncertain salvation, surrounded by thousands of refugees, and an uncounted number of the dying infected. Soon the sound of slamming car doors would be joined by that of undead fists beating against the thin glass of their temporary tombs.

"We need to get off the road," he said, jumping up onto the roof of the nearest car. The driver slammed a fist against the windshield. Tom unslung the rifle, pointing it at the driver, but the woman was still alive. She cowered back in her seat, hands raised in front of her face. He ignored her and scanned the woods.

"There's a track," he said, jumping back down.

Helena turned to the woman in the car. "You need to get out," she yelled. "Get out, get moving. Don't stay here." The terrified driver just shook her head.

Tom turned away. "What was it that woman with the RV said? We have to help everyone we can, but we can't help everyone."

They headed away from the road. There were refugees on the track. Too many, he decided, and cut a route away from the churned-mud path.

Regularly spaced pine trees had deposited a thick carpet of needles on a forest floor made uneven by up-jutting roots. He tripped twice before he found his footing, but felt easier as the sound of the slowly fleeing refugees receded. The noise from the road was barely diminished.

The ground began to rise, and he found himself walking up a steep incline. At the top, a tree had fallen, knocking into the nearest, ripping it out of the loamy soil. From the height of the splintered stump he saw the town, and the barricade on the road leading into it.

Two yellow school buses had been parked across the road. Their windshields touched. Their rear tires were sunk into the muddy ground. Razor wire glistened in front and around the vehicles, and over corrugated metal embedded in the field on either side. On top of the school buses were eight figures. They were too far away to identify any more than the long gun each carried. In front of the barricade, filling both lanes of the road, were cars and trucks of every size and make. In and around them was a swarm of people.

"Why did they come here?" Helena asked.

"I don't think they did," Tom said. "Not intentionally. Someone stopped, asking to be let in. Someone coming from the other direction did the same. When the third stopped, it blocked the road. This is the result."

There was a stretch of empty ground, about twenty feet deep, between the buses and the refugees. It wouldn't remain empty for long.

"I make it close to four hundred people within a hundred yards of the barricade," Helena said. "And only eight people to stop them. They won't let them in, will they?"

"It doesn't matter," he said. "Do you remember the compact that drove off the road a couple of miles back? That track must lead to the far side of town. They've already been overrun, they just don't know it yet."

"Overrun? You talk as if it was an invasion."

"The effect will be the same," Tom said.

"No. It doesn't have to be. They'd argue that they can't save everyone, that they can keep the people in the town longer if there are fewer people with whom the supplies have to be shared. That's not the right way to think. They can keep all these people alive today, and tomorrow that help will be repaid when the zombies come, or next week when food needs to be planted. We can't be refugees, not here in our own country. We have to make a stand. It could be here. We could clear the road, build walls far stronger than links of razor wire, and—"

There was a shot, fired by one of the townsfolk. The refugees' muttered protest, only a distant whisper, was replaced by a high-pitched howl of despair that echoed across the treetops. The crowd parted around two figures, one lying prone on the ground, the other kneeling.

The tableaux remained frozen just long enough for Tom to imagine the shouts of apologetic recrimination from the barricade; for a doctor to be called; for the injured to be tended; for the infected to be dispatched; for the refugees to be offered shelter.

There was a second shot. Tom didn't see from where it came, but it was followed by a fusillade, fired from both sides. The refugees fell, cut down as they tried to flee. One of the townsfolk fell. Then another. The refugees surged forward. Many died as they stampeded toward the school buses, but some made it. The townsfolk fled from the baying mob.

"I don't want to see the rest," Helena said, turning away. She headed into the forest.

Tom spared one last glance at the town, and the horde running toward it. Zombies were never the real threat.

Chapter 2 - What's Yours Is Mine
Centre County, Pennsylvania

"Not so fast," Tom said.

"What's to wait for?" Helena said. "We have to get out of here."

"I agree, but I don't want to twist an ankle." A memory of Bill Wright and his broken leg came to him. Of course, Bill still had access to medical care. Tom took out the sat-phone, uncertain what message he was about to send, but turned it off as soon as he saw how depleted the battery was. Bill couldn't help them. And they couldn't help the hundreds of other refugees now tramping through the woods. The sound of leaves and needles being kicked aside, branches breaking, and quiet sobbing replaced that of gunfire and screaming.

After a tense hundred yards they came to a curving track. Tom wasn't sure if it was the same one that led from the road, or if it was a trail cut by the refugees. It was full of people.

"They look like zombies," Helena said. They did, walking single file, heads bowed, eyes half shut. It was surreal. They were still human, but it was as if they'd already given themselves up to death. They pushed their way through, and kept going.

"That way's due south," Helena said when the nearest people were only vague sounds.

"You sure?"

"Yes." She looked about uncertainly. "Pretty sure. Which way?"

"East. Avoid the mountains, stick to the low ground, and we'll find a road."

"What was it you said a few days ago? That we'd all end up heading toward the same supply of water, all competing for the same shelter. That's what it's going to be like, isn't it? The survival of the most brutal."

The trite reply that life had always been like that died on his lips. "I guess so," he said. "At least, for now."

"It didn't have to be this way."

Helena set the route, and Tom was happy to let her. In some ways, direction didn't matter. They had to get away from the immediate threat, but realistically needed a car to complete the next part of the journey. He couldn't guess in which direction the nearest road lay, let alone predict the odds of finding a car.

Helena paused, leg half-raised. There were shadows ahead, not moving quickly, yet not moving toward them. He unslung the rifle. They continued more slowly. The shapes coalesced into humanoid forms. He raised the gun, but lowered it when he saw the people were still alive. There were three of them, more ill-dressed than Helena and himself. They gave his rifle a greedy glance, but made no attempt to take it. Helena steered a path away from the group, picking up the pace until they were slowly jogging through the forest. His eyes scanning for more figures, he didn't see the fallen branch. He tripped, fell, and the rifle went off. Helena spun around.

"Sorry," he said as he picked first himself, and then the gun, off the ground. They listened to the silence, and it was silence for almost a full minute as if all those currently out of sight were listening for more gunfire. The sound of movement resumed, but now he was certain that the nearest person was over two hundred yards away.

Twenty minutes later, they both heard the faint cry at the same time. It came from ahead. A man sat with his back against a tree. He had bloody scabs on his face and arms. Though the wounds weren't deep, he was clearly close to death.

"Please," he called. "Please help me."

"Drink this," Helena said, raising her water bottle to his lips. The man managed a sip, but spluttered most of it back out.

"Please," he said again. "Please help."

Tom knelt down. There was no help that could be offered. "What's your name?" he asked instead.

"Paul Zelner," the man said. "I was trying to get home."

"Where's that?" Tom asked.

"Williamsport. I have to get to my daughter. I have to tell her… to tell her—" The words ended in a wracking cough that quickly subsided. The man sagged. Tom drew the 9mm, and reached a hand toward the man's neck. The head rose, and vacant lifeless eyes stared up at him. He jumped back as the zombie hissed, raising its arm. Tom fired. The zombie died. Silence engulfed the forest once more.

"Drop that," he said, turning to Helena.

"What?"

"The water bottle. It's probably contaminated."

Clouds gathered. The wind rose. The sun moved toward the horizon. They walked as the temperature dropped. Occasionally they saw people, and even less frequently found themselves walking in parallel with, in front of, or behind a small group. It was never for long. Either the others would steer away from them, or they would cut east or west. Soon after, they had the sound of gunfire to warn them of where not to go. It wasn't close, and never more than a few shots at a time. He hoped it was people offering a merciful end to their infected loved ones, but the alternative was too vivid a threat. Every person was a potential zombie, and soon would be a bone fide thief. When the shooting stopped, something told him it wasn't the zombies that were dead.

Tom was debating the few pros and many cons of sheltering with others for the night when they heard the sounds of people.

"There's a lot them," Helena whispered, peering through the trees. "I can't hear any screaming, though. Just voices. And so many it might be safe. Do we risk it?"

"I'd say no, but if they've come from the other direction, it would be best that we know rather than creep into some even greater danger."

"Cautiously, then?"

As they drew nearer, he saw that it wasn't a single group, but a large collection of people gathered in a camping site. That was almost too glamorous a description for a parking lot, a row of cement barbecue grills, and a concrete blockhouse. From the line outside, he took that to be a restroom. It was impossible to tell by smell alone, as a rank fug hung over the entire area. There were close to a hundred people, mostly footsore, mind-numbed travelers like themselves. Other than those lining up for the washroom, they sat at picnic tables, on felled logs, or had collapsed when their feet refused to take them any farther. He scanned that last group quickly, but none appeared infected.

"Appearances can be deceptive," he muttered.

"That's a water faucet," Helena said and then asked, "What was that you said?"

"Nothing." She was right; the line wasn't for whatever was in the concrete building but for a standpipe outside. They stood by the edge of the woods, watching. A pair reached the faucet, filled their canteens, and then drifted toward the narrow road beyond the gravel-covered parking lot. The reason most people *weren't* leaving was the aroma that filled the air.

Not all the people in the campsite were recent refugees. In the parking lot was an RV, far more dented than the one that had come to their aid earlier in the day. Next to it were two cars, the type of junkers bought with the first paycheck from a first proper job. That description matched the pop-tents set up on the lot's edge. They clearly belonged to the group of six teenagers huddled around the raised barbecue grill furthest from the end. The smell was coming from there. Charred fat mixed with enough seasoning to disguise the scent of cheap meat. Theirs weren't the only eyes to be looking toward the teenagers' ill-advised cookout. Greed and hunger were written deep on dozens of exhausted faces. Perhaps it was the presence of so many others that had stopped the youngsters from being robbed. Or perhaps it was just that everyone was waiting for the meat to be cooked.

"Let's get some water and get going," Tom said.

"This is like something you'd see on the news," Helena said. "One of those reports about somewhere far away you've barely heard of."

"Yeah," Tom muttered, as they joined the back of the line. He was only half listening. There were no wires or lights, nor any sound of an electrical pump. That meant the pipe was gravity-fed. The road beyond the lot was sloped, so uphill, somewhere, was a pumping station or well, and with it was electricity. Perhaps there was a generator, still being tended. People meant vehicles, and that was what they really needed. Except there were vehicles far closer. The line shuffled forward, and he turned his eyes to the RV and the two cars. There were a few shotguns and some handguns in evidence among the refugees, but those youths didn't look armed. He could take one of their cars easily enough. Somehow it felt wrong. Taking a vehicle from an abandoned house, or even from an occupied one, didn't seem like such a great crime. The owners had the safety of being inside, even if he'd robbed them of a method of escape. Here, he couldn't help think he would be sentencing the teens to death. But wasn't his need greater? His purpose a just one? No. It was simply a justification for a truly selfish act. Yet, there was an inevitability about the coming hours. When darkness fell, a shroud would fall on the campsite, and that would be all it took for people to fall on one another.

"It's a powder keg," he muttered, and they needed to get away before it blew up.

"What I wouldn't give for a hot shower," Helena said. She spoke loudly enough for her voice to carry. Immediately ahead of them was a woman with two young girls, both standing protectively close to the woman's long skirt. One of the girls turned around.

"Or some toilet paper," Helena added. "And a clean bathroom."

The woman turned around.

"Ma'am," Tom said, as non-threateningly as he could. She took in his clothes, the rifle on his back, the sidearm in his belt, and the gun in Helena's hand before giving a tight smile and turning back around.

There was something archaic about the blouse she wore underneath the leather jacket a size too large. It made Tom think she'd been at work, collected the girls from school, and taken off without stopping to change.

"We were trying to get to the East Coast," Helena said, speaking now to the girl. "To Maryland. Tom…" She gestured at him. "Has a friend there. I don't think we'll make it now."

The woman turned around again. She was clearly suspicious of this attempt at conversation. So was Tom.

"Grandpa's in California," the girl said. "That's where we're going. He has oranges. It's warm there."

"We ran out of fuel," the woman said through tight lips, as though begrudging the utterance of each syllable.

"Near the town?" Helena asked, gesturing toward the woods through which they'd just walked.

"No. Up the road," the woman said gesturing up the hill. "Came downhill, saw all these people. You were coming from over there?"

"I don't know the name of the town," Helena began, and Tom tuned the conversation out as she gave the woman and children a sanitized version of the day's events.

He wished Helena hadn't struck up a conversation with them and felt guilty for it. Though he'd planned on leaving her at the airfield, he'd grown used to Helena's company. More than that, he trusted her, and there weren't many people on the planet about whom that could be said. The woman clearly had no one else with her to help protect the children. Helena wasn't going to leave this family to fend for themselves. The question, then, was whether he would travel with them. How far could a child walk? How fast? He looked again at the cars.

The line shuffled forward a pace. Part of him wished it would shuffle slower, but a larger part wished it would move faster. He knew what he'd have to do next. He would have to weigh one life against another. And he knew that when they were driving down the road away from this campsite, it would be his soul that would be found criminally light.

Another group of people had started a fire, this one at the grill farthest from the group of teenagers. They didn't look as if they had any food but, having made the decision that they weren't traveling further this day, had opted for warmth. Or, perhaps they were wisely keeping their supplies out of sight. A few others were surreptitiously chewing on something, but they all had the look of people getting ready to leave. Many others were already doing that. Perhaps it was the food, or the realization that there was no safety in the numbers here.

"I used to live in California," Helena said. "In L.A."

"Grandpa says that doesn't count as California," one of the girls said. "Not proper California."

Tom found he was smiling. The smile froze when there was a shout from behind him.

"Hey! No! That's ours!"

The yell came from the teenagers. The campsite went quiet. Three men had gathered close to the barbecue pit. They were older, in their early thirties. The man he assumed was the leader had speared a hot dog on a fork. Where the other two wore leather jackets, biker boots, and denim that probably had been filthy long before the outbreak, the leader was almost smart. He had a fussily trimmed beard beneath tortoise-shell glasses, wore suede brogues, a white shirt, and a windbreaker far too thin for the time of year.

Helena nudged him. "Do you see the leather jackets?"

Tom had. There was a rocker on the back, a neatly stitched patch identical to that worn by the group of bikers that had passed them on the road before they'd reached the motel.

The man took a bite of the hot dog. "Share and share alike," he said. He wasn't speaking loudly, but his voice was the only sound in the expectant campsite.

"No," the boy holding a pair of tongs said. He squared up to the man. "This is ours. You can't—"

The man's free hand moved like lightning. It slammed into the boy's face. He fell, blood pouring from his broken nose.

"If you can't hold on to it," the man said, taking another bite, "then it belongs to anyone who can take it. Nice tents. Nice cars. I think we'll call them ours."

"That's enough!" A grey-haired woman stepped down from the RV. She held a long carving knife in her hands. "This is America. We'll not have thieving and brigandry here." People hurried out of her way, leaving a path clear between her and the three men. "If you ask," she said, storming along the path, "people might share. If you try to take, people will refuse. We'll fight back. We'll stand our ground against bullies and thieves. We might be scared of those monsters, but we're not scared of the likes of you."

Tom saw the biker pull the sawed-off shotgun from under his jacket, but couldn't move in time. The man fired. The grey-haired woman crumpled into a silent, bleeding heap.

Tom had unslung the rifle, but had it only half raised when there were two shots in quick succession. The biker with the shotgun fell. The bearded man collapsed. Tom spun the rifle to point at the second biker. His hands were empty.

"Up! Put them up!" he snapped, gesturing with the barrel. The biker raised his hands.

He glanced at the ground. The biker was dead. The bearded man was clutching his thigh.

"What now?" Helena asked, coming to stand by him. There was a tremor in her voice, but the pistol was raised in a steady hand.

It was a good question. Tom looked around for the other shooter. It was one of the teenagers. She stood over the boy with the bloody nose, a monstrous revolver clutched in both hands. She was slight enough that the recoil should have knocked her back a dozen feet, yet the barrel was pointing unwaveringly at the bearded man.

"Take him and go," Tom said to the uninjured biker.

The man took one look at his injured comrade, shook his head, and started backing off into the woods. Tom said nothing. A disastrous situation had turned into a calamity, but there was a chance for order to be restored before a riot broke out. After a dozen paces, the biker turned and ran.

Tom checked that both Helena and the young woman had their weapons aimed at the bearded man before he stepped forward and picked up the shotgun by the barrel. Keeping out of the line of fire, he walked over to the boy with the bloody nose and handed him the weapon.

"You'll want to search his pockets for shells," Tom said. He looked at the young woman with the revolver. If she hadn't been in charge before, she certainly was now. "Take your cars and drive," he said quietly. "I don't know what safety looks like anymore, but it won't be found in a place like this."

"What about him?" she asked, gesturing at the man on the ground.

"We should kill him," the boy said.

"Then do it," Tom said. "You have the shotgun. No one will stop you. No police will come. There's no ambulance to take him to the hospital. No doctors to set his leg. No one here will care. But you will. Killing someone changes you. It begins a journey from which you can never turn back." He met the young woman's eyes. "The person who reaches the destination isn't always a bad one. Death is a part of life, and self-defense an unpleasant reality." He turned back to the boy. "Whether killing him is self-defense or murder is something you'll have to wrestle with the rest of your life, because it's your decision, here and now."

The boy raised the shotgun. The young woman gave an almost inaudible sigh.

"No," she whispered. "Don't."

The boy lowered the weapon and stalked toward the cars.

"What about the RV?" a voice called from the crowd. The words broke the spell that blood had woven. There was a mumbling and shuffling as nearly a hundred covetous eyes turned toward the unclaimed vehicle.

"Was the driver alone?" Tom asked the young woman.

"Yes."

The mumbling became a murmur that was on the verge of becoming a mob when Helena fired her gun into the air. Everything went quiet, but more dangerously so than before. Those with weapons had already drawn them.

"You," Helena said, grabbing the arm of the woman who'd been ahead of them in line for the water pipe. "You know how to drive an RV? You'll learn. There's room for the children." She looked around the campsite. "All the children. Quickly now."

There were only six children, all told. Helena hustled them, and the adults accompanying them, into the RV.

Tom kept his eyes on the crowd. "Get in the cars," he said quietly to the young woman. "Leave the tents. Leave everything. Get in the cars, go downhill, get away from here fast."

There was room for him and Helena in the cars, but he knew if either of them made a move to get in, the vehicles would be rushed. There was enough civility left for the children to be given this prospect of escape, and nothing more.

"Where do we go?" the woman asked.

"Away from people," Tom said. "More than that, I don't know. Good luck."

She ran to the car. It started moving before the door was even closed. The other car followed, with the RV only a hair's breadth behind. The noise of the engines receded, until the only sound in the campsite was a general sighing of disappointment, and the moaning of the bearded man.

Tom walked to the front of the line and filled his canteen with water. Everyone in the campsite was now on their feet. It didn't look as if anyone was planning to stay. A few of the quicker ones were moving toward the abandoned tents. Tom shook his head. The collapse had truly begun.

They headed downhill. When Helena spotted a track cutting off toward the east, he gladly followed her. Once again, safety lay in solitude, and they found that as the sun reached the horizon. They weren't the first people to have discovered the hunting lodge. Though it was unoccupied, it had been thoroughly looted.

"We have to stay somewhere," Helena said, picking up a frying pan from dirt-covered planks almost too crudely cut to be called floorboards.

"How far are we from the campsite? Eight miles? Less?" he asked.

"No one's followed us," Helena said. She sat down on a warped plastic chair and sighed in a way that suggested she had no intention of standing up again soon.

Tom walked back outside. Built in a clearing, there was no road leading to the lodge, nor was there electricity or water. He walked the perimeter. There was no well or even an outhouse. It was just a one-room cabin with cracked windows and a roof that was losing the battle to the combined forces of moss and lichen. Helena was right, they had to sleep somewhere, and the only alternative was the open woods. He went back inside and pushed the door closed.

Against the rear wall was an open fire and chimney. To the right were cupboards, a wooden table, and a few chairs. To the left were a trio of bunk beds, each against a wall, one set of which almost covered one of the windows. The sun was lost behind the trees so there wasn't much light for it to block.

He sat down in a chair next to Helena and stretched out his legs. The feeling was marvelous. "All right, I agree," he said. "We'll stay here tonight."

"And find a car tomorrow." With a grunt of effort, she leaned forward and opened her bag. "We'll have to. I say we eat the food rather than carrying it any further. Do you like beans?"

"Not especially."

"Sorry," she said, taking out two cans. "It's beans with sausage or beans without, unless you'd prefer the crackers without either. Do you think zombies can see?"

"What? Probably. I guess they must. I've not really thought about it."

"I meant, if we light a fire, are they more likely to come?" she asked.

"Ah." He looked at the can, and then at the door swinging open in the slight breeze. "I'm not eating them cold."

Standing was a real effort. Dragging the nearest set of bunk beds to block the door was almost beyond him. Helena used the last of her energy to break a chair into kindling.

It was in his search for accelerant that he found the newspaper. "Dated ten years ago," he said passing it to Helena for her to use to start the fire. "I guess that's the last time someone came here."

"Probably."

"No road either," he said, collapsing back into the chair. "Or maybe there's one nearby."

"Maybe. Or the owners parked in the lot by that campsite and hiked here." Her attention was almost entirely on the flames she coaxed around a broken chair leg. Satisfied the fire had taken, she sat up. "No water to wash those pans. Cook it in the can?"

It was hot, but each mouthful only reminded him of the meals he'd once eaten, the restaurants he'd visited, and the five-star meals he'd left unfinished.

"Those bikers," Helena said. "The two at the campsite, they were part of the group who passed us on the road, weren't they?"

"I think so. Or part of the same outfit."

"So we've traveled a lot of distance, all to get not very far. We did the right thing, didn't we? I mean, it was the only thing we could do."

"The children got away," he said. "We did what we could, and that was more than most. We should take it in turns to sleep. I'll take the first watch. I've some thinking to do."

She didn't argue. Huddled in the mildewed, mud-splattered jacket, he let the flames burn low. He wasn't so much lost in his thoughts as trying to prod them to life in his empty mind. It was slowly dawning how much of the world was lost, and how little of it he'd ever appreciated.

He thought it was nearing midnight when he heard the noise outside. He stood, grabbing the rifle. The sound came again. Footsteps? Possibly. Getting nearer?

"Hey. Who's that?" he called softly.

The feet stopped. He waited. The footsteps came again, this time receding back into the forest. He went back to the chair, more awake than before.

Chapter 3 - Unwelcome in Providence
February 28th, Centre County, Pennsylvania

Tom shivered awake to a dark and freezing cabin. Helena was wrapped in her coat, staring disconsolately at the cold fire.

"The lighter's broken and I've used up the matches," she said. "And the tablet's out of power. I needed the light. There was a sound outside."

"You should have woken me," he said, pulling himself to his feet.

"I wasn't exactly being quiet," she said. "Whatever was out there went away. I don't think it was zombies. Maybe a bear or something."

He opened the door. Shadows stretched in the pre-dawn light. He attempted to distinguish between the sounds of the forest and those of anything more sinister. Everything sounded sinister. A little way from the cabin was a footprint that was neither his nor Helena's, but was very human. It was the only trace of their nocturnal visitors. He pulled his coat up tight around his neck, and they walked away from the cabin.

Insects chirruped. Birds called. The sky brightened, and he began to relax.

"You're smiling," Helena said.

"I didn't mean to be," he said.

"Why? What's funny?"

"Nothing. It was more of a realization. Zombies don't set ambushes. They won't stalk us through the woods. I'm re-evaluating our chances of staying alive."

"You were right. That's not funny." Helena took a sudden detour up the slope that lay to their left. "Look," she said, gesturing toward the horizon."

"What?"

"The dawn. Look at the dawn. It was the best thing about living on a boat. Well," she added, "the best thing after the low rent. I used to wake up every morning to see the sun rise over New York. It was magical, a light show to which I was the only spectator. It's the little things like that we have to enjoy now. These brief moments stolen from time. The ones we can remember when there's nothing but darkness." She walked down the slope. "I think there's a road," she added. "About two miles that way and downhill, there's a line in the tree canopy."

It was a two-lane road with recently repaired potholes, and a complete absence of people. After a mile, they came to an abandoned car. On the verge were the remains of a small fire. As Helena checked the car's fuel tank, Tom bent down to touch the ashes. They were cold.

"Empty," she said. "They drove this far and ran out of fuel."

"So they would have stayed the night here and lit the fire for company, or perhaps to dissuade company," he said. "In the morning, they started walking. The question is whether that was this morning or some other." There was no way of knowing.

After another mile, they came to the field. Razor wire stretched across it, gleaming in the early morning light. Sometimes it was on the very edge of the road; in other places it looped back and forth across the fields. It was another two miles before they saw the town. From the decaying smokestacks, it had once been a place of industry. Now it was a fortress. His first thought was of Powell, but on the side of a shipping container, dumped across an access road, was a painted sign. "Water and food, this way." Underneath was an arrow. Following it, after half a mile, they came to another, wider road. It was similarly blocked by containers. On the roof, two people sat in folding chairs. In front of the container was a table. Littering the ground around it was a carpet of discarded cups, plates, and other travelers' discarded detritus. On the container itself was the message: *Refugee Centre. Providence. Five Miles.*

"Don't think I can recall a place called Providence in this part of Pennsylvania," he said. The two sentries on the roof of the container had stood up.

"They must have been giving food and water to the refugees. That's good," Helena said.

"Probably. Wave so they know we're not zombies."

One of the two figures climbed down. The other stayed on the container. He held a hunting rifle so the barrel wasn't quite pointing at them, but at the same time wasn't quite pointing away.

"Morning," Helena called out.

"Morning," the woman who'd climbed down from the container replied. Her tone was civil though not friendly. "Where are you from?"

"New York," Helena said. "But that was a week and a lifetime ago."

"Don't suppose this town has a bus service?" Tom called.

"There's a refugee center five miles down that road," the woman said, ignoring his weak joke. "You might find transport there."

"We're running low on water," Tom said. "Can you spare some?"

The woman unclipped the canteen from her belt and placed it on the table. She stepped back a pace. "Take it."

"Thank you," Helena said. "I guess a lot of people have come this way?"

"Some," the woman said.

There was a whistle from above. The sentry on the container was pointing toward the town. The woman nodded. "You two should go. Get ahead of the other refugees."

"Any chance of a car, or just a few gallons of gasoline?" Tom asked.

"No," the woman said. "Just water, and we can barely spare that. We can't offer you shelter. We're already full. You'll have to take your chances on the road, and those odds will be better if you get moving."

"What about a military base?" Helena asked. "Is there one around here?"

"Out here?" The woman shook her head.

Three more figures came out from behind the containers, an older man and woman in hunting gear, and a young boy. The adults were armed, though their weapons were slung. The boy carried a pot of paint and a brush.

"First refugees of the day?" the man said. His tone was affable, but there was a steely resolve in his eyes.

"And not looking to stay," Tom said.

"Do you know of any military bases around here?" Helena asked.

"Nope," the man said. "Why do you ask?"

"Because we're tracking the people responsible for the outbreak," she said. "We know they're around here somewhere. It would be a group decked out like soldiers, but small in number. Under a hundred, with light arms."

Tom frowned, but watched their expressions. No one seemed surprised.

"You can try in Providence. Ask them there," the older woman said.

That wasn't the response Tom had expected. "A lot of people have said something similar?" he guessed.

"In the hope of getting a bed," the older woman said. "We have none left to offer, and no more help we can spare. You should get moving."

"Five miles, this way?" Tom asked.

The group nodded.

"You didn't say there is no Providence," Helena said, when they were out of earshot.

"Nor did you."

"There didn't seem like much point."

When he looked back, he saw the boy painting a sign on the containers: *Warning. Quarantine Zone. Do Not Enter.* That might help keep the town safe. It might not, and it wouldn't help them.

"Why did you ask them about the cabal?" he asked.

"Because it seemed like the obvious way to find where Powell came from is to ask. A hundred heavily armed people are hard to hide, particularly when everyone would want the military to help protect them."

"And what if Powell had come from that town?"

"Then we'd have found them, wouldn't we?" she said.

The razor wire came to a ragged end at the edge of a paddock. Beyond was a burned-out brick building. The windows were sealed with heavy-duty sheet metal. The door was padlocked.

"What is it?" Helena asked, as Tom tried to find a gap through which he could see inside.

"Nothing," he said, not wanting to speak the thought out loud. They continued walking. After a mile, they came to a car that had been driven into a ditch. There were no occupants, but a little way beyond was a sign: *Providence Four Miles.*

"What's wrong?" Helena asked, as Tom glanced back toward the now-hidden town. "Tell me."

"It's nothing. Just the absence of people. Of zombies. It's getting to me."

"You're bothered by the lack of imminent danger?" She laughed.

He forced a smile, but as they continued, his mind went back to the presidential campaign.

Their opponent in the general election, Clancy Sterling, had gone to college in Pennsylvania. He'd met his wife there. She was a local, and they had long ties to the state. It had made it a real battleground. Where Tom had focused on the media strategy, Claire Maxwell had organized an aggressive ground campaign, breaking the state down into towns, and the towns into streets. In a few instances, she'd even broken the streets down into houses. It was Sterling's own fault, launching a string of degrading personal attacks on her, their children, and their quality as parents. Winning Pennsylvania had become a mission for Claire. They'd had giant maps covering their war-room, with pins, labels, and great swathes of colored cloth. Now, he was trying to recall those maps, and the section of them that dealt with this part of the state. He was certain there wasn't a town called Providence.

"Three miles," Helena said, pointing at the crude sign. In the ground behind it were the uprights for a more official sign, but that had been removed.

"We should have seen people," Tom said, looking back the way they'd come.

"What do you mean?"

"There's nowhere around here with two towns so close together. I'm certain of it. There's no Providence."

"So it was a scam to get people away from that town," she said, gesturing down the road.

48

"Except it's the kind of trick that'll work for a few hours, but not any longer. Sure, people will walk for five miles in pursuit of safety, perhaps six or seven. When they found nothing, they'd turn back. Others, following behind, would meet them, and be informed that Providence doesn't exist. They'd return to the town. So where are they? Where are the people?"

"Ah. What you mean is, where are the bodies?"

They came to the first, just after the sign announcing Providence was two miles ahead. It was a zombie with a split-open skull. Helena drew her pistol. Two hundred yards further, they came to another. It had been shot. He could see another supine figure lying on the road ahead of them, and more after that.

The bodies lay increasingly close together until they reached a spot where they'd fallen in a great ring of twisted, twice-dead limbs. At the center was a uniformed soldier. On his leg was a bandage. Next to his body was a discarded rifle. In his hand was an automatic pistol, and in his brain was a bullet from that gun.

"Looks like he was infected," Helena said. "So, he... what? He stayed behind the others, holding off the zombies, killing them one by one until they were dead, he was dying, and he had only one bullet left?"

"Looks like it." Or he could have been on his own, a solitary man trying to escape a hideous death that his injuries wouldn't allow him to outpace. Tom shifted his grip on the rifle, looking and listening for the undead.

"It doesn't seem right to leave him," Helena said.

"There's no time to bury him, and we don't have the tools."

"I didn't mean that," Helena said. "I mean that he'll lie here, forgotten."

"Are you going to forget the scene?" he asked.

"I might," Helena said, continuing down the road. "After all I've seen, and all I'm going to see, I might."

They saw Providence long before they reached it.

"You were right," Helena said. "It isn't a town."

It was a military camp, built on the highway. Or it had been. Walking sticks, bicycles, bags, and other litter formed an obstacle course as they climbed the on-ramp. The road to their left was clear. To their right were a cluster of vehicles. Not all were military. A few police cruisers and motorbikes were parked next to a very civilian tanker-truck. Beyond the off-ramp, on the far side of the highway, were tents. Monstrous things, twenty feet across, with their flaps down. Some were marked with red crosses, others decorated in a variety of camouflage patterns. What was missing were people.

"We're too late," Helena whispered.

Tom understood her disappointment. He could almost see the helicopters that had used the highway as a helipad. Where the refugees had gone, he'd never know, but they could only have missed them by a few hours.

"Maybe they left fuel," Tom said, walking toward the tanker. They had. The gauge read empty, but next to it were dozens of fuel cans. A few had spilled over, giving a filling station smell to the morning air. He picked up one that gave a pleasing slosh and made it halfway toward the police vehicles before being overcome by a wave of exhausted depression. He sat down on a stack of crates.

"The airfield lies fifty miles that way," he said gesturing down the road. "Not in a straight line, of course, but where is, these days." The fuel can gonged as he gave it a kick. "That should get one of the bikes there." He took out the sat-phone. It had enough battery left to make a call. He dialed Julio's number. "No answer," he said, putting it away. "Figures."

"What are you thinking?" she asked, sitting down next to him.

"That there's fuel here, probably more than we'd get at the airfield. There's weapons, too," he added rapping his knuckles against the case.

Helena glanced down and then jumped up. "Explosives! You're sitting on a crate of explosives!"

He shrugged. "Doesn't seem like a dangerous thing to do these days."

"What's wrong? Are you wondering how you'll find Farley?"

"No. Not quite. So we drive to the airfield, but then what? I'd hoped that I could enlist the military personnel there into helping find this base that Powell used, but is that realistic? Yesterday, we managed to drive for less than an hour before being forced to abandon the vehicle. Why should today or tomorrow be any different? I had half an idea that one of those planes might spot their base from the air, but how? What exactly would I be looking for? We've spent the better part of a week driving and walking in Pennsylvania, and we know we can't be more than a hundred miles from where Powell came from, but we've not found him. Realistically, are we going to? And what if Powell came from an airstrip? What if the reason he drove that BearCat to abduct Ayers, and to the motel, was because that was the only vehicle by the landing pad? Farley might have been there, but what if he's gone?"

"Okay." She sat down again. "So what are the alternatives? Go back to that town, try to get them to help?"

"I don't know. Farley has to be stopped. Did I do all I could to stop him? No, that's the truth, and this is the result. We're dying. The nation, the world, our species. Person by person, day by day, we're using up the supplies that are left. Soon they'll be gone, and soon after that, so will we."

"Self-pity's a luxury we don't have time for," she said. "If you want to hold yourself responsible for the outbreak, and for the cabal, fine. It doesn't change what happened, or where we are. None of us get the future we want, but the one in front of us is a choice between giving up or going on, just as it's always been. But the choice immediately in front of us is to continue to the airfield, or go back to that town and tell them that whoever was here last night has gone. Personally, I'd say the airfield because it's odd that those people didn't know that the military had left this place."

"Maybe they did, and just wanted to push the problem further down the road."

"Right, so you're voting for the airfield, too? Good. Even if the planes are gone, maybe there's some other people, or at least a proper bed and some decent food. We can get a few hours' rest and—" She stopped.

Tom had heard it, too. He stood. The sound came from the nearest tent at the base of the off-ramp. The flaps were closed, though he now wondered if sealed would be a more accurate description. The walls bulged as if someone was trying to push through them. He raised the rifle. The canvas undulated as the bulge moved toward the doors.

"Shout something," he said. "We need to know it's undead."

"Hello!" Helena called. The material tore with a rip that seemed louder than her uncertain yell. A head appeared. Even from that distance, Tom knew it was dead. Tattered skin hung from ragged muscle on a face missing nose, lips, and cheeks. He fired. The shot set off a cacophony as birds erupted from nearby trees. Beating wings drowned out the sound of the tent collapsing as the twice-dead creature disappeared from view.

"Ugh!" Helena shuddered. "Feel better? Because I don't." She picked up the fuel can. "And I won't until we're at least a hundred miles from—"

The sound came again. It was the same as before; the whispering of cloth, the expulsion of rank air from dead lungs, the snapping of metal supports as the tents collapsed. And it was tents, plural. Unlike before, this wasn't just one solitary creature. The sound came from every tent as hundreds of undead limbs pushed and tore their way out into the daylight. Tom shifted the rifle from target to target, but there were too many.

"We need to go," he said, but Helena was already halfway toward the row of vehicles. Tom backed away, unable to tear his eyes from the zombies bursting from the collapsing tents. Some wore uniforms, but most didn't. The young, the old, men, women, and children, they turned their sightless toward him.

"No keys! No keys! No keys!" Helena yelled. The words cut through the horror. He turned and ran. She was dashing between the vehicles, trying car doors, peering at the ignition on the motorbikes.

"This one," she said. Gasoline spilled around its tires as she sloshed fuel into a bike's tank.

"Slow down. We've got time," Tom said, forcing calm into his voice. "There are too many to fight, but they move slow."

She gritted her teeth, but poured more slowly, until the fuel can was empty. "Now can we go?"

He climbed on behind her. "Drive slowly," he said. "We can lure the zombies away from that town."

Even as he said it, he knew how futile it was. They might draw some of the zombies away, but not all, and there had to be thousands in those tents. If the people in that town legitimately believed that a military evacuation center existed five miles from them, then someone would come and look. They would drive to the highway, see the zombies, and drive back. The zombies would follow. Luring a few away was a gesture, and nothing more, yet it was all they could do.

After a mile, Helena began to ease the throttle. The bike sped up. Tom didn't stop her.

Chapter 4 - Airlift
Mifflin County, Pennsylvania

They were only a few miles from the airfield when they ran out of fuel. Tom knew it was only a few miles by the twin-engine jet that soared up into the sky at the same time as the motorbike's engine died. Tom squinted at the plane as it banked to the west. He'd seen that make of aircraft at a dozen regional airports over the years, but couldn't even guess at its capacity. All that mattered now was that it was lost to the skies.

"Looks like we've missed our flight," Helena said, giving the throttle another twist.

Tom climbed off the bike and gave the tires a vindictive kick. "At least it's not far to the airfield. Julio said he'd leave some fuel for us, and he's a stubbornly reliable man."

"But we can't rest there," she said. As one, they both found themselves looking back the way they'd come.

The road was deserted, but they'd passed a small pack of the undead barely ten miles before. Those lumpen creatures had been squatting motionless outside a burned-out store. He could only guess at what had once been sold there, but the zombies had been woken by the sound of the motorbike's passing. The sound of the jet engines would be another siren, luring them in this direction.

"The airfield can't be far," Tom said, unslinging his rifle. He started walking.

Another plane emerged above the trees. This was a prop that fought valiantly to get into the sky. It jerked up, and dropped down, disappearing behind a clump of red pines. Tom expected an explosion, but instead the plane reared up, clearing the trees. He raised a hand in greeting as it buzzed a wide circle, coming close to where they stood. The wings didn't waggle, so perhaps the pilot hadn't seen them. Or perhaps it was too great an effort keeping the cumbersome craft in the air to waste time on such niceties.

"Where are the fighter planes?" Helena asked, when the plane was nothing but a swiftly receding speck.

"Already gone, or being saved for last," he said. "There's only one very short runway."

"But if the planes are still taking off, then there are people still at the airfield, right?"

He didn't reply, but started walking more quickly. Soon, they were both jogging along the road. The jog had almost turned into a run when a background sound resolved into gunfire.

The airfield was attached to a farm. If flying was Julio's passion, farming was his tradition. Circumstance might prevent him from ever returning to his ancestral home, but the small farm allowed him to stay spiritually connected to the soil. Not quite a ranch, yet too well managed to be called a hobby, it occupied fifty acres north of the airfield. The livestock were gone.

Another overloaded plane staggered into the sky.

They jogged past the fields. The stubby control tower got larger far too slowly. Ahead lay a barn that dwarfed the single-level house. With his family thinking him dead, Julio had always said it was larger than he needed. Beyond the house was the double-height chain-link fence separating the airfield from the farm. Access to the airfield was through a gate two hundred yards further down the road. Barrels, tables, and other easily moved furniture added weight to the trucks parked in front of it. Compared to the barricade at the town they'd seen earlier that day, it was truly a flimsy construct. It could have been made of cement and steel and it wouldn't have mattered. The chain-link fence was broken in three places that he could see. No doubt it was breached in other places currently out of sight.

"Cars or trucks," Helena said. "Must have driven right through the fence, trying to get to the airfield."

The zombies had followed. There were some on the road, heading in the direction of the breached fence. The gunfire spoke of more creatures already inside. The fusillade was continuous; however, the volume of fire was slackening.

"There's a dozen zombies outside the front gate," Helena said.

"No vehicles in the farmhouse," Tom said. "Might be some on the airfield."

There was a sound of an explosion. A grenade, he thought.

"What about those trucks by the gate?" Helena suggested. "They might work."

"Assuming they weren't disabled in an attempt to make the barricade more formidable." But they weren't going to get on the airfield, and there was nothing for them the way they'd come. "No, there are no good choices. Let's try for those trucks."

His feet were reluctant to run. They seemed to understand what his brain refused to accept: it was futile. There were over a dozen zombies by the gate, and four more on the road between them and it. At any moment the gunfire could stop as the last remaining people at the airfield boarded a plane. The zombies would follow the sound of its engine, traipsing back out onto the road, and so right into Helena and him. There truly were no other choices. He slung the rifle and pulled out the machete, his eyes never leaving the nearest zombie on the road.

"This reminds me of a story," he said.

"What?" Helena asked.

The zombie was only forty yards away. Dressed more smartly than most undead he'd seen, it looked as if its left leg was injured. With each faltering step, it seemed like it would topple, yet it remained upright, dragging its wounded limb behind it.

"A story," Tom said, hefting the machete. It had been a noticeable weight on his belt, getting more burdensome with each step. Now it seemed flimsy and inadequate, but a shot might attract the attention of the zombies further down the road. "It was something Vice President Carpenter told me about the time when he was a general, working as a peacekeeper."

"This isn't the time, Tom," Helena said.

"The punch line," Tom said, "is that when there are no good choices left, you keep on going as hard and fast as you can."

General Carpenter's story had involved an armored convoy, ambushed by a rebellious faction that refused to obey a cease-fire. They'd been on a road that ran through a valley. Armed with decades-old equipment, the rebels wouldn't have stood a chance against the American convoy in a stand-up fight, but they had been dug in on the high ground. The convoy had got through. The other punch line, the one that had come a long silence later, was illustrated with three photographs. They'd showed the bullet holes and shrapnel scars on the vehicles. On the back of each picture, the general had written the names of the dead. The vehicles had been retrofitted, reinforced against an EMP at the expense of armor that would protect from small arms and IEDs. The story had been told as a way for the general to illustrate that if he was to join the ticket, he wanted structural reform of military procurement. That part of the story, Tom kept to himself.

He raised the machete, focusing on what he would have to do. Swing up, swing down, move on to the next. The zombie's head bobbed with each limping step, twisting its face in a macabre mockery of human exertion. Its hair was matted with mud and worse. Its chest was stained dark, but there were flecks of white paint on its once-polished shoes.

There was the buzzing whine of an engine. The zombie jerked upright. Its arms flew up and almost around in a circle as it turned its head toward the airfield. The engine-whine grew louder. Tom spared a quick glance. He couldn't see the plane, but he could see a score of the undead lurching between the buildings that shielded the runway from view. The whine turned to a roar, and Tom turned back to the zombie in front. Suddenly, there was a massive explosion. He staggered sideways. Flames licked upward from the airfield, along with a dense, choking cloud.

Helena grabbed his arm, pulling him upright. "The fuel store," she said. It wasn't quite a question, nor a statement, but she needed to say no more.

"The gunfire," he replied. It had all but stopped. Though he couldn't see the runway, he knew it must now be strewn with rubble. Whatever fighter jets or other aircraft remained, even if they remained undamaged, none would take off from here. The trucks by the gate took on a new meaning. They represented escape not just for him, but for whoever was left alive inside. A scarce resource they might now have to fight over.

With the sound of plinking, cracking metal to their left, they ran on. The limping zombie had been knocked from its feet by the blast. Its arms flailed as they drew near. Tom kicked its hands clear. There wasn't time to kill it. The zombies further down the road had seen him and Helena, and were drifting toward them. The nearest was only ten feet away. Still running, he raised the machete, swinging it down on the zombie's skull. The force of the blow split bone and brought Tom to a staggering halt. The blade was stuck. He stamped down on the creature to free it. There was a shot. A zombie fifteen feet from him spun backward. Helena stood, legs braced, carefully aiming. She fired again. The zombie collapsed, but Tom saw what she hadn't. Inside the chain-link fence, shadowy figures staggered through the smoke.

"Move!" he yelled. The zombie she'd shot was back on its feet, brown-red gore dripping from the wound in its shoulder. He ran forward, hacking the machete into its leg. It sliced through muscle. He drew the blade back as the zombie fell, and swung it down onto its head.

Helena fired again, a head shot that meant only the zombies by the gates, and those staggering across the airfield, were left.

"Only?" he muttered, hooking the machete back onto his belt. He unslung the rifle.

"The road beyond the trucks looks clear," he said as Helena drew level. He aimed. Fired. Aimed. Fired, and with each shot he took a step toward the zombies. Helena was firing, too. Part of him wanted to tell her to save her ammunition. A larger part wanted to tell her to run, to save herself, but distance didn't offer salvation, not here, not now. Alone, together, on foot or on wheels, nowhere was safe.

When the magazine was empty, there were only two zombies left. He reloaded, but slung the rifle. He had two magazines left, and they would need those if they were to see the sunset. Before he could draw the machete, Helena fired, unloading her pistol into the nearest. At least one of the half-dozen shots hit its skull, but that left the last creature. With no mud stains, or rips in its clothing, and no obvious wounds or bandages, it was only its slack-skinned rictus that showed it was dead. Tom hacked through its clawing hands. He kicked out at its knee. It staggered. He swung down, the blade smashing through its temple. It fell, taking the machete with it. He gave a tug, but it was stuck fast. Before he could pull it out, he saw the trucks, and realized what a fool's refuge it was.

The air had been let out of the tires. Cement had been poured on a mess of wood and metal in front of the vehicles. There was no escape there.

"One magazine left," Helena said.

"We need to keep walking," he said, gesturing down the road. "There's too many zombies here to look for any supplies Julio's left. We have to keep moving."

"Yeah. Keep moving. Always moving. Wait, do you hear that?"

It was an engine, coming from inside the pall of choking fumes. It wasn't a plane, but something far larger than a pickup. A fire truck appeared out of the smoke, heading straight for them. The padlock went flying, and the gate burst apart as the vehicle slammed into it the barricade. Tom leaped aside, but the truck had slowed. There was a grinding of gears, a scraping of metal, a spinning of wheels. The barricade didn't move.

"That way!" Helena yelled at the driver, pointing toward the nearest breach in the chain-link fence. "The fence is broken! Twenty-five yards. Drive that way."

The woman behind the wheel nodded. The truck reversed. Helena started to move. Tom grabbed her arm.

"Wait. Wait to see which way it goes." It might head for a different breach, and that truck represented the only way they were going to escape. The truck sped backward. There was a trio of dull, meaty thuds as it hit unseen ambulatory death, and then it changed direction.

"Come on!" Tom yelled, running along the fence, parallel to the truck.

They reached the breach, but eight zombies had got there first. They were staggering out from the airfield, toward the road. He raised the rifle, firing without aiming, downing four before the truck appeared out of the smoke. It smashed into the remaining creatures, dragging them beneath its wheels. The truck swerved onto the road, and almost into the ditch on the other side. There was a hiss of brakes, a roar from the engine, and it drove off.

"It didn't stop," Helena hissed.

The truck had crushed the legs of one of the zombies, but the creature wasn't dead. It raised an arm. Tom fired a quick shot into its head.

"It didn't—" Helena began. "It did! It's stopped."

They ran.

They undead were tumbling out of the airfield, through the now-broken gate, and out of the gaps in the fence. Some wore uniforms, some didn't, and many looked recently alive.

Helena reached the truck first. Tom had only one foot on the running board and one hand on the guide-bar before the truck started moving again, accelerating away from the airfield.

Chapter 5 - Brothers and Sisters
Mifflin County, Pennsylvania

Ten minutes later, the truck stopped at an intersection. Tom jumped down, shaking the stiffness out of his wrists.

"Never done that before," Helena said. "Not sure I'd have been able to hold on for much longer."

"I know what you mean," he said, but that minor discomfort was forgotten when he looked back the way they'd come. The intersection was on a slight rise that offered a clear view of the inferno engulfing the airfield. Dirty-grey smoke enveloped the runway. Flames had spread to the control tower, licking upward and out.

"They're not alive," Helena said. "They're not, are they? No. They can't be."

He turned his attention to the figures drifting in and out of the gaps in the fence, heedless of fumes and flames alike. There was a lack of urgency to their movement that confirmed Helena was right. They were undead.

The truck door slammed closed as the driver climbed out. She had a gun holstered at her belt, a blue scarf tucked into a black leather jacket, and an expression of tightly controlled anxiety on her face.

"Kaitlin," she said, half raising her hand. She let it fall before properly offering it.

"Helena."

"Tom." It was hard to know what to say next. "Um... The guy who ran the airfield, Julio, do you know if... if..." He wasn't sure how to finish, but Kaitlin knew what he was asking.

"Don't know," she said. "He was a pilot, right?"

"He owned that place," Tom said.

"Then he might have been on one of the planes which got out," Kaitlin said. "I'm not sure. We only arrived last night. We were the last in, so we were going to be the last out on the last plane to leave." There was a muffled explosion from the airfield. "Maybe he got out. Was that why you came here?"

"Kind of," Helena said.

The door to the cab opened. A tousle-haired girl stuck her head out. "Is this the crossroads, Katie?"

"Close the door! Go back inside," Kaitlin snapped.

"They said we had to go to the crossroads. Is this it?" the girl asked.

"Yes. Look," Kaitlin waved her arms to take in the intersecting roads. As she did, her sleeve rolled up, and Tom caught sight of the edge of a regimental tattoo.

"There was a plan in case the airfield got overrun?" Helena asked.

"Yeah." Kaitlin turned back to the cab. "Close the door. Now!" The door reluctantly closed. "Yeah, there was a plan. Kind of. If the airfield was overrun, get in the cars and trucks, and drive away. Stop here and wait for everyone else."

Tom looked back at the airfield, at the flames, the wreckage, and the distant specks shambling up the road.

"No one's coming," he said, voicing what the woman must be thinking, knowing that the sooner she accepted it, the sooner they could all continue an escape that was only half done. Helena, he noticed, wasn't looking at the airfield, but at the cab, and with a thoughtful expression.

"Give it five minutes," Kaitlin said. "We can wait that long."

The cab's door opened. This time it was a boy in the doorway. He was a little younger than the girl, perhaps eight or nine, but like the girl, he bore no resemblance to the soldier.

"Katie," the boy said, "after the crossroads, we have to go to the farm, remember? Do you remember what they said? The farm with the red water tower, that's where we have to go. Do you remember?"

"I know," Kaitlin said. "Close the door, we'll be going in a moment."

"The red water tower," the boy said, closing the door with no sense of urgency.

"They your kids?" Tom asked, though the woman looked too young, perhaps in her early-to mid twenties, and the children too dissimilar to each other and her.

"No. I mean, yeah. Sort of," Kaitlin said. She turned her eyes back to the airfield.

He understood. She'd offered them a ride out of immediate danger, but was trying to find a way for them not to travel together any further. A dozen persuasive lines jumped to the forefront of his brain, swiftly followed by just as many lies, any one of which he was sure she'd believe. That was how he'd have secured a ride a few weeks before, but the world had changed and so had he. He opted for honesty instead.

"My name's Tom Clemens. I worked for the president. We were trying to get to Washington to give him some information he really needed to know."

"About the zombies?" Kaitlin asked, giving him a more considered examination.

"Sort of. There's a conspiracy at the heart of all of this, and I was trying to stop it. Did you hear about his address to the nation? After the broadcast, we decided to come here. I thought I could enlist the help of the Air Force personnel stationed at the airfield to hunt down the conspirators."

"Oh? What agency are you two with?" Kaitlin asked.

"Oh no," Helena said. "I'm a teacher from New York. I... We sort of ended up traveling together."

"You have any I.D.?" she asked Tom.

"No, and I didn't work for an agency. I do have proof." He took out the tablet. "But the battery's dead. The journey to this farm with the red water-tower should be long enough to charge it."

There was another muffled explosion from the airfield.

"The zombies are getting nearer," Helena said. "They'll be here in another twenty minutes. We should get moving."

"Yeah." Kaitlin gave them both another brief but thorough inspection before reaching some internal decision. "Yeah, we should. Get in."

When Tom reached the door to the cab, he saw why this woman was so reluctant to offer assistance to two people who'd helped her escape the airfield. The back of the cab was filled with children.

Helena paused in the doorway, making eye contact with each child in turn. "You know," she said brightly as she climbed in, "this will be the third time I've ridden in a fire truck. The other two times were when they brought one to the school where I teach, to show my pupils what a firefighter does. Now, let me see, my students are about... your age. What's your name?"

"Soanna," the girl who'd opened the door said. "What's yours?"

As the truck begin to move, Tom closed his eyes and allowed himself to relax. Helena chattered on with the children in a way that could almost, *almost*, make him believe the world was back to normal.

There were eight children. Four boys and four girls. Soanna did most of the talking, with occasional corrections from Luke, the boy who'd opened the cab door. At eleven, Soanna was the oldest. Ramon, at seven, was the youngest. The other boys, Caleb and Tyler, were too terrified to talk. The other girls were introduced by Soanna as Emerald, Amber, and Jade.

"Are you sisters?" Helena asked.

"We all are," Soanna said firmly. "We're all brothers and sisters now."

"They're from a foster home," Kaitlin said. "Emerald, Amber, and Jade lived next door. There, a red painted water tower. That must be it." She stopped the truck by a closed five-bar gate and turned around to face the children. "You stay inside. I mean it this time."

Tom got out and walked a little way down the road, checking in either direction. He saw no zombies, but he saw no vehicles either.

"What was the rest of the escape plan after you got here?" Helena asked after Kaitlin had closed the door to the cab.

"There wasn't one," Kaitlin said. "We got to the airfield last night, and by that time there were already too many people for the planes. The seats were going to be for children and pilots, and no one else. There was a farmer there, he said he owned this place, and if the airfield was overrun, everyone should come here. He said he had a well, and a store of agricultural diesel behind the barn. If you want to call that a plan, then that's the extent of it."

"You mean it was only children on the plane?" Helena asked. "So that plane that crashed, it was… God!"

Kaitlin walked out into the road. "The real plan was to hold on for as long as possible, not to flee," she said. "Certainly not to flee before they found somewhere to land. The pilots were flying sorties every day, looking for a landing field. They hadn't found one. This guy, he had grey hair, a jet-black goatee, he was impeccably dressed—"

"Complete with mirror-polished shoes? That's Julio," Tom said.

"Right, he said he didn't know of anywhere. I guess the pilots who'd landed their planes on his airfield didn't know of anywhere either. Their passengers must have thought the airfield was just a stepping-stone to somewhere else. Somewhere safe. There was a nearly a riot last night. A group tried to storm a plane. It's why I kept the kids in the fire truck. Good thing, too. I might be wrong, but I think the fence was broken when people decided to break out. Around dawn, there was more shooting, and the planes started to take off. I think Julio and the captain had decided it was time to go. Or maybe they made that decision when the fence broke and the zombies got inside. I guess when people were told there was no seat on a plane, they stopped helping kill the zombies. I'm not sure. It all fell apart so quickly. I kept the kids in the truck, waiting to get them onto the plane, but then… you saw the rest."

Tom glanced down the road, then at the gate to the farm. "Here." He held out the rifle to Kaitlin. She frowned. "You're military, aren't you? You know how to use it, probably better than me."

She took it, though with an air of reluctant suspicion. Tom walked over to the lockers on the side of the fire truck. He slid open one, and then the next until he found the tools. He took out a fire-axe. Short-handled, with a reinforced blade and comfortable grip, it felt far more like a real weapon than the machete had.

"What are you going to do with that?" Kaitlin asked.

"Don't you hear it?" Tom asked. "It's coming from behind the house. A living person would have come to investigate the sound of the engines." He hefted the axe. "And we need to save ammunition."

The creature wasn't behind the house, but inside. Its arms waved through the broken kitchen window. Skin caught and tore on jagged shards of glass as it thrashed more violently when it saw him approach. Tom shook his head, gesturing with his axe toward the door.

"There's an open door not five feet away, and you didn't have the sense to use it. Maybe there is hope for us."

Air hissed from the zombie's snarling mouth. Tom waited until it threw an arm forward, and its head was jutting out. He swung the axe down. The blade sliced neatly through scalp and bone and brain, and came free. The creature sagged, motionless, on the window frame.

"It's dead," he called, watching brown-red gore drip from the creature's fingers down onto a plastic tray of blue-petaled bedding plants. The flowerbed under the window had been dug over, but the plants were still in their pots. That must have been what someone was planning to do, the day of the outbreak. With the edge of the axe, he nudged the plants away from the slowly dripping blood.

"Nothing on the road," Helena called back. Tom hadn't been waiting for her reply, but listening for a response from any other undead inside the house.

"I'm checking inside," he called, again listening for a response from the interior of the house. When none came, he pushed the door wide open. It led into a utility room, on the floor of which was a dead zombie dressed like the creature he'd just killed. From the clothing, the crowbar on the ground, and the pair of half-filled bags, he took them as looters rather than friends or family of the farmer who'd owned the property. It took another five minutes to confirm the farmhouse was truly empty, and that the scavengers' bags contained the best of the meager loot to be found in the house.

"Two zombies," he said when he got back to the truck. "One already dead. I killed the other. Looked like looters, or, hell, I guess they're survivors like us. Not sure how the first one got infected, but I think the other killed him before succumbing to the virus."

"It doesn't matter," Kaitlin said. "This place is too close to the airfield. We can't stay here."

"Where were you heading before you found the airfield?" Helena asked. "I mean, I take it that wasn't your original destination."

"No, we stumbled across it," Kaitlin said. "We were heading west. Just trying to get away. What about you? Where are you two going now?"

"I... I don't know," Helena said. "Tom?"

"You said there was diesel here?" Tom asked.

"Behind the barn," Kaitlin said.

"We'll need it. Fuel is hard to find. I said I'd show you some proof." He took out the tablet and sat-phone. "By the time we've found the fuel and any food left in the house, they'll have charged. While we're looking, I'll tell you what happened, and how we came to be here."

Leaving Helena to watch over the children, he and Kaitlin headed toward house. The food left in the kitchen, or that portion of it not now contaminated by the two zombies, fit into a very small box. By the time it was filled, Tom had explained about Project Archangel. The diesel was in a large storage tank behind the barn. By the time they'd confirmed there was enough to fill the fire truck a dozen times over, he'd told her about Farley, the election, and Powell. When they got back to the truck, there was enough charge on the tablet to show her the video of the journalist's murder, and a handful of documents that he hoped proved his case.

"And you're hunting these people?" Kaitlin asked.

"We were," Tom said. He looked at Helena, and at the truck, and the faces of the children. The door was open, and they were all watching, terrified and curious. "I was. I never stood much chance of finding them, and my odds now are worse. The airfield was the last idea I had. I have a cottage in Maine. There are supplies there, hidden where no scavenger will find them. It's on the other side of a bay from a fishing village that's popular in the summer, but almost empty at this time of year. It's remote, far more remote than this, and if nowhere is remote enough, I have a boat. If we fill up the fire truck's water reservoir with diesel, we'll have more than enough fuel to get there. And we could be there by tomorrow."

"And if the zombies are already there?" Kaitlin asked.

"They're everywhere," Tom said. "But where else is there? We started in New York and went west almost as far as Lake Erie. The only places that had people and walls weren't welcoming strangers. We saw one overrun. It's likely that same fate will befall the rest. No, unless you know of somewhere you'll be welcomed, then Maine, and the supplies there and the boat in the bay, is the closest I can think of to safety."

"What about this conspiracy? The people you've been chasing?" Kaitlin asked.

Helena echoed the question. "Yes, what about them? What if Powell's still alive?"

"I'm not going to find them. On the upside, they're not going to find me, either. No, they wanted to rule the world, but the world's gone. If they are still alive, they'll be in some bunker somewhere. Well, let them rule that. It's time I forget the past and see instead if we can make something of the future."

"The kids came from a foster home?" Tom asked as they filled the fire truck's water reservoir with diesel.

"Emerald, Amber, and Jade lived next door; the others came from the home," Kaitlin corrected him.

"And how did you end up with them here?" he asked.

"Does it matter?" She looked around as if she wanted to kick something. "I grew up there. Sort of. Same building, different foster parents. Me and Laurie…" She trailed off. "I got out. Joined up. She…"

"She didn't?" Tom asked.

"What? No. Well, yes. She took over the home. Ran it. She died three days ago. Ripped apart by zombies. When it all started, when the news filled with those accounts from New York, I went to see if she needed a hand with the kids. I thought there'd be some kind of plan. I thought someone would have thought of all the children. Of course they hadn't. Emerald, Amber, and Jade's mother went out looking for food. She didn't come back. I went looking for her, and I found her. She'd been infected. I killed her. That's when we left. Now we're here."

There was a lot more to the story, but the woman clearly didn't want to tell it.

"The reservoir's full," Tom said. "We should go."

Chapter 6 - A Very Grand House
Lycoming County, Pennsylvania

"I think that's got it," Tom said quietly. The motion of the truck had lulled the children to sleep.

"You think?" Helena asked.

"I've never altered the orbit of a satellite before," he said. "If I'm honest, I'm not sure that I've done it now. Theoretically, there're only a few parameters to change. Actually, it's more accurate to say that there's only a few parameters I *can* change. Realistically, I've either done nothing, or what I've done will be noticed and undone, or the satellite will crash into the atmosphere."

"But if it works?" Kaitlin asked.

"Then we should get some images of the country north and east of here, all the way to the Atlantic coast," he said. "At least, the part of it that isn't obscured by clouds."

"Good." She stopped the truck. They were on the crest of a hill. "If you're done, then it's your turn."

He checked outside the window before he opened the door and climbed up onto the roof. They'd stopped frequently, always on raised ground, to pinpoint plumes of distant smoke, scan for survivors, and to check the vehicle for damage after collisions with the undead. There had been no signs of other people, but there had been plenty of zombies. The truck was too cumbersome to steer around the undead, but it was bulky enough to drive through them, and that was what they'd done. He clambered over the ladder-platform, walking along the roof of the tender to get a better view of the road they'd just traveled. It was empty. He jumped down, inspecting the damage. There were dents and dark stains, flecks of drying gore and pieces of dead flesh stuck to the side and tires, but nothing he would call serious. He walked back to the cab.

"See anything?" Helena asked.

"Nothing. No zombies. No people."

It was more than just eerie. After being surrounded by so many refugees during their flight from the motel, finding roads almost completely absent of vehicles didn't seem natural. The few they did pass had crashed, or been abandoned with someone infected in the back who had since turned into one of the undead. There had been no contrails in the sky, or people hitching along the road. The few plumes of smoke they'd seen had been monstrous clouds, squatting over burning towns, almost as if they'd been signs warning the living away. He shook his head, trying to rid it of that grim thought.

"But there's a house about a mile ahead," he said. "Set about fifty yards from the road. It's not a farm, but it'd be a reasonable place to stop for the night."

"We've another hour of daylight left," Kaitlin said. "I'd rather keep going."

"We might make another forty miles," Tom said, "but we'll have to stop. We don't want to spend the night in the open."

"Rest tonight, and we'll be in Maine tomorrow afternoon," Helena said. "If there's no zombies in sight, maybe there's none within hearing range. A night's rest, some food, it's what we all need."

"You're in charge," Kaitlin said to Soanna. "Make sure everyone stays inside the truck." The girl puffed up with her deputized authority. Kaitlin closed the door.

"It's a nice place," Helena said.

Tom turned his attention away from the hills behind the house to give it a proper inspection. She was right. It was nice, but strangely so. The house was large. If it had been built somewhere less remote, it would have been described as a mansion. Going by the windows, there were three floors. Ivy trailed almost up to the eaves on the south-facing side, except around the windows where it had been cut back to within an arm's reach of the frame. Made of stone and brick, it had the style of a New England townhouse, but set in a rambling overgrown garden. At one time, there had been a wall ringing the grounds. In most places the stones had crumbled and were now covered by a creeping sea of grass. Where the wall still stood, it was only because of the metal brackets propping it up.

"Yeah. It's the kind of place you drive past and imagine living in," he said, "but if it came on the market, you'd never seriously consider buying it."

"Are we going in?" Kaitlin asked.

Three granite steps led up to the house. Worn in the middle by the passage of at least a century of feet, they looked far older than the building. He tried the door. It was unlocked and swung open with an almost comical creak. Inside, the light was dim. The doors leading off the hall were closed.

"Here." Kaitlin turned on a flashlight that had come from the equipment store on the truck. Dust danced in its beam as she shone it at each closed door, then up the ominously steep staircase. A floorboard gave a creak that would almost have been comical if it wasn't for the long, echoing scrape that came from somewhere inside.

"Occupied," he whispered, trying to place the sound.

"The power's out," Helena whispered trying the switch. "Do we split up to search?"

"No need." Tom stamped his foot on the floor. The response, a clattering rattle, came almost immediately, and it came from below.

"The basement," Kaitlin said.

A door at the end of the hall led to an empty kitchen. Beyond that was a door that Tom was certain led down to the cellar. Unlike the others leading from the hall, this one was locked. There was no key.

"Check the rest of the house first?" Tom suggested, more out of a desire to put off the inevitable than from necessity. It was unoccupied, and the doors were all unlocked, except for the one to the basement.

Helena shone the flashlight on the door. Kaitlin raised the rifle. Tom raised the axe and swung it down. The lock splintered. The door swung open. He stepped back, giving the soldier a clear line of fire. The sound grew louder, but not closer.

"Give me that." Wanting it to be over, Tom grabbed the flashlight from Helena and stepped through the door. The doorway was narrow. The stairs were steep. He could hear the creature, and something else. Something metal. He stopped, halfway down, tracking the light across the space. It illuminated wooden shelves, sheet-covered furniture, a rusting tool rack, and, in the corner, a zombie that had been an old woman a few weeks before. One end of a long chain was wrapped around her feet; the other was attached to the metal bracket of a workbench. The rattling of the chain grew more strident as he shone the light into her eyes. The arms clawed at the air between them, the mouth snapped, but the chain held. He scanned the rest of the room, then forced himself down the remaining stairs.

"Your life shouldn't have ended like this." He swung the axe down. The zombie was still.

"Tom? You okay?" Helena called.

"An old woman chained herself up down here," he called back. He found a rag on the workbench, cleaned the axe, and then he went back upstairs. "Must have lived here."

"Then this is a safe place to spend the night," Helena said to Kaitlin.

"As safe as anywhere," she said.

He went outside, leaving it to Kaitlin and Helena to gather the children. He walked out into the road, checking it was still empty, and then wandered the garden until he found a well-worn bench. The wood was warped, the varnish flaking. Helena found him there, twenty minutes later.

"You okay?" she asked.

"Sure."

"Why don't I believe you?"

"It's the old woman. It's all the zombies. It's all the people they were, the lives they could have led." He gestured at what he'd been looking at. In front of the bench were a row of grave markers. "Do you see the dates? They correspond to Vietnam, Korea, Germany in both wars, Gettysburg, and Antietam."

"It's a military family," Helena said. "There're photographs in the hall, and in the main room."

"It's a family that gave so much, until now there's no one left to give. How do the politicians repay that sacrifice? They conspire to rig the election, just so that history will remember their names. And it will. If there ever is a history, it will remember Farley and Sterling. It will even remember Powell, but it won't know any of these people."

"There're photographs inside of a young man in uniform," Helena said. "They look recent. You now what I think these graves show? That some died, but others came back. They went out into the world and made a life for themselves. That woman didn't, sure. She stayed and tended the family home. It doesn't mean the rest are dead, or make their sacrifice any less meaningful. That's not what's bothering you."

"It's not?"

"You think that you should still be hunting for Farley, that you've given up. You know that when we get to Maine, you might find some clues on the computers you have there, but you also know you'll never be able to act on them. You said as much and think that means you're handing the world to the cabal. You aren't. You won. The conspiracy is over, Tom. You only have to look about you to realize that Farley has lost. I think Powell's attack on the motel was a last desperate attempt at revenge after their organization was destroyed."

"And if it wasn't?"

"Think about it. It was just him and a couple of people. If the cabal was still a viable force, then where were the rest of them? No, he's dead, Tom. I bet Farley is, too."

"And what if you're wrong? What if I'm wrong?"

"You'll never know," she said. "*We'll* never know. After what they did, I want justice as much as you. Knowledge that they failed is as close to it as we're going to get. Whether you did all you could, or could have done more, it's over. You know it, and now you have to accept it. Those children need to be protected, and whether you like it or not, that's your job, now. More immediately," she added, standing up, "they need to be persuaded to wash in cold water, be fed, and put to bed. You can only mourn the dead, but you can help the living. Come on."

Leaving the children to Kaitlin and Helena, he took on the equally unfamiliar task of making a meal. He'd never cooked much, and his solitary lifestyle meant there were few occasions when he'd had someone to cook for. Since his arrival in America, he'd always had the money to eat out. More recently, he hadn't the time to shop, let alone learn. Opening packets and pressing switches was about his level of comfort. Fortunately, the woman who'd owned the house had a simple diet. There was little variety in her larder, and it gave him little choice in what to prepare. The freezer was full, but had defrosted. The stove was electric, and that had him hunting for a generator. It was in a garage to the side of the house, was powered by gasoline, and was empty. So were the fuel tanks of the two cars – one a lovingly restored relic, the other a poorly maintained runabout.

He laid a fire in a room so crammed with books that calling it a library didn't do it justice. He set a large saucepan of water to boil. Only as he was staring at the flames did he think about the water that had come out of the faucet. Another brief trip outside found a sealed well with a silent electric pump. Once the water in the pipes and storage tanks was used up, they'd have to draw it by hand.

"My specialty," he said, placing the saucepan on the table. "Pasta with red sauce."

"I don't eat that," Luke whined.

"He means ketchup," Soanna said. "That's right, isn't it? Ketchup." She gave him a pointed stare and encouraging nod.

"Of course," Tom said.

"There. See. You like ketchup," Soanna said to Luke.

"Doesn't look like ketchup," Luke said as a portion was spooned into a bowl.

"Did you know," Tom said, "that ketchup was originally a fish sauce."

"Of course it wasn't," Soanna said giving him another pointed look. "Don't be silly."

He resolved to keep the rest of his comments aimed solely at Kaitlin and Helena. It didn't matter; as soon as the food was put in front of the children, they tore into it.

"Was there a lot of food in the kitchen?" Helena asked.

"There's pasta and rice, some canned tomatoes and vegetables. The woman lived mostly on chicken, and that was in the freezer. Of what's left, there's a real lack of protein, but there's enough carbs to keep us going for a week." He took in the children shoveling food into their mouths. "Perhaps five days."

"It's a decent house," Kaitlin said. "Lots of rooms. It's remote."

"You're thinking of staying here?" Helena asked.

There was a sudden hush from the children as eight small pairs of eyes turned toward Kaitlin. The only sound came from Luke, who was humming tunelessly as he methodically chewed.

"Eat your dinner," Kaitlin said, and said nothing more until the saucepan was empty. Helena gathered the children in front of the fire to read to them from a Paddington Bear book. It was a first edition, and well-worn, as if it had been bought new and read to many successive generations of children. Kaitlin and Tom took the dirty crockery and cutlery into the kitchen.

"It's worth considering staying here," Kaitlin said. "It is remote. Unless you count when we were inside the airfield, this is the longest we've gone without seeing the zombies since we left Baltimore. Even at the airfield, we could hear them."

"On the plus side, it's remote," Tom agreed. "There's a well, but the motor's electric and there's no gasoline for the generator. I guess we could rig something up using the pump in the fire truck, but that'll use up the diesel, and we'll need that to escape when the zombies come. They will come."

"That'll be the same everywhere," she said.

"True. But if we're saving the fuel, we've got to pull the water by hand, and fetch the wood to boil it. I guess the children can help with that, but only after the three of us have killed the zombies that gather nearby." He opened a cupboard. "It'll be a bland diet, and the food will be gone in a week. So, we'll have to take the fire truck out to find more. Wherever we go, we'll have to fight the undead and kill them to stop them following us back. And what do we do when the fuel is gone?"

"And it won't just be zombies we're fighting for the food," she added. "I don't know what it was like for you, but it was people that were the real danger."

"Yeah, we saw that."

"But is Maine going to be any better?" she asked. "We'll still have to collect water, gather firewood, go out to scavenge for food, and fight off the undead. Isn't it better to start fortifying somewhere now, and hope that the zombies just stop? They have to, sooner or later."

"But can we wait until later?" he asked. "What if there are no supplies to be found anywhere nearby? That woman was infected. She managed to chain herself up and lock herself in the cellar before she died. Since we didn't see any zombies, dead or alive, around the house, she wasn't infected here. What if it happened when she went looking for supplies? I checked the two cars, and there aren't any boxes or bags in the back. So wherever she was infected, it happened before she could find any food or fuel. That doesn't speak well for our chances of finding much. At the cottage, I have a boat. If all else fails, we can fish."

"You know how?"

"Sure. More or less. Okay, if I'm being honest, I'm the kind of guy who sets up the rod as an excuse to sit and watch the water for a few hours, but I've caught fish in the past. The boat would also allow us to go up and down the coast, moving from place to place, looking for supplies, and moving on when the zombies arrive."

"And if the food's all gone? If we don't find any, anywhere?"

"We keep following the coast," he said. "Hell, we can even strike out to sea and make for Britain if we have to."

"In a rowing boat?"

"It's a little larger than that. Britain's evacuating the cities to the coast. It might hold on longer than anywhere else." Of course, there were other problems with going to that country. "Look, I'm not saying it will be easy, or that there won't be a million other problems we've not even thought of. We can't stay here. It's better to leave now, take all the supplies we can, drive north, then east, get to the cottage and take it from there. Maybe you're right, maybe in a week or a month, the zombies will stop."

"And maybe they won't," she said. "I don't like the uncertainty."

He took down the jar of coffee beans. They were an exotic blend in a small jar, suggesting the old woman didn't drink more than a cup a day. The grinder was electric. He picked up the pepper mill, and unscrewed it, emptying the grains onto the counter. "No more pepper. No more spices. No more anything except that which we can grow." He filled the pepper mill with coffee beans and began to grind it over a bowl. "No more coffee. Now, that's going to be the real challenge."

"You don't know of any military bases or bunkers or somewhere we can go?" Kaitlin asked.

"I worked on the campaign," Tom said, "not in the administration, but I know the location of plenty of bunkers. I don't know that they'd let us in. What about you? You're military. Were you on leave?"

"Retired," she said. He glanced at her. She seemed too young for that. He put it down to military cutbacks. Whatever the story, by the way she bustled around the cupboards, she didn't want to talk about it.

"Did you vote for him?" he asked instead. "For Max?"

"No," she said after a moment's pause. "I voted for General Carpenter."

"Ah. Well, that's why we wanted him to be on the ticket."

"I almost stayed home. Every election seems to be the same. You get these grand promises, but they never come true. Something always comes along to derail them. Nothing like this, of course." She closed the cupboard. "That, at least, is one thing to thankful for."

"What?"

"No more elections. We'll leave at first light. Go to Maine, and who knows where after that."

The children were asleep before Helena reached the last page. They looked peaceful, lying on the floor and sofa, cuddled together. The moment lasted until Helena put another log on the fire. The flickering flames cast weird shadows, making everything look primitive. Reading by firelight, sleeping when it was dark, and all in the same room for warmth.

He took his mug to a dark room on the other side of the house. He opened the curtains and sat, watching the night outside, sipping the peppery coffee.

Chapter 7 - Toll
March 1st, Lycoming County, Pennsylvania

"What are you looking at?" Luke asked.

Tom jumped down from the truck's roof. He'd retreated outside when a mutiny had erupted over sharing a toothbrush. From the sounds inside the house, it was still going on. "What do you see?" Tom asked, holding out the tablet.

Luke squinted at the screen. "A… is that a fire truck?"

"Precisely," Tom said. "That's us. That image was taken by a satellite. Up in space," he added.

"I know what a satellite is," Luke said. "That's how we talked to Katie when she was away. Wait…" He stared at the screen, then the sky. A look of puzzled wonder spread over his face. He jumped up and down, waving his arms, all the time trying to see the screen.

Tom smiled, but after a few seconds, relented. "It's not live," he said. "The picture was taken just after dawn."

"Oh." Luke stared at the screen, one arm waving slowly back and forth. As the concept sank in, he lowered his hand. "But that *is* our truck?" he asked.

"That's us, yes," Tom said.

"Cool!" He ran inside.

The satellite was three degrees off the course Tom had thought he'd programmed, and it was traveling too fast. It wouldn't be long before its orbit decayed and it burned up in the atmosphere. However, it had done what they needed. He had images of most of the route north. To be more accurate, he had pictures of the places they very definitely wanted to avoid. The area around Crossfields Landing was still a mystery, but he thought they could reach it long before nightfall.

He put the tablet away and climbed back up to the truck's roof. He was under no illusion that life would miraculously improve when they reached the coast. Life was going to get a lot harder before it ever got better. What was galvanizing him was a new sense of purpose. He'd woken with a clear and achievable goal: get the children to Maine. Beyond that, his future was a blank canvas, and that was an entirely new and unexpectedly liberating concept.

Movement caught his eye. On the road, two hundred yards north of the house, a slouching figure shuffled toward them. The sight soured his mood. He jumped down and picked up the fire-axe.

"Luke said you've got a satellite image of us," Helena called from the doorway.

"Yeah, I'll come inside in a moment." He waved the axe down the road. Helena nodded and closed the door.

How swiftly death had become commonplace, Tom thought as he walked onto the road to await the staggering creature. Dealing with the undead was a morning chore. His sour mood turned dark. Not just a chore for the morning, and not just for *this* morning, but for how many days to come?

It was a man, wearing a police windbreaker over a suit. An expensive one, he realized, as the zombie drew nearer. Mud splattered the once-polished shoes, gore covered the buttons, and ragged tears marred the perfect creases.

He took a step toward the zombie, waiting until it raised its arms, until it opened its mouth, until it grew more animated, clawing and thrashing at the air as it got closer. Closer. He swung. The axe hit the creature squarely above the nose. For a moment it was motionless, those dead eyes meeting his. Then it collapsed. Using the axe as a lever, he rolled the body to the side of the road.

Yes, his future lay before him as an open book, but he felt he could already see what events would dominate the individual chapters.

"That's the route," Tom finished. "As I say, I don't have the last fifty miles, but this will get us to the coast."

"Use the highway to get to the interstate in New York State, and then avoid any major roads as we go east into Maine. Especially Route 2," Kaitlin summarized, looking at the lines drawn on the roadmap. It was a touring guide to the northeast, short on details but big on adverts. The soldier threw a glance at the children, all jockeying for a better position from which to view the map. "It's easy enough. We should be there long before nightfall. Okay, kids, I've a game for you. It's called find and keep."

"You mean find and go seek," Luke corrected her.

"No, find and keep. You have to find blankets. The winner is whoever can carry the most. Here's a hint, they're easier to carry when they're folded. Go on."

Luke scuttled off. The others followed, though Soanna wore a far too grown-up expression, as if she realized that it was a chore rather than a game.

"Is there any news? Any messages or anything?" Helena asked when the children were gone.

"Not really. The World Wide Web is gone," Tom said. "There are a few networks still operational, but they're full of people asking whether a sanctuary exists anywhere in the world. A lot of people are talking about Britain. They've been broadcasting that there are no reported cases of infection there. It was for domestic consumption, but radio waves carry, and other people have heard. There's anarchy from the Volga to the Pyrenees. Russia's gone quiet, so has China. Korea's in flames, and Japan's just as bad as anywhere else."

"What about closer to home?" Kaitlin asked.

"Nothing concrete, and nothing official," Tom said. "There's no rump government issuing emergency decrees, and no one's trying to hold the nation together. I'm taking that as a mixed blessing. It means Max is almost certainly dead, but it also means Farley has failed in his bid to seize power."

"Found one," Luke said, running back into the room, trailing a blanket in his wake.

"Folded, Luke, folded," Kaitlin said. "And we should see what else is here that we can take."

The house, originally built in the time before steam, and rebuilt before the automobile supplanted the railroad, had more supplies than they had room for. The difficulty came in choosing what was most important. The tool lockers were already full and had little space for more. With the children in the back of the cab, each clutching as many blankets as they could find, there was room for the food and not much else.

"What's that?" Helena asked, as he carried a box out toward the truck.

"Candles," Tom said. "I found them in the pantry."

"Candles?" She smiled. "Seriously?"

"What?"

"Batteries use up less space and they'll last longer."

There was logic in that, but when he put them back in the house, he did so with reluctance. What they might not need now, they certainly would in the future.

The children's chattering excitement, a residual by-product of a night of relative safety, abruptly stopped when they drove past their first zombie, two miles from the house. After that, they saw them more frequently, and always moving toward the truck. At first, Tom thought they'd escaped the house just in time, but then realized they were heading toward the sound of the engine. He wondered whether they'd made a mistake leaving that property.

At first, Kaitlin was able to drive past the undead. Then they started coming across the vehicles. One after another, abandoned on the road. Their undead former occupants crawled across broken glass and over twisted metal as they tried to reach the truck. Kaitlin stopped trying to dodge them and, with gritted teeth, drove over them instead.

"You sure about the route?" Kaitlin asked an hour later as she weaved around another van, stalled in the middle of the road.

"Another mile, and we'll hit the highway," Tom said.

"You sure?" she asked again.

"There was a sign," Soanna said. "I saw it. One mile ahead."

"One mile," Tom echoed. He'd seen the sign himself, and that was all he had to go on. The stalled cars weren't on the pictures the satellite had taken. There was no way that the rusting row of abandoned vehicles had appeared during the time they'd been driving that morning. Wherever that picture was of, it wasn't here.

"One mile," Kaitlin muttered. There was a screeching grind as the truck shunted a car out of the way. An undead arm stretched through the broken windshield, giving them an almost languid wave as the vehicle was shoved against another. Jade gave a muted whimper. Emerald and Amber swiftly copied suit. Soanna responded by bellowing an absurd nonsense rhyme. Tom joined in, loudly and off-key, making up words for those he didn't know. The caterwaul didn't quite drown out the sound from outside, but the absurdity distracted the children. They screamed the rhyme, giving vent to their fears until, just as abruptly as it had slowed, the truck sped up.

"We're through. We're through," Kaitlin said, as they accelerated onto a highway gloriously, wondrously free of vehicles.

Tom closed his eyes, and relaxed, only realizing how tense he'd been as his muscles slowly unwound. A few hours north, a few east, and they would be at the coast. Whatever happened after that, the traveling would be over.

"There's something ahead," Helena said.

Tom opened his eyes. Images of the choppy Atlantic waves were replaced with a line of police cruisers parked across the road. Beyond those, vehicles lined either side of the shoulder. Parked in front, at the side of the road, was a tow truck. Kaitlin brought the fire truck to a halt, with the blockade still a quarter mile ahead.

A figure appeared from behind the tow truck, walking out into the middle of the road. They waved their arms in what might have been a friendly gesture before crossing to one of the cruisers. There was a muted hum of an engine, and the cruiser pulled out, leaving a gap in the barricade.

"They're making a space for us to drive through," Helena said. "Or are they getting ready to pursue us if we drive away?"

"We can't outrun them," Kaitlin said. "And we can't risk them shooting at us."

"When you can't go back, what's left but to go on?" Tom said.

Kaitlin started the engine. When they were two hundred yards from the barricade, the police car reversed into the gap, stopping with the engine facing them. Kaitlin kept going, her fingers tapping on the steering wheel, her eyes on the shadow of the driver in that police cruiser. One hundred yards from the barricade, she slammed her foot on the brake. They waited.

The driver of the police cruiser got out. It was a woman in civilian dress. She stood by the vehicle, one hand on the door, the other on the roof. A man walked from the tow-truck toward her.

"Only two of them," Tom said.

"There's three," Kaitlin said. "Third one is in the tow-truck. In the cab."

"You sure?" Helena asked.

"Positive. I saw the sunlight reflect from a scope."

"You mean a sniper?" Helena asked.

"It might mean nothing," Tom said. "I better go and have a word." He leaned forward, putting the 9mm into his waistband. He smiled at the children, but couldn't think of any believable words of comfort. "Get ready to reverse and get off the highway as quickly as you can." He climbed out, walking away from the truck.

"Howdy," he called at the man and woman, keeping his tone friendly and his smile wide. "Makes a change to see people. Living people, I mean." He kept walking. "There's been nothing but zombies for the last hundred miles." He half turned around, waving back down the road. As he did so, he noticed the pieces of burned rubber and the scorch marks on the asphalt. He turned back to the two people, angling his path so that he stopped twenty yards from the woman, thirty from the man, and seventy from the tow-truck. "No, nothing but the dead. It's terrible. Truly terrible."

The woman stepped away from the cruiser. She had a pistol holstered at her belt, the button undone. The man was similarly armed, with his hands held braced on his hips.

"Where are you from?" the woman asked.

"Originally?" He decided this wasn't the time for the truth. "The military camp at Providence." He watched their expressions. Neither seemed to recognize the name. "A couple of hundred miles that way?" he added. "You know, part of the relief effort, get people off the roads and back inside? No? You guys don't look military."

"I'm Captain Hennessey," the woman said. "This is Lieutenant Danvers. We're police, and in charge of law and order in this county."

"Have to keep the road clear," Danvers added.

"Sure," Tom said. The man's statement begged the question of whom they were keeping the road clear for. Not wanting to feed him his lines, instead Tom asked, "You seen many zombies today?"

"Nope," Danvers said. He was biting his lip almost as if he was trying not to smile.

"Well that's something," Tom said. "Maybe we've outrun them." Now that he was closer, he could more clearly see the vehicles lining the highway beyond the police cruisers. A few looked damaged. A minivan and a pickup were both missing their front wheels. That sense of unease, of cautious paranoia that had been his constant companion for most of his adult life, was telling him this was all wrong. Three people weren't enough to operate a roadblock. Any town nearby would want passing motorists to keep going. And then there was Danvers's expression. The man seemed to be enjoying himself. No, this wasn't some official police blockade, but a robbery.

"It's a good thing you're keeping the road clear," Tom said, turning around, and taking a step to the side. He turned back, glancing at the tow truck. He couldn't see the sniper. "We'll need that if we're to get everyone to the joint-government defensive works they're building on the far side of the St Lawrence River up near Montreal. It sounds like our government's working with the Canadians to draw a line and make a stand."

"They are?" Danvers asked. "Where did you hear that?"

"On the military frequencies. Aren't you listening to those? We've been in contact since we left. Most people flew, of course, but it's easier to drive the trucks and tanks. You'll need to move a few more cars so the military vehicles can get through."

Danvers looked as if he was about to acquiesce. Hennessey didn't.

"Ain't seen any planes overhead," she said. "How far behind you are these tanks."

"A couple of miles," Tom said.

"No. I don't believe you," Hennessey said. She turned to face the tow truck. Danvers's hand moved toward his holster. Before Tom reached for his own weapon, there was a burst of gunfire. Bullets smacked into the tow-truck, riddling the paintwork. It was Kaitlin. There was no more time for thought. Tom dragged his gun clear of his belt, dropping to one knee. Hennessey had drawn her weapon. She managed one shot toward the fire truck before Tom fired. Hennessey fell. Tom shifted aim. Danvers was running. There was another burst from the truck, cutting him down.

Just as quickly as it had begun, the fire fight was over. Tom ran toward the bodies. Hennessey was dead. He kicked her gun away. Danvers gave a coughing hack, a bubbling rasp, and was still. Tom turned toward the tow-truck, but Kaitlin was already halfway there, the assault rifle raised. She reached it, took one look inside, and yelled, "Clear."

She moved around the vehicle with a quick professionalism, obviously searching for any other members of this little gang. Tom doubted there were any. He walked back to the corpses, curious as to who these people really were. Starting with Hennessey, he searched her pockets until he found a wallet. In it was a photo I.D.

There was a chugging roar from the fire truck as Helena started the engine.

"Stop!" Kaitlin yelled, waving at the truck. Something was wrong, though Tom couldn't tell quite what. Kaitlin ran across the road toward the truck. Helena turned the engine off. She stuck her head out of the cab.

"What?"

Kaitlin pointed at the roadway. Tom crossed over to the soldier. She was standing by a lump of broken tire.

"I've seen this before," she said. "You see the edges? The tire didn't break. It's been cut."

"Why?" Helena asked.

86

Tom knelt down and looked inside, knowing what he would find. "It's an explosive. Remotely detonated."

"Careful," Kaitlin said as Tom gently removed it.

"Looks like an incendiary," he said.

"You know explosives?" Kaitlin asked.

"I know enough to disarm this one. It was a childhood interest," he added. "That explains the scorch marks on the road, and the damaged vehicles beyond the line of police cruisers. Set off the explosives, and destroy the tires, bringing any vehicle to a halt. That would make it easy to rob them."

"Robbery?" Helena asked. "So they were thieves?"

"No." Tom held out the I.D. he'd taken from the dead woman. "Captain Hennessey. She really was a cop."

"The guy in the tow-truck didn't have a rifle. The light was reflected from a pair of binoculars." Kaitlin held up a phone. "It's the detonator."

The thieves' horde – mostly food and a small amount of ammunition – was in a blue panel-van parked at the front of the line of disabled vehicles. To the side of the road beyond were the bodies. There were thirty-seven, rolled into a ditch.

"There's a lesson here," Tom said. "I'm not sure precisely what it is, except that each hour that passes, this world gets increasingly more dangerous."

"We should leave that stuff," Kaitlin said. "It might be booby-trapped. I don't want to risk it, or waste any more time here."

As she went to move the police cruiser, he found pen and paper, and left a note for anyone else who came that way.

"This vehicle may be booby trapped. The people here were using the police cruisers to stop people and rob them. We killed them."

Chapter 8 - Shopping
Tioga County, Pennsylvania

"There's a sign for a grocery store," Luke said. "Can we stop? We need toothbrushes."

"It's too dangerous," Kaitlin said.

"We do need to refill the fuel tank," Helena said softly. She'd taken over driving. It was a case of on-the-job-training that had made the last thirty miles a less than smooth experience.

"I think I've found the store on the satellite," Tom said.

"We're not going inside," Kaitlin said. "I mean it."

"What if there's a delivery truck parked in a loading dock," Tom said, passing the tablet over. "Do you see it?"

Kaitlin took the tablet and peered at the screen. "The truck might be empty."

"It might be full of toys," Luke said.

"We don't need toys," Soanna said.

"She has a point," Kaitlin said. "Where's the nearest town? How do you zoom out on this?"

Tom took the tablet back and zoomed out. "The town's about five miles away. No smoke. No obvious signs of life. Not that that tells us much."

Helena stopped the truck as the grocery store came into view. It was a low, one-floor building, with space for a hundred cars in the parking lot, though it was now almost empty.

"Yeah, you see the way those two cars are slewed across two parking bays? That matches the image exactly." Tom said. "So there should be two vans and one rig parked out the back. Let's check the fuel. See if we've enough diesel for two vehicles. If we don't, then it's academic." He climbed out and waited until the door was closed before he spoke again. "I understand your reluctance," he said.

"I don't think you do," Kaitlin said.

"We need more supplies. Assuming that everything is still in my cottage, then we've got enough for a little over a week. We'll have to go out for more, and whether we do it in this truck or find some diesel-powered car, the engine will make a lot of noise. The zombies will hear. They'll follow us back. We'll have to fight. If we bring the supplies with us, we don't have to go out again. Look, it'll take twenty minutes to see what's in those vehicles. There're no zombies down by the store and none on this road. The kids will stay in the fire truck. Someone can stay with them. They won't be at risk."

"We do have enough fuel to bring another vehicle," Helena said. "I say we do it."

"It's up to you," Tom said.

"Fine," Kaitlin said after a moment's deliberation. "But just to check if there's something actually useful in those vans."

They parked the truck on the road by the entrance to the parking lot.

"I can't see any monsters," Luke said.

"You stay inside the cab," Kaitlin said, getting out. "All of you."

"We're always inside," Soanna said. "And I need to use the bathroom."

"When I get back," Kaitlin said.

Helena and Tom followed her outside.

"Fill up the tank," Helena said.

"You're going?" Tom asked.

"I want to talk to Kaitlin," Helena said. "You can keep an eye on the kids. It'll be good practice."

"Just keep them inside the truck," Kaitlin said.

The children stared at the two women walking across the parking lot. Then they turned their eyes to Tom. They all wore matching expressions of suspicious calculation. It was off-putting, so he turned away from the truck, taking in his surroundings. Except for the broken window at the front of the store, and the complete lack of traffic on the road, it looked much as it must have a month before.

As he began the laborious process of refueling the truck, he calculated how much fuel they'd used, and how much they'd need. He decided they had more than enough to get to the cottage. Did a fully laden delivery van weigh more or less than a fire truck? He wasn't sure, but they should be able to get at least one van all the way there. Even if the van had to be left by the side of the road somewhere, they could go back and collect it at some later date. There were plenty of other grocery stores between them and the Atlantic coast, but each day that went by increased the chance that they'd be looted. Who'd notice another vehicle abandoned by the side of the road? It wasn't just food they needed, but clothing, toiletries, bleach, tools, and... and the list was endless.

The tank was full. He replaced the cap. The one thing they wouldn't find in the store was more fuel. He had a small stash at his cottage for his boat, which would stretch a lot further if they used it on land, but that would mean relying on sail if they took to sea. He sighed. Each solution begat a new problem.

"Perhaps you're thinking too much," he murmured. He walked back to the cab and opened the door.

"I hope you're enjoying our road trip," he said. "I guess we're missing a dog, although I don't suppose many of you have read *Travels with Charley*."

Seven faces stared blankly back at him. Seven.

"Where's Soanna?" he asked.

"She went shopping," Luke said.

"Shh!" Amber hissed. "You weren't meant to tell."

"What do you mean, shopping?"

"For toothbrushes and stuff," Luke said.

Tom scanned the parking lot. There was no sign of the girl, nor of Helena and Kaitlin.

"Stay here." He closed the door and ran toward the store.

The two cars near the entrance were empty, their doors closed and windows intact. Someone had driven them here, so where were they? He should have thought of that before. Something far larger had been driven through the plate-glass window. The vehicle was gone. Had the car's passengers left in that other vehicle?

Glass crunched as he stepped inside. Immediately in front were the registers. Beyond those were acres of shelves. Even accounting for the items on the floor, most of the store's goods had been taken. From the way that the only untouched shelf in sight belonged to a display of winter soup mix, he guessed it was the locals.

A sound came from further inside the store. He raised the axe, lowering it slightly as he registered that noise as an old familiar one. He moved toward it as the sound resolved into the squeak of a trolley's wheel. He rounded an aisle, and saw Soanna, pushing a trolley.

"What the hell are you doing?" he demanded.

She jumped, spun around, and looked apologetic for a fraction of a second. Then she gave him a glare, swept an arm along the nearest shelf, knocking a row of shampoo into the trolley. "What does it look like? I'm shopping."

The trolley was half-filled with a random assortment of toiletries, toothbrushes, and soap. He opened his mouth and closed it on the angry retort. It was the wrong reaction. The time when children could just be children was gone, at least for now.

"It was the people from the town who came here," he said instead. "You saw how they left the soup behind? So everyone who came here had to know what it tasted like, and decided it wasn't worth eating, even when there's so little else. Has to be local people, and they had to have come together. It says a lot about the town and its hygiene that they left all the toiletries behind."

"Yeah. I s'pose."

"There was some toilet paper near the registers," he said. "I say we get that, and then your trolley will have more in it than we have room for in the truck. Agreed?"

"Okay," she said, clearly suspicious at his placatory tone.

"You're the oldest," he said, grabbing the trolley and pushing it along.

"You mean the others will copy me? They won't. I told them to stay in the truck, so they will."

"Right. Just like you did when Kaitlin told you? They look up to you, and you need to look out for them. Right now, they're on their own, unguarded."

"That's your fault, not mine," she said.

"How about we say that we're both equally to blame, and that we've each got a lot to—" He stopped. He heard a sound, and now he was listening to it, he realized it had been there for some time. A clink of metal, then a bang of wood. Clink. Bang. Clink. Bang. He turned around. It was coming from the rear of the store. At the far end of the aisle was a pair of double doors marked staff only. Through the handles on this side was a chain. The sound came when the doors were pushed, and the chain hit them.

"Quickly. Zombies. Must be trapped inside the storeroom." Then he thought of Helena and Kaitlin. "Very quickly! Go!"

"But my trolley!"

"Leave it. No time."

He pushed her in front of him, and almost straight into the arms of a zombie. Its clawing arms swiped over her head, catching in his coat. He slammed his palm against its chest. It was like hitting wood.

"Run! Run!" he bellowed.

Its mouth snapped down as he brought his forearm up, knocking its hand free of his coat. Its other arm slapped into his side. Tom staggered back, wincing with the pain. He punched and pushed, but the snapping mouth got nearer. He grabbed and twisted, and managed to throw the creature against the nearest bank of shelves. They collapsed, and it slipped, falling to one knee. He backed off, turned, and ran after Soanna. When he stepped outside, he remembered the pistol in his belt. He drew it, turned around, watching, waiting. He saw the zombie lumber past the registers. He raised the gun, backing off a step, and lowered the weapon. There was no point wasting ammo. He turned and ran. Soanna was almost at the truck, and past the point where Kaitlin crouched, rifle raised. He glanced again at the store. The zombie had reached the shattered window. It tripped as it tried to walk through the broken frame, slamming face first onto the ground. He jogged back to the truck.

"The delivery vans were empty," Helena said as they drove back onto the highway.

"There wasn't much left in the store," Tom said. "It was stripped nearly bare."

Kaitlin's jaw was set. She said nothing. Nor did the children, and Tom couldn't think of anything he wanted to say. It was Soanna who finally broke the silence.

"It wasn't completely bare," she said. She dug around in her pocket. "I got toothbrushes." She held up three of them.

Chapter 9 - Caught
Broome County, New York State

"This'll do," Kaitlin said, bringing the truck to a halt. It was half an hour since they'd left the interstate behind, but probably only ten miles in distance. Tom put the sat-phone and tablet on the armrest. He'd been trying to work out where they were and had narrowed it to three different sections of rural road. The precise location wasn't important, but puzzling over it offered a distraction to the children. They were more subdued than before, feeding off Kaitlin's tight-lipped anger. Part of that was caused by Soanna's excursion into the store, part of it was everything else they'd seen. Tom got out. Helena followed. Kaitlin closed the door to the cab, this time without admonishing the children against leaving.

"There's not as much damage as I thought," Helena said, examining the front of the truck. "We've lost some lights, but how much night-driving are we going to do?"

The exit from the interstate had been full of the undead. They wouldn't have taken it if the road ahead hadn't been packed with more of those monstrous creatures. A long column, thousands strong, had been drifting south. They'd made it to the off-ramp just ahead of that hideous pack and found it almost as densely packed with the living dead. They'd driven through and over them, running them down, crushing them against the stalled vehicles lining the ramp, but they'd made it.

"I'll get the crowbar and clean the tires," Helena said.

The door opened.

"Can we use the bathroom?" Luke asked.

"No bathrooms here," Kaitlin said. "Just plenty of trees."

"I'm going to take a walk up the hill," Tom said, gesturing to the sloping rise to the right of the truck. "I'll give you a hand in a moment."

He walked across the verge, and onto the scraggly grass. The ground was soft, damp, with a few brighter shoots among the darker wintery blades. There were buds on the bare branches of a tree whose type he couldn't guess at, and the sound of a bird, trilling softly somewhere out of sight. Spring was on its way, but that gave him no peace.

Soon after they'd joined the interstate, a pair of motorbikes had overtaken them. One of the bikers had waved, but neither had stopped. They'd hashed over the possible meanings of that gesture because it was their only distraction from the surrounding horror. Just before the interstate exit, they'd seen both bikes, lying on the road. There was no sign of the bikers.

He reached to top of the incline. It wasn't a hill, just a foreshortened slope at the edge of farmland. In front lay acres of fields. Small green shoots sprung from ruler-neat rows, stretching off into the distance. Beyond, a trio of giant metal columns jutted up above the beginnings of a town. They might be steam-pipes, and the poles visible beyond the row of trees at the field's edge might be football posts. Perhaps they weren't. At another time, it might be worth investigating. Now, it was too dangerous. He thought of the zombies on the interstate. Where had they come from? How had so many people become infected all in one place, or had they? Did the zombies attract one another? Perhaps they'd been at some camp, similar to Providence. He hoped not.

"Hey." It was Soanna.

"Don't you ever stay put when you're told?" he asked.

"No one said I had to stay in the truck," she said. "Besides, it's safe, isn't it?"

Helena had begun to follow the girl up the hill. Tom waved that it was okay.

"As safe as anywhere," he said. "Which isn't very safe at all. There really could be monsters hiding behind the trees. You need to understand that."

"If it's as safe as anywhere, then I'm as safe here as in the truck," she said with frustrating logic.

"You know what I mean," Tom said. "But I don't think you understand it yet. You will. Do you know anything about farming?"

"Of course. Is that a farm?" she asked. "What's it growing?"

"No idea." Nor did he know when the crop would be ready for harvest, or even if it was edible. "We can get fish from the sea, but in a few months we'll have to come to places like this and pick the food. There'll be no more grocery stores, no more cardboard packaging. No refined sugars and added salt. Salt, now how do we get that? From the sea, I suppose. One more chore to be added to the long list."

"Salt? I thought that was bad for you."

"You can't live without it. They used to use it as currency, did you know that? It's where the word salary is derived from. There's so much that will have to be done, and so much that we don't even realize." He could almost hear her brain trying to process what he'd said.

"So we have to come back here to pick this field when it's all grown?" she asked.

"No, probably not. It'll be too far for us, and it's too close to that town. Whoever's there will harvest it."

"I can't see anyone," she said.

Nor could he. There were no zombies, but at the same time, no one was standing guard over the field.

"Are we going there?" she asked. "To the town, I mean?"

"It's too close to those zombies on the interstate. No, we'll go to the coast. We'll stick to the plan. But as we get nearer, we should keep an eye out for fields and livestock. That's a thought. Maybe chickens or... or..." He trailed off. His ears had caught something. "Do you hear that?"

"What?" she asked.

"Shh! Listen." The sound seemed to be coming from everywhere at once, and it took a moment for him to understand what it was. "Helicopter. It's a helicopter." It was coming from the south and approaching fast. He saw it. A black speck, growing larger as it drew nearer.

"Is it the Army?" Soanna asked.

"No. That's a civilian model." Or he thought it was. There was something red on the tail-wing. He raised his arms, waving at the others by the fire truck. "Helicopter," he yelled, though surely they would have realized.

He turned back to watch it get closer. It was a civilian model. The tail wing was emblazoned with the logo of a Pittsburgh broadcaster. "Must be heading to the town." And coming from somewhere else. That meant that the town was in contact with somewhere. Perhaps it was worth going there. Perhaps... and then he realized that he was wrong. The helicopter wasn't heading to the town. The craft hovered over the field, and came to a sudden, thudding landing, side on to them, less than fifty yards away. The doors opened. He saw the figures inside. The guns. The uniforms.

"Run." He yelled at Soanna. "Run. Go. Back to the truck!" He grabbed her arm, pushing her down the incline, but he didn't follow.

In the back of the helicopter were three figures in military fatigues, all wearing headsets that obscured their faces. The rifles two of them carried were pointing at him. He stood his ground. He wouldn't draw in time. But they weren't firing, either. Not yet. He might be wrong. This might be help. It could be anyone. A figure jumped out of the helicopter, and ran, head bowed, until he was clear of the blades. Hope died as the figure took of his helmet. Tom saw the shock of blond hair above a familiar face, partially covered in a bandage.

"Powell," he hissed. He turned around. Helena and Kaitlin were halfway up the incline. "Powell!" This time he bellowed it. "Run! Go!"

Helena stopped, her face going pale as the meaning sunk in. She grabbed Kaitlin's arm, and Tom turned back to face Powell. The man was saying something, but the words were caught by the rotors. Powell motioned to the pilot. The rotors slowed and then stopped.

"Far better," Powell said. "How are you, Mr Clemens?"

"By the look of it, better than you," Tom said. "You get those wounds at the motel?"

There was a roar from the fire truck's engine.

"Sir, the others," one of the guards said.

"Leave them. We'll get them later," Powell said. "It's not as if they matter. They don't matter, do they, Mr Clemens?"

"I thought you were dead," Tom said.

Powell raised a hand to the bandage on his face. "It is remarkable what the human body can withstand. But I knew *you* were alive."

"How?" Tom asked, though he could guess the answer. Arrogant stupidity had blinded him to the obvious, but he wanted to keep Powell talking so the others could escape.

"What comes down must go up," Powell said. "We followed the data trail. Interfering with a satellite? That's a federal crime."

Tom nodded. The sound of the truck grew more distant. "So what, then? Aren't you going to shoot me?"

"Believe me, Mr Clemens. I would like nothing else," Powell said. "In fact, I would like a lot more. My masters, however, have decreed otherwise. I told you before there was someone who wanted you alive. He still does."

"Who?"

Powell smiled. "Come with us and find out. If you don't, I will kill you, and then hunt down your friends. A vehicle like that really isn't hard to track."

Tom eyed the two gun barrels. His choices were limited. He'd have to dive to the ground, roll down the hill, and hope he wasn't shot before he found cover. He'd have to fight back, and he didn't have the ammunition to do that for long. He might kill Powell, but he might not, and he probably wouldn't get the other two. If Powell was dead, they might leave and give up searching for him. They might not. If he went with them, he would meet Farley, and there might be an opportunity to kill the man, and perhaps destroy the rest of the cabal. That was what he'd wanted, to end the conspiracy for once and for all.

"Who gets to live forever?" He raised his hands and took a step toward the helicopter.

"Stop," Powell said. "I know you're armed. Slowly, drop your weapons."

Tom carefully extracted the 9mm and dropped it. He took another step.

"Wait. Search him," Powell said to one of the guards.

The man stepped behind Tom. Metal prongs bit into his side. There was a moment of white-cold pain, and then nothing but contradictory sensations.

Chapter 10 - An Old Friend
Location Unknown

By the time Tom regained his faculties he was in the helicopter. His hands were bound with plastic ties, and his pockets felt suspiciously lighter. The chopper hovered in the air as Powell gave orders through a headpiece. Then it swung around, heading south. Tom relaxed. Helena and the children were safe. Then he rid his mind of them, and focused instead on Powell, and the confrontation with Farley that he knew was about to come.

Powell opened his mouth, yelling something that was lost in the roar of the helicopter's rotors. Tom shook his head. Powell shrugged. There was another stinging jolt as he was stunned again. He slumped in his seat, head lolling on his chest. Keeping his eyes closed, he marshaled his strength.

The flight took longer than an hour, but less than four. He tried to recall what little he knew about helicopters, and their range. He knew the difference between a Huey and a Black Hawk, and that this was neither. A hundred miles, two, it didn't matter. They were taking him to Farley. Soon, it would all be over.

Finally, the helicopter began its descent. It wasn't the military base he'd expected, but an abandoned factory. Giant, rusting pipes disappeared into broken-windowed buildings out of which decaying chimneys jutted, smokeless, into the empty sky. Though there was an unrecognizable, faded logo on the tallest chimney, there were no signs or company names that might give a clue as to where the place was.

"Out!" Powell yelled.

Tom pushed himself out of the door, and onto a weed-covered helipad. There was at least three years' growth of moss on the ground, but a helipad meant the site had once been economically important. He scanned the horizon for signs of a town. Or the landing pad meant that it was somewhere so remote that the employees slept on site.

A barrel was shoved into his back, and he was pushed away from the helicopter. Wherever he was didn't matter; he wasn't going to escape.

Beyond the helipad was a parking lot containing three APCs, two police cruisers, a tanker, and a portable power plant – a giant generator hauled by a twelve-wheeled rig. It was the vehicles next to it that caught his eye. Two ancient four-wheel-drives, and three six-wheeled deuce-and-a-halfs. They were all painted green, not with a camouflage pattern, but in a cheap, dark-forest color. Set against the far more modern armored personnel carriers, they looked incongruous. There was something puzzling about the vehicles which were almost as old as him, something that nagged at a recent thread of memory.

"I said move!"

He staggered onto the asphalt. It was clear where they wanted him to go. Cables snaked from the power plant into a two-floor building that looked less decayed than the others. Two people came out of a set of double doors repaired with plyboard. Like Powell and his goons, they were dressed in military uniform, complete with rank and insignia. He doubted the ranks were real, but the rifles were. For each vehicle to have a driver, there had to be at least twelve people on site, not counting those who'd just arrived. Realistically, he should expect twice that number. However, there were no machine-gun nests or searchlights, no patrolling guards, or even snipers on the roof. He thought back to the few certainties he'd uncovered regarding the cabal. Though the leadership had sufficient influence to enlist official support, he'd always suspected there were fewer than a hundred and fifty members, and perhaps a lot less. It could be that they were all here.

He was shoved inside the building. There was no reception area, just a long corridor with doors leading off it. He couldn't tell what was inside, or whether they'd been offices or workshops. Though each door had a window, some were covered in board, the rest were coated in a thick layer of grime. Halfway down, and on either side of the corridor, were a set of closed fire doors. The only light came from irregularly positioned freestanding electric lamps.

"I like what you've done with the place," Tom said. "It's very homely. So where's Farley?"

Powell gave a short laugh completely absent of humor. "Secretary Farley? Oh dear. Put him in the hole. There is a lot we need to discuss, assuming you survive the night."

This wasn't how he'd imagined it. He'd assumed he'd be put in a room with Farley, that there would be a moment where the two of them were mere feet apart. He would attack, and that was as far as he'd thought. There was something sinister in Powell's words, a barely contained glee that could only have one meaning.

He counted the paces as he was prodded down the corridor. Not because he thought escape was likely, but to take his mind from the evil fate awaiting him. One of the guards opened the fire doors on the left. With the encouragement of a rifle barrel, he was pushed through. Outside a padlocked door halfway down the corridor were a table and chair, and a guard who looked like he'd been sleeping just minutes before.

"He's the fresh meat, is he?" the recently sleeping sentry asked. He grinned as he reached into his left pocket for a key. A look of puzzlement crept across his face when he didn't find it. The hands began a patting search of his uniform. There was an exasperated sigh from behind Tom. Any relief at discovering he had an incompetent jailor was tempered by the very sturdy fitments to which the padlock was attached. The key was found. The padlock unlocked.

"Gag him," one of the guards behind him said. "Don't want you to scream." Rough hands tied a foul rag over his mouth. His hands were still cuffed with the plastic ties, but they were in front not behind. Before he'd made up his mind to make his stand here and now, a gun was pushed against his temple.

"Enjoy," the jailer said. The door was opened, and Tom was shoved into the pitch-dark room.

Two stumbling steps from the doorway, the floor disappeared. He tumbled down the unseen staircase, coming to a halt in a heap on a landing halfway down. There was a cruel laugh from above before the door was closed, plunging the room into absolute darkness. Tom growled in anger and pain. The stench from the rag almost made him retch. He reached up and pulled it off. The smell wasn't coming solely from the gag. There was an earthy odor to the room, of damp, mold, and rank sweat.

Hands outstretched, he searched about until he found a railing and pulled himself up. Shuffling his feet, he mapped out the landing. It wasn't large, perhaps three feet square, at a point where the stairs bent at a right angle.

As the sharp pain from the fall resolved into a dull ache in his knees and shoulders, there was a sound from below as of a figure slowly straightening. Fear swept over Tom unlike anything he'd ever known. There, below him, invisible in the dark, were the undead. The soft crack of air in a knee joint sounded louder than thunder. The low exhalation of breath more violent than a tornado. If he was going to die, he'd go down fighting.

"Come on, then. You want to fight? Let's go."

There was a cough that turned into a brief laugh. "Fight?" The voice was male. "I'd rather not." Male and familiar.

Tom froze. "Who's there?" he asked.

"I could ask the same question, but I think I know the answer. They said they were going to bring a friend. I should have guessed it would be you."

"Max?" Tom asked, he couldn't believe it. He didn't want to believe it.

"Hello, Tom," President Grant Maxwell said.

Question after question flooded Tom's mind, but it was a statement of the obvious that battled its way to his lips. "You're alive," he said.

"Alive? Yes," Max said. "Though in very reduced circumstances."

"How? I mean, why? I mean, why didn't they kill you?"

"Because they have plans for me, Tom. They have plans for you too, I suspect."

Tom reached out, found the railing, and descended the stairs. He reached out until his hands found warm flesh. "Max!" He awkwardly gripped his friend's hands. "I'm sorry."

"Me, too," Max said. "The stairs are cleaner than the floor. Perhaps we should sit there." They sat down.

"How long have you been here?" Tom asked.

"That depends on the day. Did you see my speech? My address to the nation?"

"I did. It wasn't your best."

"It was a mistake. I should have cancelled it when the plane failed to arrive. I couldn't say what I wanted, so tried to come up with words that would unify the nation, would offer comfort and strengthen resolve. I don't think I managed it, but when that zombie cut it short, I was hustled from the podium and into the motorcade. It was only as we were driving away that I realized I didn't recognize the agents. I felt the jab of a needle, and woke up here. Wherever that is. Any ideas?"

"It might be Pennsylvania. It might not. It's an old industrial site in the middle of nowhere."

"Ah. So how did you end up here? How did they catch you?"

"I was using satellite images to find a safe route to the coast. They tracked my usage. It was Powell, the man with the white hair, who caught me. He was the guy who framed me for murder. He killed the journalist in my house back on the day of the inauguration. I almost killed him on the day of your address, but he was calling himself Herold back then."

"Shame you didn't manage it. But he told me his name was Spangler. I think that's what he said. We didn't have a long conversation. I suppose I don't know anything that they don't. I think he just wanted to meet me so he could say that he had. Spangler, Herold, and Powell? That's familiar, though I can't place why, and not that it matters now."

"Have they questioned you much?" Tom asked.

"They've barely asked me anything at all," Max said.

"What about Farley, have you seen him? Is he here?"

"Farley?" Max sounded surprised. "He's dead, Tom."

"He is?"

"Two days after the outbreak in New York."

"That's impossible," Tom said. "Then who's running the cabal?"

"You thought Farley was behind it? He wasn't. Two days after the outbreak, he went off the grid. His security detail lost track of him for two hours. He was found in his car. It had crashed."

"Maybe that's what they told you," Tom said, "but that doesn't mean it's true."

"He was still alive. They took him to the hospital. I saw him there. I was with him when he died, and he did die, Tom."

"I… I was sure it was him," Tom said. "I was certain he was the one behind all of this."

"You were wrong. A week after I asked him to be secretary of state, he came to me asking for the offer to be rescinded. He had cancer."

"You didn't say," Tom said.

"No. He didn't want anyone to know, and that was why I couldn't withdraw the appointment. Imagine what it would have looked like. Offering him the job was meant to shore up party unity. Rescinding it would have led to an outright civil war." Max gave a bitter laugh. "A poor choice of words. I told him that as long as his treatment wasn't affecting his work, then the job was his, but that if he felt he couldn't do it, he'd have to resign and say why."

"He *was* involved," Tom said. "I know it. He *was* part of the conspiracy. More than that, he was at its very center. It's why he was chosen as a candidate for the election."

"The manner of his death suggests he had a change of heart. He was on his way to meet with someone in the Russian embassy when his car crashed. We thought Russia was behind the outbreak before we discovered it was North Korea. I think he went to confirm they had no better idea of how it had begun than we had. Although, here and now, talking to you, the idea of North Korea being behind this is laughable. Under any other circumstances, I wouldn't have entertained the idea for a second."

"If Farley came to you after the election, then he can't have been part of this plot," Tom said. "I know that the cabal's plans were brought forward, and I thought it was because I was closing in on them. Perhaps it was because they were worried Farley would confess all he knew. Although, why not simply kill him?"

"Does it matter?" Max asked.

"Yes. When I learned General Carpenter was dead, I assumed Farley was working his way down the line of succession. If anything, his death confirms that's precisely what someone else is doing. What about the speaker, or the president pro tempore?"

"The speaker went missing," Max said. "I... I don't remember when. There's a lot I don't remember. I've had time to think over the last few days. It began on the day of the inauguration, which means they had it planned long in advance, perhaps even before the last ballot was cast. At some point after I'd taken the oath, and before I saw you, they drugged me. It made me... erratic. There's a lot I don't remember. Those memories I do have aren't clear, but cloudy, as if I were trying to peer into the depths of a murky pond. I don't know how that initial dose was administered, but I think the rest were in my toothpaste, or the soap, or something in the residence. When I moved down to the bunker, I came back to myself. Not completely, I'm still not what I was, and of course, now it's too late. I'll never see Claire, Jane, or Rick ever again. I'll never be able to take back what I did, what I said. I'll never be able to apologize to Claire, but I can apologize to you. I'm sorry, Tom."

"What for?"

"For not listening to you. You know what Claire said? She said she trusted you, and I should do the same. They showed me proof that you were behind the bombings on the day of the inauguration. She didn't believe it when I told her. I said... well, it doesn't matter now. Whether the words were unforgivable or not, there will be no opportunity for apology, only redemption."

"Not Farley, not the speaker, not General Carpenter, so who?" Tom asked. "Who else was there? What else can you remember?"

"Signing pieces of paper. I can remember maps in the situation room. Walking the corridors at night and... I think there were phone calls. At least, I remember talking into the phone I can't be sure there was anyone at the other end. After a night in the bunker, I became aware of how abnormal I felt. That's when I learned how close my country was to destruction. Contradictory orders had been given, apparently by me. Governors had been told to deploy the National Guard to protect the small towns while Homeland had been given control of local police units and told to deploy them around state capitals. The military was dispatched to the middle of nowhere, with orders to hold the high ground. I don't think they had any better idea of what that meant than I did. That was the point, I think. Enough orders were given that it appeared there was a national strategy, yet in truth it just delayed any real response to the crisis."

"Delayed it long enough for the country to tear itself apart," Tom said. "We could have stopped it in Manhattan. It could be over by now if the police hadn't been drafted out of the city, and if the military had been deployed."

"I know. You don't think I know? I have to live with that. I'm the president that destroyed the country, destroyed the world!"

"That's not what I meant," Tom said. "The military and police were removed so they could be kept safe and redeployed when you'd been replaced. That must have been the plan, but they've left it too late. I saw what it was like out there. Tens of thousands of refugees tearing towns apart in search of shelter from just as many zombies, and there were more of the living dead every day."

Max sighed. "And all my fault. That's not self-pity. It's a simple statement of fact. I could have stopped this. I didn't."

Tom wanted to say that it wasn't too late, that it wasn't over, but their dark prison was no place for wishes and platitudes. "You said something about a plane that didn't arrive," he said instead.

"What? Oh. Yes. It's a very strange thing, becoming president. Before the glow of victory has a chance to fade, you're taken aside and told some very hard truths about our nation, and about the world. Things that you suspected, things you even guessed at. Being shown the files, the photographs, the intelligence reports, it made suspicions a nightmare reality. There are so many contingencies. None for zombies, but plenty for things that are just as bad. Nuclear war is only the start. You know there's a plan for invading England? It was created during the Second World War and updated during the Soviet era. The word liberation features prominently, and it is listed as a training exercise, but it came in useful when I had to speak to their new prime minister. Did you hear that Quigley, their foreign secretary, has taken over?"

"I did. He's a vile man."

"Indeed. Farley told me about Archangel, about this plan to create a super-vaccine. I hadn't worked out what to do with the information. When I went down to the bunker, and removed myself from whatever poison they were doping me with, I discovered that Quigley was promising the people of Britain a dose of this vaccine during an evacuation of their cities. Apparently it works against the undead. Not in all cases, but in enough. I threatened him with those invasion plans unless he handed it over. I told him that if he didn't share it, I would take it. That was what was on the plane. One hundred thousand vials of vaccine. I was going to use the address to announce the vaccine's existence. I thought knowledge of it would hold the nation together long enough for order to be restored. The plane didn't arrive. I changed what I was going to say. Now I'm here."

"It wouldn't have mattered if it had arrived," Tom said. "That zombie was infected deliberately. Your speech was sabotaged."

"I know, and I also know it no longer matters. Not now. They plan that I should become a zombie and be filmed killing others. That's why I'm still alive. They want the manner of my death to add legitimacy to my successor, whoever that is. I imagine you have some similar role to play."

"That's truly evil," Tom said. "And I'm not going to sit here waiting for it." He pushed himself to his feet.

Max grabbed his arm and pulled him back down. "Wait. There's very little in this room, believe me, I've searched every inch of it." He stood. There was the sound of shuffling steps, then a clink of metal. Max sat down again. "Here, this is all I found. No, don't move your hands." A moment later, the plastic ties were cut. "It's a pipe," Max said. "I've been sharpening the edge against the wall, but I have no intention for this particular democracy to commit suicide, not when there's some fight still in me."

Tom grinned. "I'm not sure that's precisely what John Adams meant. There's twelve vehicles out front, so at least twelve people here, plus

Powell, his two guards, and the pilot of the helicopter. There's likely to be more."

"And we'll deal with them one at a time. They open the door to drop in food and water. When they do, there are always two of them, and they're cautious. At all other times, there's only one jailer on guard outside, I'm certain. Do you know what time it is?"

Out of reflex, Tom's hand went to his pocket to retrieve his phone. "No, but it was about an hour from sunset when they brought me in here."

"We'll wait six hours. I'll hammer at the door. You stand behind it. When it opens, we'll make our move. Take the jailor's weapons and see how far we get."

The rush of enthusiasm that came from having planned an attack began to wane. Time dragged and was hard to keep track of.

"I'd say it's been about an hour," Tom said.

"About that," Max agreed.

"I think *I* should apologize to *you*."

"I agree, but was there a particular transgression that came to your mind?" Max asked.

"I won't apologize for asking you to run for office, nor for helping you win the election," Tom said. "There might have been a time when we could have debated the relative merits of that, but after all that's happened, I'm certain I was in the right."

"So what do you want to apologize for?"

"I should have told you everything right from the beginning," Tom said.

"That might have been best," Max said. "If you had, I'm not sure I'd have believed you. When did you know?"

"About the depth of the conspiracy? I still don't know it all, but it was shortly before I asked you to stand for the presidency. I'd discovered hints of it before then, and that confirmed I'd been chasing these people, or running from them, for my entire adult life."

"Hm. So when you asked me to stand for the governorship, that wasn't connected?"

"Honestly, and if this isn't a time for honesty, when is? Honestly, no. I wanted you in the governor's mansion partly because I thought it would be useful, partly because I saw the race as a challenge, but mostly because I despised your opponent."

"Not because you thought I'd be a good leader?"

"Sorry,' Tom said. "You did a good job, though. And when I was looking for a presidential candidate, yours was the only name on the list."

"You won't be insulted if I say I wish it wasn't?"

Tom smiled. "Hey, it could be worse. Even if you count your address as the end of your presidency, you ruled the country for nearly nine hours longer than William Henry Harrison."

"So mine wasn't the shortest presidency in history, even if it might be the last. Another bittersweet victory. Were you really born in Britain?"

"I was. They told you that?" Tom asked.

"They showed me a very large file. The contents were not pleasant."

"Like what?"

"No, I won't say. Most of it will be false. Some might not be, and I don't want you to have to lie. I certainly don't want you to admit any of it is true. I will assume it was all a fabrication. And I'll accept your apology, but there's one thing. Claire, and the children. If you get out of here and I don't, go to Vermont. She took Rick and Jane there after I... Just go there, and if she's alive, tell her I'm sorry."

"Of course."

"I think it's time," Max said.

"Let me knock," Tom said. "They threw me down here expecting us to fight. I'll say you're dead."

"No. It's my duty to do that. You stand behind the door. Ready?"

"Here we stand," Tom said.

"No, Tom," Max said. "Here we fight."

Tom went up first, the metal bar gripped tightly in his right hand, his left feeling for the steps in front. He reached the door, extending his hand and moving his feet, searching out how much space he had. Before he'd finished, Max hammered on the door.

"He's dead," the president yelled. "He's dead."

"What?" the jailer called out.

"I said he's dead," Max said. "That's what you wanted, isn't it? I killed him. So what now? What next?"

"You killed him?" the jailer asked. There was a brief silence that stretched long enough for Tom to think they'd made a mistake. There was no reason for the guard to unlock the door. Max would be told to wait until morning, or—

There was the sound of a key in a lock, a metallic click as the padlock was removed, and another as the bolt was thrown back.

"Stand back!" the jailer barked. The door opened. The corridor was so brightly lit in comparison to the pitch-dark cell that Tom was nearly blinded. He swung the metal pipe at the guard's shadow. He missed the man's head, but the pipe crunched into his collarbone. The man screamed. Tom swung again, slamming the metal bar down on the man's skull. The screaming stopped.

"I've got his rifle, get his sidearm. Quick," Max said.

Blinking, trying to bring the shifting, pulsating shapes into focus, Tom pawed at the man's clothing until he found the belt, the holster, the pistol. He drew it. "Got it."

"Now!" Max ran out into the blinding light of the corridor. Tom followed, blinking in the harsh white light that surrounded them. It was too bright. Far too bright.

"Oh, well done," Powell called out. Max staggered to a halt. Tom did the same, trying to see the man. There were two walls of light, twenty feet from the door, on either side. The lights were dimmed. Behind the lamps, on both sides of the corridor, were five guards, all armed with assault rifles, which were pointing at him and Max. Powell stood, arms folded, to the left.

"Quite a show," Powell said. "Thoroughly entertaining, though I did hope you'd be a little more inventive."

"I guess you were right, Tom," Max said. "This where we stand." He raised the rifle. Tom spun around, not aiming, just pointing the pistol in the guards' direction. He pulled the trigger as Max pulled his. Nothing happened.

"Is there anything else you'd like to try?" Powell asked in that same self-satisfied simper. "As I say, it was an entertaining show, but as it's at an end, it's time for the next to begin."

"There are cameras in there?" Max asked, gesturing at the cell.

"Of course," Powell said.

"You let us kill that man," Tom said.

"Is he dead?" Powell asked. "Well, his blood is on your hands. The circumstances that put him into them were on his. Within our cause, dedication must be absolute. Now."

Something hit Tom in the chest. He vaguely registered the wires snaking back to the guard's weapon before the pain began.

When he came to, he was back in the cell. The dead guard was gone. So was Max. He could be absolutely certain because the lights were on. They didn't go out.

Chapter 11 - Questions
Time Unknown, Location Unknown

Tom sat on the bottom step, his eyes closed, his mind on the past. The lights hadn't been turned off since the ill-fated escape attempt. There was a blanket in the room, though the harsh lighting emitted so much heat that it was unnecessary. Following what Max had said, he'd ignored the half-empty bottle of water until thirst forced him to take a sip. Fear and exhaustion joined paranoia, making him certain the water was drugged, and that he shouldn't drink any more. Thirst crept up on him, a tidal force that couldn't be denied. He took another sip and regretted it immediately. The cycle continued until the bottle was empty. Other than his growing thirst, it was hard to tell how much time had passed. He wasn't hungry, so guessed it was less than a day, but he was tired of guesses. Assumptions, theories, and one plan after another had led him here. Plans were for the living, and his life was over. As he waited for the end, all he had for company were regrets.

As he was beginning to think they would let him die of thirst, the door opened. Powell stood framed in the doorway, almost as if he was posing.

"Mr Clemens," he said. "I'd like a word, if you please."

Seeing no advantage to rebellion, Tom pushed himself to his feet and climbed the stairs. Before he reached the doorway, Powell backed into the corridor.

The table and chair were gone. There were two guards. One wore a corporal's chevrons and carried an assault rifle. The other had sergeant's stripes and a stun-gun.

"Please place your hands behind your back," Powell said, again with that tone of mock civility.

"Where's Max?" Tom asked.

"Like yourself, he is a late addition to our drama," Powell said. "Both of you are desperately miscast, yet we must each play our part. Opening night approaches, and there's no one else to stand in front of the curtain."

There was a trace of the south in Powell's accent. Not much, but enough to suggest he'd been born there but raised somewhere else. Tom found himself smiling. Details like that were useless. Even if he were to escape, and somehow find out where the conspirator had been born, what good would it do?

"You're smiling," Powell said. "That's good. An audience always appreciates confidence."

Tom's hands were cuffed, and he was prodded along the corridor to a room beyond the fire doors. Twenty feet deep by thirty long, windows lined the exterior wall, but each was covered in thick black sheets. As in the corridor, light came from the freestanding electric lamps dotting the room. In the middle was a solitary wooden chair, facing the windows.

"Sit down," Powell said.

Tom did. His hands were cuffed to the chair's leg. Powell walked back out into the corridor and returned a moment later with a video camera already attached to a tripod. He positioned it in front of Tom.

"I've wanted to talk to you for some time, Mr Clemens," Powell said. "Of course, my interest is merely the curiosity of one professional with the work of another. My superiors, however, have some more pressing questions, and those must come first." He turned the camera on. "And the first regards your interest in Dr Ayers?"

Tom blinked. Of all the possible questions, he hadn't been expecting that one. "Who?"

Powell gave a jerk of his head. A fist slammed into Tom's side, doubling him forward.

"What aroused your interest in Dr Ayers?" Powell asked.

"Never heard of her," Tom spat.

Powell gave another jerk of his head. A fist punched into Tom's chest. It hurt, but he tried not to let it show.

"You really aren't as smart as you think you are, Mr Clemens," Powell said. "Perhaps there isn't that much I can learn from you. You've never heard of her? *Her?* How do you know the good doctor is a woman? Answer the question. Why were you interested in her?"

"Who said I was?"

"That won't do," Powell said.

This time the blow came before Tom could open his mouth. It hurt, but he'd been beaten before. He could take the pain, and he knew he'd have to. This was just a warm-up.

"You sound like you're from the south," Tom said. "Tennessee? No, it's further north. Virginia?"

A fist slammed into Tom's jaw.

"Not the face!" Powell snapped at the guard, and this time there was genuine fury in his voice.

Tom spat blood onto the floor. "Why not in the face?" he asked. "Why am I still alive?"

"Did Farley ever confess anything to you?" Powell asked.

"Farley's dead, isn't he?" Tom asked.

"Answer the question."

"Or what?" Tom asked. "You'll kill me?"

"There are worse things than death, Mr Clemens," Powell said. "And you are about to find out what they are."

"Well, get on with it, then. What are you waiting for?"

Powell smiled. "Tell us about Dr Ayers."

"Tell me about Farley."

Powell sighed and turned off the camera. "One hour," he said. "And remember what I said about the face."

The guards took it in turns. Left, then right, chest, stomach, legs. Tom told himself not to scream. The pain went on, growing, until he had to give it vent. He began singing the national anthem. He made it almost to the end of the first verse before one of the guards changed aim and punched him in the face.

"Not the face," the other one hissed. "You heard what he said."

Tom spat a gobbet of blood onto the floor and grinned. He sang more loudly. The beating didn't start again. Instead, he was taken back to his cell.

Time passed. The door opened. A bottle of water was thrown in. The door was closed. More time passed. He tried to keep track of how much, but it was impossible. The lights never went out. He couldn't even find where the camera was hidden. The door opened. A pouch of un-hydrated rations was dropped on the landing. The door closed. More time passed. Another bottle of water. Some time later, another pouch of food.

In total, six bottles of water and three packets of rations were dropped inside before the door opened, and a guard barked, "Outside." It wasn't Powell.

Stiffly, Tom pushed himself to his feet. The guard was the one with the sergeant's stripes. Tom didn't recognize the man standing behind him. He couldn't remember how many faces he'd seen. It no longer mattered.

"More questions, is it?" Tom asked.

"Out," the sergeant barked.

Again, his hands were cuffed, but he wasn't going to fight. Not yet. At best, he'd be able to take one of them with him, and that one was going to be Powell. He'd have to get through the coming torture, and this time he was sure it would be more thorough than an inexpert beating. Water boarding, stress positions, worse. He'd have to take it, and be ready when the chance came.

He was taken to the interrogation room and tied to the same chair. He couldn't quite say why, but something made him think that there were fewer people on site than before. He heard footsteps outside. The door was behind him, and he had to force down the impulse to turn to see who approached.

"This is him?" a woman asked.

"It is," a familiar voice said.

A chill shot down Tom's spine. He knew that second voice. He knew it well. The figure stepped around the chair, and Tom saw him properly.

"Hello, Tom," Charles Addison said.

Tom said nothing, just stared up at Max's chief of staff.

"Well?" Addison asked. "Don't you have something to say?"

"Life is full of myriad possibilities, yet none so strange as this," Tom replied.

Addison frowned. Tom forced his lips into a smile.

"Shouldn't we get on with it?" the woman asked.

"Yes. Of course," Addison said. "Why were you interested in Dr Ayers?"

"Why were you?" Tom replied.

"We don't have time for this," the woman said.

"No," Addison said. "We have time enough. Go on, Tom. You have questions, so ask them."

"Your presence gives me most of the answers I need," Tom said. "There's one thing I'd like to know. Who's in charge? Who are you working for? You're not in the line of succession, so you can't take the presidency."

"Actually, that's not true," Addison said. "Before he died, President Maxwell appointed me to his cabinet. It's all very official."

"You got him to sign something when he was drugged?" Tom asked. "That won't stand up. The Senate can't have approved it."

"Senate? Stand up?" Addison laughed. "In what court do you think it will be challenged? There is no Senate to ask for confirmation, let alone give it. Now, Dr Ayers. Why did you trek three hundred miles to see her after the outbreak?"

"I thought she might have answers," Tom said. The pieces were starting to slot into place. "Wait. Before he died? You've killed Max?"

"No, *you* killed the president, Tom. It was rather tragic, and the manner of his death was somewhat theatrical. I believe you were trying to make a statement of some kind. Knowing that your plan had failed, you took this final revenge on the cat's-paw you manipulated into office."

"He's dead?" Tom asked again.

"You should know," Addison said. "You killed him. That is what the history books will record."

"You think there will be history books?" Tom asked. "There won't."

"Enough," the woman said. "Why did you go to Ayers's home?"

"How did you know I went there?" Tom asked. "Satellites? Cameras? That has to be it. You were keeping watch on the property? Why? You'd already taken her."

"Just tell us, Tom," Addison said. "We asked her, and she has no idea why someone like you would want to speak to her."

Tom frowned. "You asked her why I went there? Why did you go? Wait." He laughed. "No. Tell me it isn't true." He laughed again.

The woman gave a frustrated growl. A fist slammed into Tom's side. The laugh turned to a coughing rasp.

"How can she help us, Tom?" Addison asked. "She doesn't seem to think she can. What does she know that will stop the outbreak?"

"You found the laptop," Tom said. "The one I left in my apartment. The one I used to look up her address. I didn't wipe the memory. That's why you went there. That's why you took Ayers. I was following you, but you were following me. Oh, come on, Charles, you have to laugh at that."

"But why did you go there?" Addison asked, desperation clear in his voice.

"Because I thought she might know how to stop it," Tom said. "I take it that she doesn't?"

"It's as I told you," the woman said. "He has nothing useful to say."

"So she doesn't know anything?" Tom asked. "No one does, do they? This thing that's been unleashed, you can't stop it. Whatever your plans were, they're in ruins. It's over. It's done. You betrayed Max for nothing. You betrayed your country. Your species. You destroyed us, Chuck. There won't be any history books. Not anymore."

Addison opened his mouth to reply, but left before saying anything. The woman followed. Tom tensed, waiting for the torture to start. It didn't. He was taken back to his cell.

He'd read somewhere that a beard grew at some fraction of an inch per day. He rubbed his chin's bristly growth, trying to remember what that number was, but his mind began to drift. Where had he read that? It was a magazine. Was it in a waiting room? A dentist's, perhaps. Or a barber's? He always enjoyed haircuts. Not the actual cutting of his hair, but there was something tranquil about sitting in a chair, unable to do anything except think for twenty minutes.

Now he had nothing to do but think, and he'd been in the cell for longer than twenty minutes. Twenty days? No. It couldn't have been that long. Perhaps five days. Probably less than seven. There were now twenty empty bottles of water, but he was sure that they were bringing them at uneven intervals. They'd delivered the unheated ration packs five times since Addison had questioned him. That was where he'd gotten the idea that it had been five days.

"Addison," he hissed.

With hindsight, it seemed almost obvious. Almost. The chief of staff could relay orders on behalf of the president. Legitimacy would be provided by whatever documents Addison persuaded the drugged Max to sign. There was nowhere to which Addison didn't have access. However, had the outbreak not occurred, his association with Max would have tainted any chance Addison had of seizing power. There had to be someone else involved, someone far higher up the chain of succession than an emergency cabinet appointment. Similarly, if Farley had decided to confess all to Max, then he would have warned the president about Addison. Unless Farley didn't know. Addison had to be a recent recruit to the conspiracy, and one that Farley wasn't aware of. Again, that confirmed there was someone else, someone high up. Or more than one.

What Powell had said came back to him. His talk of parts and plays had been more than a verbose brag. It contained the key. The pieces fell into place, and he understood the events as they'd happened, and what they meant, and how they no longer mattered. The cabal had splintered. Addison *was* a recent recruit to the cabal, but was using the chaotic nightmare to seize power for himself. Hadn't Max said the speaker of the house had gone missing? Farley had been murdered. Addison and Powell had killed the other members of the cabal. The tenuous legality of an emergency cabinet appointment wouldn't stand up under any normal circumstances, but under these, with a fragmented nation, they might. There had to be more to it, something else he was missing, but it didn't matter. The crucial piece of information was that Addison was doing what Tom had wanted. He was destroying the cabal.

A smile spread across his face. Addison was here. He wasn't in a bunker directing the military that he'd deployed out of harm's way. Addison was grasping at straws, seeking an end to the undead, and had wasted his few resources in pursuing Ayers and Tom. The coup had failed. Perhaps the generals and admirals had already disregarded his cabinet appointment. Perhaps the Secretary of Agriculture had taken the oath on the deck of an aircraft carrier. Perhaps a real relief effort was now under way. Perhaps. It was a pleasing fantasy that, even now, Special Forces were hunting Addison and Powell. A strike force might by winging their way to this very spot. At any moment the door would be broken down and... and, no. It might just as easily be a missile, but was more likely to be nothing. He was being kept alive for a purpose, and it wasn't so that he could be rescued and turn witness against the cabal. There was some part of the puzzle he'd missed. Something he'd overlooked, something that gave Addison hope that his schemes were not yet ash.

Hope? What hope was there? The world was in ruins. Addison was clinging onto a fantasy of power no more realistic than Tom's fantasy of rescue.

The door opened, a bottle of water was thrown in. Tom watched it bounce down the stairs, coming to rest on the landing.

The memory of when he'd first met Addison came back to him. It had been in Vermont, in the house Claire had inherited from her father, the day after he'd asked Max to run for the presidency. Claire had been the one who needed persuading. She'd had to put her career on hold while Max was in the governor's mansion. She was a doctor of archaeology, and Max's entry into politics had added a political subtext to any dig on which she went. Instead, she'd taught, written, and raised their young children on the understanding that when his term as governor finished, so would his political career. Tom still was unsure precisely what he'd said that had changed her mind. It was Claire who suggested they ask General Carpenter to join the campaign as an advisor on the military. Max had proposed Addison.

No, Addison couldn't have been involved in the cabal before then. He would have had no worth to them. Perhaps he was wrong. He'd been wrong about Addison's character. He'd not liked the man, but then, there were few people whose company he did enjoy. Addison was competent, and Max had trusted him. It was for that reason Tom hadn't investigated the man's background more thoroughly.

Who was the woman who'd been with Addison? He hadn't seen her face and didn't recognize the voice. He'd never know. He found he was smiling again. The cabal had fractured, and Addison had no idea how to stop the zombies. That was his ray of comfort, that the living dead tearing the nation apart would doom the conspiracy. It would doom him, too. He would die, but not in the cell. They were keeping him alive for some evil purpose, but whatever it was, it lay outside. That was when he would act. He'd kill Addison. That would be his revenge.

Revenge. It had consumed his life, and the thought of it brought forth an image of his parents. The memory was from six months before they died. His father had arrived home unexpectedly, a Chinese takeaway in his hands. His arrival had defused the fight brewing between Tom and his mother. They'd sat at the kitchen table while his father told stories about driving a delivery truck through Europe. The stories were lies. His father hadn't been in Europe, and he wasn't a long-haul trucker. He was a government agent. An occasional assassin and frequent thief who did jobs too unglamorous for spies, too low-reward for mercenaries.

Tom hadn't found that out until much later, and that particular truth had set him on the path that led him here. The stories his father had told were a lie, but that didn't mar the memory. It was one of the few happy ones he had, and so he turned his mind away from the conspirators, and to it. He let the image of his father, his mother, and his infant brother fill his mind.

The door opened. Another bottle of water was thrown in. Tom ignored it.

Chapter 12 - Confessions
March 12th, Location Unknown

The door opened.

"It's time, Tom," Addison said.

"You're on guard duty now?" Tom asked. "Are your troops deserting you?"

"Don't make this harder than it needs to be," Addison said.

Tom pushed himself to his feet and limped up the stairs, playing up how frail he felt. It wasn't much of an act. "What day is it?" he asked as he neared the top.

Addison took a step back before he answered. "March twelfth."

Tom nodded, but found he had no interest in the answer. The date was unimportant. There were three guards in the corridor. All had weapons drawn. It was only Addison whose hands were free. Tom held out his arms, wrists together.

"No, Tom, there's no need to tie you," Addison said.

"There isn't? Then why don't you shoot me here?" he asked.

"We're not going to kill you, Tom," Addison said.

Tom didn't believe him.

"Take him. Get him cleaned up," Addison said.

"That way," the guard with the corporal's stripes said. He gestured down the corridor, in a direction opposite to the room in which Tom had been questioned. The hallway was long and ominously unlit, save for a shadow of light from an open door at the far end. No, he didn't believe Addison for one second. He cleared his mind, preparing himself. It was impossible to know when the moment would come, but when it did, he would be ready.

The room had been emptied. Heavy curtains covered boarded-up windows. Was that to stop the undead from seeing the lights from inside? Or to stop people? Or to stop satellite surveillance? Unless he was going to break the glass, it didn't matter. In the middle of the room was a table.

On it was a pile of clothes. Next to it was a bucket. On the table, next to the clothes, was a bar of soap.

"Wash, and change your clothes," the sergeant said.

Tom turned around. "Seriously?"

"Wash. Change. It's not complicated," the man said. His rifle was held across his chest, but a private had his pointing at Tom's head. The corporal held the stun-gun, aimed at Tom's chest. Addison hadn't followed them. Tom wondered why.

Waiting for the trick, he stripped off his dirt-encrusted rags. He took his time. Three guards was too many. He might manage two. One would be better. He threw water and soap on his body, getting as much on the floor as on himself. Any hope they might step nearer to hurry him along, slip on the suds, and present him with his opportunity didn't pan out. The guards stood in the door, seemingly disinterested.

The clothes were a suit and white shirt. They weren't his, and weren't a great fit, but it gave him the shape of what was going to happen next.

"Don't I get a tie?" he asked.

There was no answer from his guards.

"What about shoes? No?" He put his boots back on and pulled on the jacket. "What now?"

"Wait," the sergeant said.

Tom sat on the edge of the desk. "Which one of you killed the president?" he asked. There was no answer, nor even any reaction from the three men. "You know this is folly," he said. "The world's tearing itself apart, and you're trying to build a castle on quicksand. Addison just wants power, you know that, right?"

No answer.

"He's killed everyone else between him and the top. All the other members of the cabal. He's killed politicians and journalists, scientists, and anyone else who witnessed what he's done. He'll kill you, too." Nothing. "But of course, you know that, don't you?" There was a slight flicker as the corporal glanced at the sergeant. "Yes, of course you do. Addison didn't kill them himself. It was you. You're the assassins, aren't you? Did

122

you plant the bomb on Air Force Two? Did you kill the speaker? Did you kill Farley?"

"Shut up!" the corporal hissed, raising the stun-gun. Before he could fire, the sergeant grabbed the barrel, pushing it up to point at the ceiling.

"Look at the water, you fool," the sergeant said. "He wants you to fire." The room was sloped. The water was slowly tricking around the feet of the guards.

"So you killed them. How?" Tom asked. "It's not as if I'll be able to tell anyone."

"You want to know?" the sergeant asked. He took a step forward. Another. "All right." He moved lightning fast, slamming the butt of the rifle into Tom's stomach. Tom doubled over.

"They need your face and mouth," the sergeant said. "No one said anything about the rest of you." He drew a long knife from his belt. "You don't need your fingers. You don't need your legs. If I were you, I'd shut up."

Tom picked himself up, made a show of brushing an imaginary speck off the suit, and perched again on the edge of the desk. He was revising his plan of attack.

It was two hours before Addison returned.

"Is it done?" the sergeant asked.

"Everything's in place," Addison said. "The message has been sent. There is no turning back. In a few hours, it will be over." There was something about the tone. Now that Tom was listening for it, he heard the slight edge of deference in Addison's voice. The guards didn't work for him. Presumably they worked for Powell. Tom found himself smiling again. He could guess who, after himself, would be the next person for these people to kill. Addison wasn't long for this world. He took comfort in that.

"Good," the sergeant said.

"Bring him," Addison said.

"Where's Powell?" Tom asked. "I hoped I'd get a chance to say goodbye to him. Or is he already dead?"

123

Addison turned around and walked down the corridor, but Tom caught the look between the corporal and the sergeant. It wasn't much, but it was something.

He was directed out of that room, and toward the one in which he'd been so briefly interrogated. The chair was gone. In front of the heavy black curtains were a wooden desk and an office chair, with the camera facing them.

"There is a script on the desk," Addison said. "You are going to sit at the desk and read the script into the camera."

Tom walked over to the desk. The chair would be too heavy to throw. "Why didn't you kill me?"

"We might, Tom," Addison said. "When the time is right. For now you should glory in the wonder of being alive."

"You've been spending too much time with Powell," Tom said. "You're starting to sound like him. Where is he? Or have you already killed him?"

"Still trying to sow division?" Addison said. "Read the script, Tom. Learn your lines."

There was nothing else on the desk. More to buy time, he picked up the sheet of paper, and scanned it. "I'm accepting responsibility for the bombings last month."

"You are the chief suspect," Addison said. "The evidence has already been gathered. Future generations will need a villain. Who better than you?"

"You want me to say I created the virus?"

"No," Addison said. "You *hired* the scientist who did."

"Ah, yes. You mean Ayers?"

"That is a fortuitous piece of luck," Addison said. "We won't name her immediately, of course. The hunt for her will be a useful distraction as we rebuild."

"Rebuild?" Tom laughed. "And it says I killed Max and General Carpenter, and others in the line of succession. You don't want me to name them? No, wait, let me guess, you're not sure that they're all dead. That's it, isn't it? You don't want me claiming responsibility for the death of someone who might be alive." That small flame of hope flickered back into life. Not for him, but that there still might be some group who could organize a recovery. There might still be a chance for people like Helena, Kaitlin, and the children.

"You have the script. You'll say what's on it," Addison said. The nervousness was clear in his voice now. Tom decided to amplify it.

"Max was your friend," he said. "You've known him since high school. How could you do this to him?"

"Politicians don't have friends, just favors they haven't called in." It was another uncharacteristic line, something rehearsed.

"How long have you planned this?" Tom asked. "Since Max won in November, right? You're the reason the plans were brought forward, or to be more accurate, you're the one who brought them forward. You knew that when Max went down his chief of staff would go down with him. They might have offered you power, but you knew that you would die. So you acted first. You came up with your own plan. That's why I wasn't killed. You wanted me alive because someone close to Max has to be blamed. If it's not you, then it had to be me. That's it, isn't it?"

Addison sighed. "Answers only lead to more questions. Politics is a play acted out on the world stage. We are but players doing our part. Yours is to accept responsibility. Do you deny you have none?"

"So it should be you standing here, making this confession?" Tom put the script down. "And if I don't want to say any of this?"

Addison smiled, as if he'd been waiting for those very words. "I said that this is being enacted on a world stage, Tom. Is there no one, anywhere in the world, for whom you would not sacrifice yourself? Now. Next month. Next year. You see, that was always your problem. You never took the long-term view. Even as we speak, the crisis is coming to a head. In a few short hours, our enemies will be destroyed. The military, currently deployed to stand guard over remote rail and road links, will begin the battle for our towns and cities. To retake the nation will require sacrifice. To ensure that it is made willingly, the people will need a purpose. What better one is there than hunting the man who destroyed the world? When the dust has settled, when these creatures have died, their bodies burned, hatred of you will unite us. It truly is a higher calling, Tom."

"I'd say you're insane, but you're not," Tom said. "You're just desperate. Your plans have fallen apart. None of that will come to pass."

"Read the script, and you will live, for now. If you do not, then the only person on this planet you care about will die."

They would kill him anyway, that was obvious. There were too many in the room for him to make his move. He should have struck earlier. Now, he might have left it too late. He picked up the script again. "You'll release all of this gradually?" he asked, thinking furiously, trying to spot the escape route he'd missed, the angle he'd overlooked.

"Precisely," Addison said. "A few million are dead. A few million more Americans will die in the days to come, but the world will belong to the survivors. There will be no foe. America will rise, higher and further than before. We shall be a beacon in the wilderness. The beginning of a new history. Read the script. We both know you will. Your protest has been noted, but you have no choice."

Tom let his shoulders slump. "Do you have a pen?"

"What?"

"I'd like to make a few changes."

"You'll read it as it is."

"Look, Chuck, I get how you want this to play out. You want to keep me alive just long enough for my death to bring a nation together. You've not seen what I have. The country is tearing itself apart. I don't think it can be saved, but this twisted ruse of yours might actually work. You won't be the one to lead the country, even if you won't accept it, but the people will need a villain, so let it be me. But it needs to be done properly. This?" He waved the piece of paper. "No one will believe it. Let me make a few changes."

"Like what?"

"Like saying I made two unsuccessful attempts on Max's life before I killed him," Tom said.

"Why?"

"Because you don't want to create any conspiracy theories that he was in league with me. You want him to be an unwitting dupe. The unwilling pawn that had kingship thrust upon him. What you've written will give rise to doubt, which will lead to insurrection and war. That will prevent a crop being planted, and starvation will bring an end to civilization before the year is out."

"Here." Addison pulled a ballpoint pen from his pocket and threw it to Tom. "You understand that it's a recording. It's not going out live. Go too far off script, and we'll start again."

Tom shrugged. "I'll be dead. I don't care what people think of me. I do care that there are people left to think something." He made a few random notes on the piece of paper. The pen wasn't a great weapon. He'd only get one shot, one thrust at Addison's throat.

"And here," he began, gesturing at the paper, hoping Addison would take another step nearer, but before he could continue the door opened. A man with a beard too scraggly for the uniform came in.

"What?" Addison asked.

The bearded man held out a handset. "You have to take this."

Addison took the receiver and held it up to his ear. "What?" he exclaimed. He stepped out into the corridor.

"So," Tom said to the guards that remained. "What do you think the odds are that he'll kill you before you have a chance to kill him?"

They didn't reply. One was watching him, the other two were glancing at the door, just as curious as he was as to who that call was from, and what Addison was being told.

"So who are you, really?" Tom asked. "You're not military. Mercenaries, is that it?" They didn't give a response. "It's a funny thing, truth. It always has a way of getting out. The more elaborate the lies, the more easily they fall apart."

He was talking to himself. He looked at the pen. It wasn't mightier than the sword, and certainly not the assault rifle. The energy that had been driving him a moment before had gone. It was over. He wasn't going to read the script, and so they would shoot him and fabricate some other story. It hardly mattered. He'd tried to save the world. He'd failed, and done it in a spectacular fashion, but at least he'd tried.

Addison came back in. "Change of plans. Harris, start the chopper. No, wait, we can't fly. Those APCs, are they shielded?"

"You mean it's happened?" the sergeant asked. "I thought you said it wouldn't. That it couldn't."

"Well, it has. The APCs, they're meant to be shielded. Can we use them?"

"No, that's why we've got the old trucks," the sergeant said.

"Then we take those, and leave now," Addison said.

"Should have done that this morning," the sergeant said. There was no trace of respect in his voice. "What about the prisoner?"

"Bring him," Addison said.

Tom slid his hand, still holding the pen, into his pocket. Wish for a miracle, and it might just happen. He forced his face into a scowl to hide his utter jubilation at the unexpected reprieve.

Chapter 13 - Fire, Returned
Location Unknown

His hands were cuffed behind him with plastic ties. It was done with such haste that they weren't tightly bound. Given time, he thought he could work them loose. As he was hustled from the room, he realized it wasn't because the guard aimed to help him escape, but that the soldiers wanted to leave the facility as quickly as possible. Addison had asked the sergeant if the vehicles were shielded. Taken with all else they'd said, the puzzle began to rearrange itself so the pieces formed a new, more terrible picture.

Two other guards ran past them. "Are we going to the base?" one called.

"No. The mine," the sergeant replied.

Tom was shoved outside, toward the green-painted vehicles. Two of the police cruisers were missing, but there wasn't time to see anything more before he was pushed inside a battered four-by-four. The interior had been refitted, but that couldn't disguise that it had been built in the 1970s. In fact, the dashboard looked as if it had been replaced with controls that were a lot older.

"Retrofitted against an EMP, right?" he asked. "This is Prometheus. The Russians and Chinese are finishing what the zombies began." That was the apocalyptic nightmare he'd been trying to thwart before the outbreak, and which he'd almost forgotten when the dead began attacking the living. "That's it, isn't it?"

"Shut up," the corporal said.

The sergeant was by the door. "Hell if I'll wait. In!" he bellowed at the third guard. The man got in the driver's seat, the sergeant in the passenger side of the cab. "Go!"

"We were meant to—" the driver began.

"Let him burn," the sergeant interrupted, "because I'm damned if I'm going to burn with him."

"You said we're going to a mine? You think there's any that'll be deep enough?" Tom asked.

The corporal slammed his rifle into Tom's face. He rocked back in his seat, forcing the pain down, using the motion to try to free his hands. There wasn't enough give. A hood was thrust over his head. It didn't matter. He let his head loll forward, pretending he was insensible, as he worked on the plastic cuffs.

The vehicle bounced along an uneven surface, picking up speed, lurching left, then right. Were those turns? The vehicle hit something, and bounced up and down. Was that a pothole? Were they even on a road? Or had they collided with one of the undead?

"After today," the corporal said, "this is it. It's gone on long enough."

"You know what the boss said," the sergeant replied.

"I don't care. This isn't what we were paid for."

"Fine, if we survive the next hour, you can do what you like," the sergeant said. "But you've got to tell— Watch out! Zombie!"

The truck swerved, but not enough. There was a jarring jolt as something hit the front. As the corporal swore, Tom shifted his leg, moving his hands to where he could just, *just* reach the pen. With the next lurching bounce, he pulled it from his pocket. Gripping the pen awkwardly between fingers and palm, he stretched his wrists so the plastic ties were taut. Stabbing the pen into his wrist as often as into the plastic, he worked at the cuffs.

The vehicle took a steep turn, and he shifted his feet, bracing them on the floor. There wouldn't be time to take the hood off. He'd have to dive sideways, wrestle the rifle from the guard, and fire blindly at the driver. If he survived the crash, he'd... he'd worry about that if he did.

"How long?" the corporal asked.

"Twenty minutes," the driver said.

"I meant *until*," the corporal said.

The vehicle rocked. Tom pulled, and the plastic snapped. His hands were free. He took a breath, waiting for the next jolt.

"We've got time," the sergeant said. "Plenty of time. Plenty of—"

Tom was thrown forward. Everything went white. The truck slewed to the left and slammed to a halt. Someone screamed. It wasn't Tom. He pulled off the hood, shaking his head to try to get rid of the ringing in his ears. The corporal's head lolled forward, blood dripping from a savage gash on his temple. Tom grabbed the man's rifle, aiming it at the truck's cab. The driver was moaning. The sergeant was unconscious. Tom put his shoulder to the door, pushed it open, and fell outside. He staggered to his feet and froze. A mushroom cloud squatted over the land, not nearly far enough away.

Part of him had known that this was going to happen. That this was why they had wanted these ancient vehicles that had no circuitry for an EMP to fry. The sight still cut him to the quick. A bomb had been dropped on America. But how far away? Ten miles? Twenty miles? Thirty? He couldn't tell. He couldn't think.

His mind stayed blank until the sound of an engine drowned out the now-hoarse screaming from the guard. The approaching vehicle was getting nearer, though it was currently hidden by the slope of the rutted track.

He turned away from the cloud, looking at the truck, the track, and tried to process what he had to do. Get away. It was that simple. The bomb had fallen too far away for the blast to kill him, but the radiation might. The shockwave had caused the crash. Either that or it had been caused by the flash, though the bomb had fallen behind, and was too far away to cause anything other than very temporary sight loss.

The truck's door opened. The driver had a hand against his head, but either his concussion was clearing or his sight was returning. His hand dropped to his belt. Tom raised the rifle and fired a three-shot burst, cutting the man down. The engine noise was getting nearer. He needed to get away, and escape the radiation. He wouldn't do it on foot, or in this truck. Smoke and steam billowed from the engine. He was on a track, not a road, that was barely ten feet wide. The truck had crashed into a thicket of trees on the left-hand side. He ducked down, moving behind the thicket, waiting for the vehicle to get nearer. Nearer. The truck came into view. It stopped the moment that the driver saw the crashed vehicle. Tom judged the distance as close to thirty yards. He could make out the driver and one passenger, but there wasn't time to waste confirming whether there was anyone else on board. There wasn't time for anything, not anymore. He raised the rifle. The passenger door opened. A uniformed guard stepped out, weapon raised. Tom aimed.

The ground shook. He was thrown from his feet. His first thought was shockwave. His second, that it was another bomb. His third was attack. He picked himself up and ran toward the second truck. He fired from the hip, aiming at the guard on the ground. One burst. Another. A third. The man was still. The driver's door was opening. The man stumbled onto the track, a pistol in his hand. Tom shifted his aim, cutting him down. Not bothering to check they were dead, he jumped into the truck. He tried the ignition. For a moment he thought it wouldn't start. It did. He slammed a foot on the gas. The truck jerked forward, butting into the crashed vehicle. Metal screeched as it was pushed aside. With the left-hand wheels on the muddy slope, he drove past the stalled vehicle, and onto the clear track. He didn't ease off the gas until the crash was no longer in sight. When the road curved, the mushroom cloud was still visible.

"Think. Think. Think."

But saying it didn't help. Mushroom cloud, fallout, radiation, blast radius, flash, the words lined up in his brain, but without meaning.

"Two shockwaves. Two." So there had been two bombs. He looked for a second cloud, but couldn't see one, and now that first was lost from view. Without it filling the rearview mirror, his mind began to clear. Maybe the second time the ground shook wasn't due to a shockwave but an earthquake caused by the first detonation. Or it was conventional explosives. Or it could have been a missile taking off from an underground silo. Or—

"No. Think. What do you know?"

That he'd seen a mushroom cloud. He'd felt the shockwave. There had been a flash.

"And what does that mean?" He knew, in theory, a one-megaton bomb could cause temporary flash blindness for up to thirteen miles. Had it even been a flash? Had the driver been blinded, or had his hand been

132

raised to his head due to a concussion or something else? He had no idea. Certainly the two who'd been in the vehicle he was now driving had been able to see. Did that mean it was more than thirteen miles away? Now that he tried to remember, he couldn't recall whether it was thirteen miles or thirty. Of course, as he didn't know the size of the warhead, it didn't matter. Of course it didn't. If you could see the mushroom cloud, you were far too close.

He glanced in the mirror again, a reflexive instinct to see if the cloud was still there. What he saw was worse. One of the deuce-and-a-halfs was on his tail. Barely a hundred feet behind, it was closing fast. He pushed the gas pedal down until it touched the floor, and almost lost control as the track abruptly kinked hard left, then just as hard right. By the time he'd regained control, the six-wheeler was twenty feet closer. He could see the outline of a driver and passenger.

The track had to lead somewhere. Of course it did. It led to wherever the guards had been taking him. The place to which they were going that would be secure from the fallout. They'd said something about a mine. It could be around the next bend. He had to get off the track, onto a road, and far upwind of the irradiated particles drawn up into that malignant cloud. That was easy to say, and impossible to do. Trees surrounded him on each side. The six-wheeler was closing.

He spared a glance around the cab. There was a bag in the foot well. Waiting for the next relatively straight section of track, he grabbed it. He had to wait another minute before he could check the contents. There was a chrome-plated .45, a few spare magazines, a book and... and he glanced back at the track just in time to avoid a tree stump.

"Personal possessions." That's what the bag contained. No grenades, no explosives, nothing that might rid him of his pursuers.

Perhaps they weren't pursing him. Perhaps they were just trying to get away as fast as he. That hope lasted until they reached another straight section of track. With the six-wheeler only sixty feet behind, the passenger pushed a rifle through the window and opened fire. Tom didn't hear the sound of an impact, but it told him they weren't going to give up.

"All right, so think. What do you know? Fallout. Got to get away from it. But what goes up doesn't come down immediately." He had time. Not long, but he was in a vehicle that was easily managing forty-five miles an hour on rough terrain. Assuming that he wasn't driving straight into the blast-area of another bomb. No, he couldn't think like that. He was alive. If he wanted to stay that way, he had to deal with his pursuers.

He slammed his foot on the gas pedal, almost losing control as the vehicle took a steep turn. The moment the six-wheeler was out of sight, he stamped on the brakes. Pocketing the .45 and grabbing the rifle, he was out of the vehicle barely before it had stopped. Leaving the driver's door open, he ran around to the passenger side. He'd chosen the spot poorly. There was little cover, and no time to find anything more concealing than a rhododendron.

The six-wheeler rounded the curve. The driver braked, but not in time. The vehicle crunched into the back of Tom's truck. He winced, praying that it was still drivable as he took aim. The driver jumped out, a rifle raised, aiming toward the woodland on the driver's side of the vehicle. More slowly, the passenger got out. Tom breathed out and fired. One burst at the driver, and the man flew backward. Tom shifted aim; the passenger had dived to the ground. Tom fired, emptying the rifle into the man.

A third person jumped out from the cab on the driver's side. Addison, an automatic rifle in his hands. Tom's finger curled around the trigger, but the magazine was empty. Addison fired. Bullets smacked into the ground a few feet in front of Tom. He rolled into the sparse undergrowth as leaves and bark rained down upon him. He grabbed the .45 from his pocket, and crawled through mud and dirt for a dozen feet. He stopped. There wasn't time for subterfuge and misdirection. This had to end.

With a roar, he pushed himself to his feet and charged. Addison was half in, half out of the vehicle, reaching for something inside. Tom fired. One of his bullets hit the man in the thigh. Addison screamed, fell to his knees, clutching his leg. Tom slowed his run to a walk and stopped five feet from the man. He glanced around. The two guards were dead. No one else appeared from the truck.

"Tom. Please," Addison said. "We have to get away."

Tom raised the gun.

"Please, Tom. It doesn't have to end like this. I can tell you everything. I can tell you how this all began, who was really behind the outbreak."

Tom backed away a step, his eyes darting between Addison and the back of the truck, until he reached the rear. He looked inside. It was empty.

"Who?" he called to Addison. "Who was behind it?"

Addison had curled up, almost into a ball. "I'll tell you, Tom. I'll tell you."

"Who?" Tom yelled, even though he knew the man was talking just to stay alive.

Addison straightened. Tom saw the gun in his hand. He fired. The first bullet took the man in the arm, the second in the chest, the third in the head. Addison collapsed in an inelegant heap.

"I can truly say that the world is better off with you dead," Tom murmured. A wave of regret washed over him, mingling with the adrenaline coursing through his veins. He leaned against the vehicle and heaved.

"Escape. You have to get out of here," he told himself. Pausing only to grab the rifle from the dead guard and take the ammunition from his webbing, he ran back to the truck. It started, though with a rattle. He drove away.

Chapter 14 - Outrunning Death
Location Unknown

He had to get away. The speedometer hit twenty. Thirty. He had to get away. The truck bounced over ruts, slewed through puddles, and churned up mud. Forty. Fifty. He had no destination in mind, just a need to outrun the lethal particles that, even now, were settling back to ground around the impact site. Fifty-five miles an hour, and the track widened, the trees thinned. He could see the edge of a pasture ahead, and beyond it the silent chimneys of something industrial. Was it the place where he'd been held prisoner? No. There were twelve stacks clustered in two groups, each with red and blue stripes painted near the top. Sixty, but no speed could be fast enough. Sixty-five. The wheels hit mud. The vehicle spun, tipped, and he thought it was going to roll. It didn't, but he eased off on the gas.

Addison. He should have searched his corpse. There might have been a clue as to the location of the mine. Perhaps an explanation as to how the outbreak began. He doubted that. The man knew nothing. What Tom really wanted was an explanation as to why Addison, a man he'd thought of as brusque but decent, opinionated but well-meaning, arrogant but dutiful, had turned on his friend and his nation.

"You're not going to find it. Not now, not ever. Some questions don't get answered." But as he said the words, he realized the truth lay in the man's actions. It was power, pure and simple. The same force that had driven Farley until fear of imminent death had made him recant. No more explanation than that was needed. And he realized how true that was. A smile formed on his lips. It wasn't an expression of joy, but of satisfaction. The cabal was dead. The conspiracy was destroyed. From the moment Farley had washed his hands of it, they'd acted in desperation and haste. Addison had been recruited to take the blame. When he'd realized that he was destined to be the fall guy, he'd hatched his own plans. It was over.

"Addison's dead." He hunched over the wheel, focusing on the track, turning his head this way and that as he tried to dispel the image of the man's corpse. The conspiracy was far from the most important thing in his world. The shockwave that had knocked him from his feet hadn't accompanied a flash, and he'd seen no other mushroom cloud. Perhaps it was an earthquake, or a secondary explosion, or the result of conventional ordnance.

"Or it could have been an asteroid. You don't know. You can't guess." The real question, then, was what the target was. The facility where he'd been held captive? He wasn't sure. That mushroom cloud might have been squatting over it. Without knowing how fast they'd been driving, he couldn't be sure. He couldn't even be sure how long it was after they'd left the prison before the bomb fell. What other target could there be? And then, that second explosion could have been the mine being destroyed. It had to be. His smile grew, but only until he remembered that Max was dead, and though the cabal hadn't won, the mushroom cloud meant the whole world had lost.

A deer ran across the track. Blood ran down its flanks from an arrow protruding out of its haunch. He swerved and stopped, watching it bound away into the trees. An arrow meant a hunter. He opened the door.

"Hello!" he called. Someone was in the woods. Someone trying to fill the pot for a desperate family.

"Hello!" he called again. There was no answer. He wanted to search for them, but knew he couldn't. There wasn't time. "No. No time for sorrow. No time for regret."

Yet it took a real effort to drive away. He kept his eyes open, hoping against hope he might see a figure run out onto the track. When it met a two-lane road, and he'd seen no one, he abandoned that hope.

A mile after he joined the road, he finally saw people. A group stood by a stalled car. One of them raised her arms in a wave.

"No uniforms," he said, slowing. After all he'd been through, he knew it could still be dangerous, but he didn't care. Another was waving now. People. It was like cold water on a hot day. Then the others raised their arms, and he realized they weren't waving. They were undead. The zombies lurched out into the road, staggering toward him. Frustrated anger bubbled over as he slammed his foot on the gas, driving straight at the creatures. At the last minute, he swerved, clipping the grasping hand of the nearest zombie. It went spinning, but he didn't look back to see it fall. Eyes fixed on the road ahead, he drove.

Zombies. Nuclear war. A conspiracy that had destroyed any chance of a recovery. It was all too much to take in.

"So break it down," he said, speaking out loud to push despair away. "There was one cloud. There might be more, there might not. It might just have been the cabal that was targeted. No. Forget the guesses. Focus on what you know."

What did he know? He'd tried to stop the world tearing itself apart and had given little thought to what would happen next. The mushroom cloud was formed of radioactive debris dragged up from the impact site. The length of time it took for it to settle depended on weather and wind, but if you couldn't escape the fallout, you should shelter for at least three days.

"Fallout." He brought the truck to a screeching halt. He had to get upwind of the cloud. He'd been driving away from it, but had he been traveling in the wrong direction?

He looked for trees, but the only ones he could see were bare of leaves. He stepped outside, turning his face this way and that, trying to feel the wind. He ran to the roadside and tugged out a handful of grass. When he threw it in the air, it scattered in every direction. He grabbed another clod, a third, a fourth, ripping the grass from the ground until his hands were covered in dirt. A sob escaped his lips, echoed by a rasping sigh from the other side of the road. A zombie limped across the asphalt. One foot still wore an expensive hiking boot, the other trailed a sodden sock. He pulled the .45 from his pocket. Aimed. Fired. The zombie crumpled.

"Stop. Think. Smoke. Wind. Fire, that's it. Matches. I need matches."

The vehicle had been stripped of almost anything of use, but in a half-empty toolbox he found two road flares. He sparked one, threw it out into the middle of the road, and watched the smoke billow up and then toward him. The bottom dropped out of his world. The smoke changed direction, drifting back the way he'd come. He watched it, not even daring to breathe, expecting it to change direction again. It didn't.

Minutes passed.

"Take it," he finally said. "It's the only reassurance you're going to get." What he needed was a Geiger counter. What he needed was to get somewhere safe. He didn't know where that was, except it wasn't here on this lonely road. He got back in the truck and started the engine.

"Three quarters of a tank," he said. "Okay. Good. So where to?" He stopped himself from answering the question, at least aloud. Talking to himself was one thing, questioning himself was something else.

"Start with where you are."

It took five miles before he was sure he was heading north.

"And in an electronics-free truck retrofitted to survive an EMP." He found he was laughing again, and knew it was hysteria, but he didn't try to stop. He'd survived. He'd been barely twelve hours ahead of Powell in New York, but he'd escaped. He'd been captured by Addison and escaped again. He'd escaped being framed for murder, being trapped by the undead, and now he'd escaped a nuclear bomb. If there was a winner in this horrific apocalypse, it was him. The laughter abruptly died as he realized that there wouldn't be just one bomb. There could be another just a few miles ahead. There could be thousands, and nowhere on the planet would be safe.

"And there's nothing you can do about it. You're alive. Alive and free. Free." He repeated the word. It was true. Ever since he'd watched his family home burn to the ground, he'd been on the run, living in the shadows. Now his life, however much of it was left, was finally his own.

Chapter 15 - Unlucky Survivor
New York & Vermont

After five more miles, he saw a sign for the interstate, and it was wrong. It was for the I-87. He was in northern New York, not far from the border with Vermont. He'd thought he'd been held captive somewhere near Dr Ayers's home and the motel where he'd confronted Powell.

"The sign's right. You're wrong. Live with it." Certainly there was no mistaking the next sign pointing to Plattsburgh and the Canadian border. That brought him to the question of where he was heading. There was only one answer to that. East to his cottage. There were no military installations near the village of Crossfields Landing, and no other obvious targets. Get to the cottage, get to the boat, get out to sea. Could he get to Maine? The fuel gauge read three-quarters full. He let himself breathe out with relief. He might make it.

Avoiding the interstate, he stayed on the smaller county road. He wasn't the only one. Cars, trucks, vans, even a limo, were parked, abandoned, or had crashed. As he passed, he kept the speed low, his eyes watching for movement, for people stranded by an EMP, or simply lack of fuel. He was more than willing to give someone a ride. He was eager, not just for company, but to know that he wasn't the last person alive. But the few shambling figures he saw wore the ravaged features of the undead.

The stalled traffic grew worse, lining both sides of the road, reducing it to one lane, then to less than that. Metal scraped against the side of the truck as he forced his way past one car after another. The shambling figures drew closer as he was forced to slow. Hands and fists beat against the bodywork, and the road ahead filled with those twisted mockeries of humanity. Finally, he was forced to give up, reverse, and go back.

It took another half hour before he was on a clear road, heading toward the Lake Champlain Bridge and the border with Vermont. Frustration added to growing uncertainty of what he would find at journey's end. His only comfort was the fuel gauge.

"Three quarters of a tank. Should be enough." Something was wrong. "Three quarters?"

After he'd crossed the bridge and entered Vermont, he was sure. The needle on the fuel gauge was stuck.

The truck ground to a halt twenty minutes later. There were no cars in sight, no buildings, or even a distant trace of smoke from a welcoming fire. A light dusting of snow covered the ground. It was barely deeper than a heavy frost, but it hadn't melted. All he had for protection was the cheap suit Addison had provided. It didn't take him long to make an inventory of everything else in the truck. One road flare, the .45, the rifle, a half-filled canteen, and two candy bars that only brought on a sudden wave of hunger. He ate them both and didn't feel satisfied. He wasn't going to survive a night outside, though from the position of the sun, that was still some hours off.

"No point putting it off."

Yet he hesitated. He knew he couldn't linger, but he felt he was missing something.

In the bag in which he'd found the .45 was a cheap paperback. He stared at the front cover on which a cowboy rode across purple sage toward a distant homestead. He wondered at the nature of the assassin who'd thought it as much a necessity as the gun, before tearing out the blank page from the back. He wrote a short note:

"This vehicle might be contaminated by radioactive particles. It was close to the location where a bomb was dropped. It was south of here. I'm not sure where."

He hesitated, uncertain why he was leaving a message, and finally decided that it wasn't for anyone who might come this way, but for himself.

"It survived the EMP, so if you have a Geiger counter to check it's safe, and fuel to put in the tank, it should work. Good luck. Stay safe." After another, brief hesitation, he signed it *Sholto.*

It was a name he rarely used, a pseudonym that was more of a private joke than a secret identity. More thought had gone into its selection than the name he most commonly used. Tom Clemens had been chosen simply because he'd read a lot of Mark Twain during his first few years in America. Sholto was different. Within it was a message the recipient had failed to understand. Now, here, it became something else.

"A new name, for a new world, for however long I survive in it."

He left the note on the passenger seat and opened the door. The cold hit him like a wall. It almost made him retreat back inside. He slung the rifle, slammed the door closed, thrust his hands into his pockets, and forced himself to walk.

His head bowed forward as the residual warmth ebbed from his body. After what felt like an age, he finally allowed himself to look around. The truck was still in view. He'd only managed a few hundred yards. Forcing one foot in front of the other, he trudged on.

As it often had during his captivity, his mind turned to Britain. Had it survived the bombs? Had London? Had Bill? There was no way to answer that. Instead, he flicked his eyes left and right, looking for buildings, for cars, for anywhere that might offer shelter. Occasionally he heard noises that might have been nothing, or which might have been the undead, but he saw none. Nor did he see any cars, abandoned or moving. At first he thought that was strange, then he wondered if he was already dead, walking some twilight path in the realm between life and death. His numb brain toyed with the idea until the empty fields became a desert; the cracks on the road became carved intentions.

"Remote," he growled, realizing he was slowly freezing to death. The rest of the words wouldn't form, but that was the real answer. This was a place people from the cities would have fled to, not one from which the locals would escape. He knew that might be wrong, but he had to focus on reality, lest his fantasy became true.

The sun was lost behind a thick bank of dark blue clouds, so he wasn't sure how close it was to nightfall when he saw the farmhouse. The building wasn't immediately ahead of him, but just visible beyond an unplowed field. Behind it were other rooftops, but he couldn't tell if they were barns and outbuildings, or the beginnings of a town. There was no smoke, no lights, no sound other than his stuttering breath. The temperature was plummeting. He had to take shelter, and trust to the kindness of strangers. Even as he thought the words, his hand came out of his pocket to tug on the rifle's strap. The cold wind biting into cracked skin made him aware of the gesture, and of what his instinct was telling him. Trust wasn't the right word. Hope for kindness. Expect the opposite.

The field's uneven ground slowed him. His feet felt like leaden weights. Before he was halfway across, he knew he wouldn't be able to pick up his pace. The farmhouse was where he would stop regardless of what he found there. Three-quarters of the way across the field, he heard an irregular banging. Someone fixing the fence that seemed to get no closer? He couldn't see anyone, and, of course, no one would bother with routine chores at times like these. Chopping wood? Perhaps, but the sound didn't seem right.

He reached the low fence separating the yard from the fields. The sound was still there, but there was no sign of people. He opened his mouth to shout a greeting, but all that came out was a shallow plume of vapor. It took him three tries to climb the fence, and he almost lost his footing as he clambered over. The sound was louder, and he recognized what it was, and realized he should have known long before. With frozen fingers he fumbled the rifle off his shoulder. His vision blurred as he raised the weapon, scanning for the zombies he knew were nearby. Dreading the coming confrontation, he crossed the yard, nearly slipping on the icy concrete. The sound grew louder. He turned the corner and saw them. Six zombies beat their fists against the door and walls at the front of the house. He watched, his brain slow to process the scene. Their hands left dirty stains against the winter-worn paint as they tried to reach through the walls. Were they farmers? Locals? They were dressed casually, but only one wore a jacket. The others were in shirtsleeves. On the arm of the nearest, a bloody bandage unraveled with each downward swing. Frozen neurons sparked. The zombies were trying to get into the house. There were people inside.

"Hoy!" he croaked. It was barely a word, and it came out weak, inaudible against the undead's pummeling racket. Rage blossomed, sending a last reserve of furious heat through his numb limbs.

"Hey! Hey you!" It was barely loud enough to carry across the yard, but it was loud enough. The bandaged zombie turned its head.

"Yeah," he murmured. "That's right." He aimed. Fired. The shot missed, but the sound carried. Almost as one, the other five turned away from the house, and toward him.

He fired again. The bandaged zombie fell backward as its brains sprayed over the creatures behind. The zombie in the quilted jacket stumbled into the body, falling to the ground, but that still left four, and they moved as if they were heedless of the cold. He shifted aim.

"Haven't you heard?" He fired. A zombie fell. "The cabal's dead. It's over. You can stop."

But they didn't stop. The three creatures staggered closer. Tom tried to take a step backward, but his legs wouldn't move. He fired. A zombie in a red flannel shirt collapsed. He shifted aim, fired, missed. He could see mud and blood and worse clotted inside those gaping maws. He fired, not aiming now, just emptying the magazine into the hideous creatures. More by luck than aim, one of the shots slammed into the brain before the rifle clicked empty. He dropped the weapon, fumbling for the .45, but his fingers wouldn't work. He couldn't get it free.

"Down!" a voice called. "Drop. Get down!"

He let himself collapse. It wasn't hard. There was a booming roar. The zombie fell. Tom rolled across the icy yard away from the creature. He pushed himself to his knees. An old woman stood in the doorway to the house, a shotgun in her arms.

"You okay?" she called.

Tom forced himself up. "Yeah. Yeah, I think so."

"You're alive. I didn't think any—"

Before Tom could warn her, before he could draw his pistol, the zombie in the quilted jacket reared up from the ground and clamped its mouth on her leg. The woman screamed, firing the shotgun at point blank range. The slug took the zombie in the back, but the creature didn't stop. Tom stumbled over to her and dragged the zombie off. Its left arm was limp, its legs didn't work, but its right hand reached for him. He dragged the pistol out and fired into its skull.

144

"She killed me," the woman said, staring at her bloody leg. "Louise killed me."

"Inside," Tom said, pushing the woman back through the open door. The warmth of the interior was like a blow.

"She killed me," the woman said again.

"Bleach," Tom said, leaning against the wall. "Clean the wound." The words came out stilted.

"There's no point," the woman said, limping away from him, down a short hallway, and into the kitchen. It was lit by the flickering glow of a wood-burning stove and candles that gave off a heady floral scent. The windows were covered with thick blankets.

Tom dropped the .45 on the countertop and pulled himself over to the sink. He opened the cupboard underneath and found a bottle of disinfectant.

"It won't work," the woman said. "We tried it on Fred."

"We've got to try," Tom said. He pushed himself back to his feet, and saw stars. He had to grab the counter just to keep his feet. "Got to try," he said again.

The woman gasped as he doused the wound with the bleach, but she didn't protest. There had to be something else he could do, something more scientific, but his strength was now completely gone. Dropping the bottle, he collapsed into a chair, next to the woman.

"You should get your gun," the woman said, gesturing to the counter, eight feet away. "I'm going to turn. It always happens."

Tom nodded, but didn't move. The woman stood, limped over to the pistol, and put on the kitchen table, next to his hand.

"Where did you come from?" she asked.

"South," he said. "Pennsylvania. I saw a mushroom cloud. Felt the shockwave of another bomb. Or I thought it was Pennsylvania. It might have been New York. I'm not sure."

"Nuclear bombs?" The woman limped over to the stove and moved a kettle onto the plate. She sat down again. "The power went out this morning. Fred said they'd try using bombs on the zombies. I said it was madness."

"I don't think they were using it on the zombies," Tom said. Though, of course, he had no way of knowing that. Perhaps someone had. "I guess it doesn't really matter. You didn't see any mushroom clouds here. No bright lights?"

"Nope. Just the power going out."

She looked down at her leg. Tom did the same. Something in her words slowly fed a thought that blossomed into a question. "You're on the electrical grid, here?" he asked.

"Fred's place is," she said. "That's five miles west of here. I've got a generator. Took all the fuel to his place. All the food, too. Abigail Benford," she said. "My name. What's yours?"

"Tom Clemens," he replied automatically. "Except it's not. My mother called me Thaddeus."

"Oh yes? And what do your friends call you?" she asked.

That was a hard question to answer. "I don't know if I have any left," he said. "But if I do, I guess he'd call me Sholto."

"That's worse than Thaddeus," she said. Her eyes went back to her leg, and then to a clock on the wall. It had stopped. "Took Fred an hour to turn. Took Louise only a minute."

"You might be the exception," Tom said.

"You mean that I might be immune?" Abigail said. "We talked about that, when we were waiting, watching, hoping that the world would right itself. Thought it just might before Maxwell gave his speech. Should have known the world couldn't get back on its feet. Nuclear bombs? You say you saw two of them?"

"I saw one mushroom cloud. Felt the shockwave of another. They had to be close. Not sure if the second was nuclear. Don't know. But I saw one mushroom cloud. I know that."

"Huh. And that was this morning?"

"Yeah. I'm not sure what time it was."

"Have you changed your clothes?" she asked.

"What?"

"It's what they told us, back when we thought the Ruskis were going to drop the bomb. Radioactive particles stick to your clothing. You have strip and wash, but don't scrub so hard you break the skin."

The fallout. He remembered now. He'd known it. He'd said as much on the note he'd left on the truck. He stood.

"There's clothes upstairs. The cupboard in the second room off the landing," she said. She looked at the .45. "Maybe you should take the shotgun with you."

The clothes were worn, old, and in the back of a cupboard in a spare room. Her brothers, maybe? He didn't want to know. Back-story just meant more people who were dead. He went into the bathroom and ran water over his hands. There were no flash burns on them, nor on his face. Perhaps that bright light had been nothing more than him hitting his head as the truck crashed. Or was that just what he wanted to believe? A wave of nausea swept over him. For a moment he thought he was going to pass out, and caught hold of the sink for support. The moment passed. He rinsed himself with cold water. It wasn't much better a wash than he'd managed with the bucket and bar of soap that morning. Morning? It seemed far longer ago than that.

In darned socks, mended jeans, and a thick shirt, he picked up the shotgun and went back to the stairs. He paused halfway down, listening. There were sounds from the kitchen, of metal knocking against metal, but somehow he didn't think it meant Abigail had turned into one of the undead. She hadn't. She stood by the stove, stirring something in a pot.

"You look just like him," she said, turning to look at his approach. He didn't ask whom. "Sit down before you fall," she said. "I hope you eat beef stew, because that's all we've got. Not much of a last meal for either of us. Came from the school." She pointed at the industrial-sized can sitting on the counter.

"I've spent the last week... No, it was longer than that, but I've spent it a prisoner of the people responsible for all of this," he said.

"You have?" She turned around. "How so?"

"I was trying to stop it. I failed."

"Ah." She gave him a more measured look, then turned back to the stove. "It was Fred's idea that we should all sleep under the same roof. Security in numbers, you see."

"Against the undead?"

"No. Against the refugees. They didn't come. Not in any great number. We saw a few cars, and saw off a few small groups, but the hordes we were expecting never arrived. You know why?"

"The roads south of here are blocked," he said. "All it takes is a couple of vehicles to run out of fuel and you get a bottleneck that no one's going to unstopper."

"That's pretty much what we thought," she said. "After we'd seen no one for a couple of days, Fred went out looking for supplies. He got bit, but made it back. We thought he was immune until he died. I went out this morning. We needed more food. It's amazing how much gets eaten when there's nothing else to do but play cards. I thought the school would be better than the town. It was. Lots of food in the kitchens. Enough to keep us all fed until harvest. When I got back, there were zombies outside the house. Don't know where they came from, or how they got there, or why they arrived just then. Doesn't matter, does it? We shot them, but Louise had been bitten. We tried cleaning the wound, bandaging it and… Well, you saw them outside, you can guess the rest. I got in the truck and came back here. I suppose I should have kept going, but to go where? This is my home. Our farm. Don't suppose there'll be a harvest, not this year, nor any year hereafter." She took out a bowl, filled it, and placed it in front of Tom.

"You're not going to eat?" he asked.

She opened a cupboard, took out a dusty bottle, and poured herself a very small measure. "Nope." She took a sip, put the glass down, and leaned back in her chair. "Some strange world, this one," she said, closing her eyes. "Tell me about these people holding you prisoner. They were responsible for all this? The zombies? The bombs?"

He swallowed another mouthful of stew. "It's a long story," he said, deciding that he would tell her the entire truth, right from the beginning.

"It began with my father. I suppose calling him a government assassin is closest to the truth. It wasn't glamorous enough work to call him a spy."

Abigail grunted. Tom looked at her. Her eyes opened. There was no life left in them. The zombie's arms swept across the table, knocking over bottle and glass. Tom stepped back, grabbing the shotgun. He aimed it straight at her head, and hesitated, but only for a second. He pulled the trigger. Nothing happened. Neither of them had reloaded the weapon.

Abigail lurched out of her chair, arms outstretched. Tom jabbed the shotgun at her. There was little force to the blow, but it was enough to knock her back in the chair. He grabbed the .45, and fired. She died.

He stood there, watching undead brain drip down the calendar behind her shattered head, obscuring the red-ink hearts denoting dates to remember and which would now be forever forgotten. The gun felt heavy in his hand. Infection. Radiation. It was all too much, yet he couldn't give in, couldn't give up. He put the gun on the table, went upstairs, washed, changed, and then sat down on the bed in that small room. The future, however brief it might be, weighed heavily on him. So heavily that he soon fell asleep.

Chapter 16 - The Dark Night
March 13th, Addison County, Vermont

He woke, cold, shivering, hungry, and thirsty. The moon was high outside. The yard empty of the undead. Slowly, almost unwillingly, he made his way downstairs. The fire in the stove had gone out, and he didn't want to light it again. He didn't want to spend any time in that grim room. He went back to the bathroom, filled a glass with water, and downed it. He drank another, intending to fill his stomach with water, but the flow turned to a trickle, and stopped with the third glass only half full. Of course, there was no electricity for the pump, and he'd used up all that was in the pipes.

He had to go back into the kitchen now, this time to fetch the shotgun. He cleaned it with a rag soaked in disinfectant, unsure whether he was scrubbing away the infected blood or the invisible radiation. Except, was it likely to be contaminated? Was the pistol? It had been inside the truck, hadn't it? And he'd driven away from the mushroom cloud before the irradiated particles thrown up during the explosion had a chance to settle back to Earth. That was why it was called fallout, wasn't it? It had to fall. He wasn't certain, and after being wrong about so many things, didn't want to bet his life on the small chance he was right.

The shells were in a cabinet in the living room. The gun loaded, he went outside. The night was clear, the road empty. All was still. Almost too still. Where were the bats and moths, the rodents and all the rest scurrying about their nocturnal business? He crossed quickly to the truck. On the passenger seat was a box. In it were three cans of stew, identical to the one in the kitchen. There were no keys. They were probably on Abigail's body. He wasn't going to leave before dawn, so that could wait. He took the box back inside.

Again, he hesitated. Unwilling to go back in the kitchen, he started a small fire in the living room, using a polished brass tray as a fire pit. Opening the window to let the smoke out, he heated stew, still in its can, on the flames. As fire turned the label to ash, it struck him again how ill-prepared he was for this new type of life. It wasn't just his ignorance of radiation, medicine, or survival. What did he know about farming? Perhaps this part of America had no nocturnal animals. His ignorance was astonishing, but he knew that in the coming months he'd either learn or die.

"Months? Okay, yeah, maybe not months, but it might be. It might be years. You're alive now, so what next?"

In some ways it was the same question he'd been asking himself since the outbreak, but now it was brought into sharp focus. The cabal was dead. He could assume more than one nuclear bomb had been detonated, and that the United States wasn't the only target. There was a chance that more bombs would fall, and in the coming weeks the planet would become a radioactive desert.

"But what if it's not?"

Then he was alive, and if he didn't starve, freeze, get ripped apart by the undead, or get a lethal dose of radiation, he might still be alive in a week's time.

"Maybe, and you might as well assume you will be. So what are your priorities?"

The stew began to bubble. He had to go back into the kitchen to find something with which to take it off the heat, then again to get a spoon and bowl from the cupboard. As he methodically ate his way through the can, he felt sympathy for the students at whatever school it had come from.

"A high school might have a Geiger counter, and that's what I need." It might not, but a police station would, or a firehouse, or an airport. The undead were everywhere, starvation and thirst would dog his footsteps from now on, but radiation could be avoided if he found a Geiger counter. He'd find a police station in a town, and he'd find a town by following the roads. And then...

"Maine?"

His cottage was the obvious destination, but then what? He put the bowl down. He'd eat the rest before he left, but right now he couldn't face another bite. He knew he wasn't going to sleep, so went back upstairs, found a blanket, and brought it down to cover Abigail. Before he did, he retrieved the keys from her pocket. Covering her with the sheet seemed a tokenistic gesture. It was like how Helena had wanted to bury the police officer near Dr Ayers's house. It meant nothing to anyone else, but it was the least he could do, and because it was the least he could do, he had to do it, lest he lose some last part of himself.

He went out to the truck. There were a few gallons in the tank. Not enough to get him to Maine, but enough to get him to a town. Find more fuel. Find a Geiger counter. And then…

"Britain?"

Maybe. Unless it had been destroyed. It was a dream, an obligation, and one he'd left too late. His chance was gone. The thought of obligations reminded him of Max, and the promise he'd made.

"Claire." Max had said the First Lady and their children were at their house in Vermont. That couldn't be far from here. There was little chance she'd survived, but he'd promised he would look. He would keep his word, and so close this last chapter of his old life, leaving him a truly blank slate, and a fate of which he alone would be the master.

More pertinently, the Secret Service had set up a command post there after the election. There would be a supply of fuel, weapons, and, probably, a Geiger counter.

He sat down in the living room, to wait for dawn.

Chapter 17 - The Long Day
Addison County, Vermont

He woke from a light doze with a vision of a street he'd not walked in decades, and a face he'd not dared meet in person. The idea energized him in a way that the now-cold stew couldn't. There was coffee in the cupboard, but he didn't want to waste time making it. He paused in the doorway to the kitchen, staring at the .45 on the table. He couldn't risk taking it, nor the assault rifle that still lay where he'd dropped it in the yard. He doubted either was radioactive, but at the same time, didn't want to stretch his already taut luck.

There was paper in the drawer of a very old-fashioned hall table, on which was an equally old-fashioned phone next to a very new cell-phone charger. He scrawled a note and taped it to the hallway floor by the entrance to the kitchen. He pinned a second note to the front door.

"There's a .45 on the kitchen table. It may be radioactive, and this property might be contaminated. One zombie inside. Dead. She was the owner. Abigail Benford. Her death was quick. Her last act was one of kindness. May that be a lesson to us all." He signed both notes *Sholto*.

He left the two cans of stew in the hall, but took the box of shotgun shells and a short-handled axe from the tool shed.

It was only as he was pulling onto the road that he realized the truck worked. It was an old model, with a missing radio, and no visible electronics on the dashboard. It was possible that there was simply no circuitry for an electromagnetic pulse to fry. He glanced back at the house, now receding in the distance. Abigail had said that the power had gone out at the other house, the one from which she had fled, but that could have been the mains supply, and it was five miles away. It was possible that he was beyond the effects of an EMP. He tried to think if he'd seen anything electronic in the house. He couldn't remember. He should have tried the phone, or looked for a flashlight. Certainly, he should have looked for that. The house grew smaller in the rearview mirror, but he didn't turn around. He didn't want to go back.

"Should have looked for a compass, too," he muttered. He'd taken a road map. According to it, he was twenty miles west and forty south of Claire Maxwell's home. Within two hours, he'd have access to all the electronics he could want.

He gave the fuel gauge a tap. The needle gave a reassuring bounce. He had enough to get to the house, and there he should find all he would need. Much to Claire's irritation, a fuel tank had been installed, along with the guard post that she called a barracks. The house was her retreat from the world, and very much a place for her to escape from the political life the governor's mansion had thrust upon her. Perhaps she was still there. Perhaps the Secret Service agents were there as well. He doubted it. Another doubt crept in, of the odds that the house might have been targeted by Russia or China. That was even less likely. Alive or dead, she would be irrelevant to the grander global game of politics. That didn't mean it hadn't happened, but he tried to not to think of that, or of what he might be driving into.

More likely, she and the children had been hustled onto a helicopter and away to a bunker. It was equally probable that after the Secret Service had left, locals would have gone to the house to strip it bare, so when he saw the sign for the filling station, he decided to stop. When he saw the nozzles hanging loose by the pumps, he almost changed his mind. He brought the truck to a halt by the side of the road, grabbed the shotgun, and jumped out.

"Hello!" he called. There was no reply. Beyond the pumps was a small, weather-beaten store in serious need of a lick of paint. Parked behind that, he could see the hood of a black sedan. Shotgun raised, he walked toward the vehicle.

"Hello!" he called again, now listening for the dry wheeze of the undead. He didn't hear that, either. The sedan was a high-end model, and a rental according to the sticker on the rear windshield. Mud splattered the wheels and coated the doors. Someone had driven it all the way from Arkansas. The backseat was filled with wrappers and empty fast-food cartons.

"An airport?" Perhaps that had been the starting point. A plane forced to make an emergency landing after the airspace was closed. A passenger, desperate to get home, but wise enough to see the world had changed, had grabbed anything on sale from any concession stand willing to take their money. The car must have been the last one in the lot. Or perhaps it had been driven here by someone who worked the car rental business at the airport.

"Or perhaps not. It doesn't matter."

And it didn't, he was just delaying going inside. That wasn't because he thought he'd find the undead – he no longer feared them – but out of a reluctance to finish this last part of his journey. There was another possibility waiting for him at the house in Vermont. Claire and the children could be dead, murdered by the cabal. The more he tried not to think about it, the more that possibility became a certainty.

"Hello!" he called, slamming the butt of the shotgun into the wooden door at the back of the store. There was no response from inside, but the door was firmly locked. He went back to the front. This door was open and creaked as he pushed it aside.

The interior was unlit. The three banks of shelves were mostly bare. What remained was an odd assortment of dish soap, brake fluid, and shoe polish. Six stools were lined up along the narrow counter at the rear of the store, near a solitary register. Behind the counter was a door that led to a small kitchen. He tried the light switch and was unsurprised when nothing happened. The faucet over the small sink had been left on to run dry, presumably by some previous scavenger. He turned the faucet off. Pausing only to glance longingly at the short menu advertising maple syrup with everything, he went outside and perched on the hood of the truck.

No zombies, which was good, but no people, which was a mixed blessing. The countryside seemed so lifeless. It was almost as if he was existing outside of time, as if nothing was real unless it was within his field of vision. That thought lasted until he heard the sound of an engine.

Two cars sped along the road toward him. Both were old model trucks like the one he'd taken from the farm, though both appeared to be in better repair. He tried to remember how to look friendly but dangerous.

The trucks came to an abrupt halt. Even if he'd still been carrying that assault rifle, he'd be no match for the six soldiers who jumped out. He thought of the cabal and their propensity to wear military uniforms, but three of the soldiers here were women. He'd not seen any among the guards at the industrial site, nor with Powell. The one with Addison had been an exception. It wasn't much of a lead on which to place his life, but against six of them, violence wasn't an option. He decided to play peacemaker instead. He slid the shotgun back into the truck.

"Hi," he said addressing a man with sergeant's stripes on his sleeve. By far he was the oldest in the group. There was a trace of grey in his stubble. Of the others, three were male, but he doubted they could raise more than a few scraggly whiskers.

"Good morning, sir," the sergeant replied with that gruff civility a non-com always used when addressing a civilian. "Is this your filling station?"

"I was just passing through," Tom said. "On a search for gasoline."

One of the privates had a small box in her hand. She was waving it around as if it were a talisman.

"Is that a Geiger counter?" Tom asked. "Would you mind running it over me?"

The soldiers, as one, took a step back.

"I was upwind of a mushroom cloud," Tom said. "Somewhere in... I thought it was Pennsylvania. It might have been New York. I was trying to get away and didn't pay attention to where I was until I reached Vermont."

"Dawson!" the sergeant barked. The soldier with the Geiger counter snapped to attention before she understood the meaning of the command. The device held at arm's length in front, she approached Tom. The machine clicked softly, but no more rapidly, as she got nearer.

"Best check the truck, too," Tom said.

"Clean," Dawson said. "It's clean."

Tom gave an involuntary laugh of relief. "Thank you," he said. "Thank you. That's a pretty ancient Geiger counter. Looks like it came off the Ark."

"We got it from a high school," the sergeant said. "It works, and that's what counts. Where did you see this mushroom cloud?"

"Pennsylvania or New York State, I'm not sure," Tom said. "I think it was about twenty miles south of me. Maybe less, maybe more. A minute or two after, I felt a shockwave, but that might have been from a secondary explosion."

"You didn't see a second mushroom cloud?" the sergeant asked.

"No," Tom said, "but there were too many trees and hills to see much. I started driving, and I... I don't remember much until I ran out of fuel. I walked, and I... I don't remember much of that, either. I reached a farmhouse. The owner was infected. She died. Now here I am. Is there anything you can tell me? I'm guessing from the Geiger counter that other bombs fell."

"I'm afraid so, sir," the sergeant said. "I'm afraid so. All right, you lot, you know the drill. Hernandez, Dawson, watch the south. Janson, Brooker, take the road to the north. Watch. Listen. Sir, is there anything inside the store?"

"It's been stripped," Tom said.

"I meant anything... moving."

"Ah. No."

"Clark, you know what to look for. Snap to it!" The privates deployed. "Jim Russell," the sergeant said, holding out his hand.

"Sholto," Tom said. "Thaddeus Sholto."

"Sholto? What's that, Dutch?"

"British," Tom said. "It's good to meet you, but where did the bombs fall?"

"Twenty miles north of the Canadian border."

"In Canada? What's there? A military base or something?"

"Nothing. There's nothing there," Russell said. "I don't even think there's a town. If there was, there certainly isn't anymore."

"Or we zapped the missile's targeting chip," Private Dawson called. "We can do that, can't we?"

"You're meant to be watching the road," Russell barked. "Obey your orders, or you'll feel precisely what the American military can do!"

The private scurried further down the road.

"Where were you heading?" Russell asked.

"Maine, I think," Tom said. "The Atlantic coast. I… it's hard to know what to do, or where to go. What were you doing in Canada?"

"Guarding the border. That's where we were deployed. The entire brigade was there. If you can call it a brigade. Our orders were to stop the infected, isolate them, but let the rest of the refugees through. It didn't matter which direction people were traveling."

"Canadians were heading south?"

"And that tells you what a futile exercise it was," the sergeant said. "But orders are orders, and I didn't see any Canucks with whom I could clarify them. It wouldn't have mattered if there were. No one told us what to do with the infected."

"Were there many?" Tom asked.

"Hard to say. We stopped a few cars where people had noticeable bites, even a few where they had some zombie chained up in the back. Those were mostly children." He shook his head. "But we couldn't really do anything. This was a four-lane road, and there were ten of us. Me, this lot, and four others. All nine of them were only a few weeks out of basic training. It took half of us to stop a car while the other half stopped the next one. By the time we'd dealt with the occupants, a dozen other vehicles had rocketed past."

"What did you do with the infected?" Tom asked.

"What could we do? We stood over them with our rifles, waiting with their families, at least, when the families stayed. A lot of times they didn't. And then we shot the zombie. You heard the rumors about immunity?"

"No."

The sergeant gave a sad smile. "There are two rumors. One is that there's a safe haven just a little further down the road. I've heard that on every continent, and in every conflict where I've been deployed. Refugees always tell themselves safety lies ahead until, in repetition, that prayer becomes an expectation that's almost always unfulfilled. The other rumor is that people are immune. Everyone we stopped seemed to believe it, but it was always something they'd heard from someone else. Never saw it myself. They always died, always came back, and I always put a bullet in their skull. After the sixth, I told them not to stop any more vehicles. We just kept the road clear. Even that was almost more than we could do. We stayed because those were our orders. And then the bomb fell. Now there are five of these kids left. I don't know who ordered us north, or why, but it's almost as if they wanted to destroy any chance we had of stopping this."

Tom sighed. His chances of survival weren't great. No one's were. The truth had to be told, and this soldier deserved to know it.

"The orders came from the White House, but not from the president," Tom said. "There was a coup of sorts. A conspiracy that began before the election. Farley and Sterling were both involved. Whichever of them won the election, the cabal would own the White House. It's why Grant Maxwell ran. When he did, and when it became clear that he'd win, the conspirators recruited Charles Addison, his chief of staff, to their cause. He was to be the fall guy, and when he realized, he created his own plot, bringing the cabal's plans forward. After it had begun, he killed off the other members of the conspiracy, drugged the president, and had himself appointed to the cabinet. He had the crazy idea that in the chaos of the nation's collapse that would be viewed as legitimate. Then he began killing those in the line of succession. I don't think he killed them all, but the president's dead. So are the VP, the speaker of the house, and the secretary of state. You, and the rest of the military were deployed to rural and remote areas so that you'd be relatively intact after the country had fallen apart. He intended to use you to regain the nation and, through that act, secure his place as leader. Except the bombs fell."

"Addison? Seriously?"

"The plan is as deranged as the man was. I don't know who was behind the outbreak, except I think it was a pre-emptive retaliation in response to the cabal's earlier plans. They created a vaccine that would be effective against most of the world's most deadly diseases. They intended to blackmail the planet and destroy those parts of it that wouldn't bend the knee. As I say, deranged."

"How do you know this?"

"I tried to stop it," Tom said. "I failed. They captured me, and I was held in a cell with the president. They killed him."

"And the conspirators?"

"Addison killed most of them. I shot him in the shadow of that mushroom cloud."

"Then it's over?" Russell asked.

"All that's left is what we can create from the ashes."

"Why did—" Russell began, but stopped and shook his head. "I don't care. You can't promise no more bombs will fall?"

"No."

"They say the devil is in the details, but if a missile might already be winging its way to this very spot, the details don't matter. You said you're heading to the Atlantic coast?"

"I think so. What about you?"

"South and west. Might have to change our plans, but we'll stick with them for now."

"Sarge!" Private Jenson called. She was pointing down the road.

"Zombie?" Russell called back.

"Yes, Sarge."

"Then shoot it. It's time we left. You could come with us."

Tom considered it, but there was his last obligation to Max. "No. There's a place I want to go. That I want to see."

"I understand. Good luck to you."

"And to you," Tom said.

The private fired. It took her three shots to kill the staggering creature. The soldiers piled back into the trucks and drove away.

Tom had considered asking them to come with him to Claire's house. He was glad he hadn't. Telling the sergeant the truth, or at least that brief summary, had been wise. If they met others, the story would spread. Perhaps it would prevent any remnant of the cabal from seizing power. A moment's reflection told him that wasn't the case. Somewhere, someone would be in a bunker, sworn in when all those above them in the line of succession were assumed dead. Perhaps there were dozens of presidents now, each in their own isolated refuge, all thinking themselves the sole ruler of these devastated states. It hardly mattered. The bombs had wrecked civilization. The zombies would prevent it being rebuilt.

He climbed back in the truck and drove north. He thought about the email he'd sent three weeks before, the warning sent to military commanders and journalists the world over. Perhaps some had read it and heeded its message. Maybe one of them had deliberately changed the targeting on a missile, and that was why it had struck the middle of nowhere, just north of the border. Or maybe not.

"But you're still alive."

Chapter 18 - Family First
Washington County, Vermont

Claire Maxwell's father had been a pilot in the USAF. He'd won the house in a poker game, the legality of which had created a lawsuit that had dragged on until shortly before his death. Claire had said she thought her father had only clung onto life to confirm he really had won. That spoke volumes about the relationship she'd had with the man, so it had always surprised Tom that she'd not sold the property. He suspected it was something to do with her husband's move into politics. The rambling house offered a home that a governor's mansion never could. She was the brains in that particular couple, and excelled at personal politics, but she'd never enjoyed it. Her PhD was in archaeology, and her heart was forever in the classical world. Before Tom had asked Max to run for the presidency, she'd said that she didn't mind him trying politics while the children were young, but as soon as they were old enough to join her excavating ruins, he'd have to resign. After he'd announced his bid for the presidency, she'd smiled and waved, and accompanied him on the campaign. She'd given interviews, and posed for photographs, but he'd always thought she wouldn't have minded if Max had lost. His victory had meant any trip to Italy or Greece could only ever be a state occasion and a media circus. A journey to Afghanistan or the Middle East would be impossible.

The previous owner of the forty-acre property had called it "the compound." Tom had been there a few times before the campaign, and a few more during its early days. Back then, Max had been manufacturing credentials as a candidate local to the northeast, rather than as some way-way-out-of-stater.

He got lost twice before he spotted the double-thick chain-link fence topped with razor wire. He slowed, following the road around the property, stopping briefly when he saw the first guard tower. It was empty. He drove on to the main gate. It was closed, but the sentry box next to it was empty. Tom stopped the truck and got out. He didn't shout or sound the horn. If there had been anyone nearby they would surely have heard the engine. There was nothing but silence. He grabbed the shotgun, knowing that the worst of his fears were fact. He didn't want to confirm them, but knew he had no choice.

His boots clicked on the freshly repaired road as he crossed to the sentry post by the gate. Inside, a man in a suit and tie was sprawled in a chair. His eyes were open, his shirt stained from a neat trio of bullet holes. He'd been there long enough for something to gnaw on his fingers. Not a zombie, but something smaller. Precisely what, Tom couldn't guess.

Shotgun raised, he stalked toward the house. He saw the second body fifty feet from the gate, lying on a path to the side of the road. It was another Secret Service agent, though she was dressed in more practical, rugged outdoor gear. He recognized the face as someone on Jane's detail. The agent had been shot in the chest, again three times. Tom stared at the corpse, telling himself he was piecing together the details, collecting evidence. In truth, he was only putting off the inevitable.

He didn't recognize the third body. Unlike the first two, this one was dressed in military uniform. He rolled the corpse over. It was a man in his late twenties. He'd been shot once in the stomach, and then again in the head. Tom's brain leaped to a conclusion, but he didn't want to give voice to it, not yet.

Tom walked up to the house. There were two bodies just inside the hall. One was a man dressed as a soldier. He'd been shot once in the face. The other was the head of Claire's detail. He stalked through the house, going from room to room, up to the attic, then down to the basement, seeing everything, but not allowing himself to feel a thing. After half an hour, he'd found twelve more bodies. Three wore uniforms, the rest were Secret Service agents.

There was a surveillance post in the basement. From the position of the two agents, dead in their chairs, both facing the now-blank screens, they'd been killed before they'd seen anything to make them raise the alarm. It suggested they'd died first, and that the cabal had someone working on the inside. Perhaps more than one person. With Addison's involvement, that was more than likely. Missing, however, were Claire, the two children, Jane and Rick, and six members of the protection detail. He went to the back door and looked outside. Behind the house were two old barns. On the path leading to them were two more agents. He pushed open the door and walked toward the buildings. There was an inevitability to what he would find, but it wasn't inside either of the barns.

Between the barns was a narrow path. Two more agents lay dead along it. The fifth was at the edge of the trees just beyond the buildings. He followed the trail of disturbed leaf litter, occasionally spotted with blood, until he found the sixth agent.

He stopped. There was no obvious trail leading into the woods, but he knew that Claire and the children hadn't escaped. The chain-link and razor wire built to protect the compound also turned it into a prison. The agents had done their duty, and died to save their protectees, but there were no vehicles in the driveway, nor on the road leading to the property. However the cabal's soldiers had gotten here, some had driven away. They wouldn't have left until the job was done. Claire's body, and those of the children, would be in the woods somewhere nearby. He didn't want to find them.

He went back to the house and sat in the kitchen – one of the few rooms without a corpse. He'd promised Max he would come and look for Claire. He'd come here and done that small thing, and it didn't seem enough. On the counter was a photograph of the family, taken before the campaign stylists had gotten their hands on them. They looked happily ordinary, smiling, at ease. The Max in the picture was a far cry from the ragged man he'd seen in the corridor outside their cell. He tried to remember when he'd last seen Claire and the children. He guessed it was a few days before the inauguration, though he couldn't now remember. Rick had been excited about living in the White House. Jane had been permanently grumpy since realizing, sometime before Christmas, that a move to Washington meant she'd be leaving her friends behind. Claire had been worried, Tom remembered that. Not for herself, but for her family, and how the next four, or perhaps eight, years were going to change them. He put the picture down.

There was another possibility, of course; that the cabal had captured Claire and taken her and the children away. He forced himself to his feet and went looking for the generator. With power restored to the property, he went back to the basement and searched through the security footage.

He saw a Jeep and truck, both painted in desert camouflage, drive up to the gate. It opened. They drove through. The agent in the sentry post must already have been dead. The two vehicles stopped just beyond the guardhouse. Men in uniform jumped out.

By that stage, someone working for Addison must already have killed the agents in the basement. Quite what alerted the rest of the security detail that these weren't the real military didn't matter. He skipped forward to the end, four hours after the murderers arrived, and saw four soldiers walking slowly back to their vehicles. Claire and the children weren't with them.

Tom cycled through the other cameras, trying not to look at the faces of the Secret Service personnel as they died, until he found one positioned on the rear wall of the house. He saw Claire and the two children being hustled toward the barn. He saw an agent turn around and then collapse. Claire disappeared. Tom changed the view until he found a camera on one of the barns. He saw Claire and the children, together with an injured agent, run into the woods. A moment later, three of the uniformed men ran into the forest after them. It was thirty minutes before they returned. Their weapons were held casually as if they were certain there was no threat facing them. He'd seen enough, yet he still hadn't seen it all.

He forced himself back outside and into the woodland. He walked in a straight line from the barns until he reached the fence, doubling back, trudging through mud, searching for the bodies. Hours passed. A light rain began to fall, and he still hadn't found them. The rain grew heavier. He ignored it. Lightning cracked and thunder roared.

"They're dead," he said. He knew it. Their bodies lay somewhere in the grounds. He tried to tell himself that if he hadn't found them, they might still be alive, but he knew it wasn't the case. If they were alive, then the cabal would have destroyed all evidence they'd been there. The bodies of their dead would have been taken, the camera footage destroyed. That it hadn't suggested a supreme confidence that could only have come from success. He'd promised Max he'd come and look for them. He had and wished he hadn't. He trudged back to the house.

Listlessly, he searched the kitchen for food. There was lots. More than he could possibly eat, and most of it canned or packaged. He had no appetite. He forced himself to wash, standing in a hot shower, methodically scrubbing at his skin. Max's wardrobe provided him with clothes.

He went back to the kitchen. The idea of cooking was beyond him, but he was ravenous. He opened a pack of cereal that was more chocolate than grain and ate it dry, watching the rain fall outside.

Chapter 19 - The Prisoner's Dilemma
March 14th, Vermont & Maine

By dawn, the storm had passed on, leaving the skies almost clear and Tom no reason to stay. Before he left, he walked to edge of the woods, but didn't venture in. Perhaps Claire and the children had escaped. Not destroying the evidence could have been an oversight on the part of the cabal's killers. He decided to believe the fantasy and take comfort in it.

There was enough food in the compound to feed forty people for a month, and enough fuel to get a convoy to Mexico. He loaded up a Secret Service SUV with enough to get him to Maine, and a thousand rounds of ammunition for a carbine he'd taken from a locker in the surveillance room. After a moment's consideration of the number of people once living on the American continents, and so the number of zombies he might now face, he added a thousand more. What he didn't find was a Geiger counter, or much by the way of medical supplies.

"So look for a hospital, and find both," he murmured as he finished loading the SUV, though beyond aspirin and bandages there was little medical equipment he knew how to use. He left the rest of the ammunition, and everything else in the house, for anyone who might come after him. He hoped that it would keep them alive, but he didn't leave a note. He no longer saw the point. He drove east.

America stretched out before him. Ruined. Broken. Lifeless. Empty fields, abandoned homes, crashed vehicles; the scenery changed, yet stayed the same. He told himself that there *were* other survivors. The soldiers were proof of that, yet it wasn't enough. He needed there to be some other, more immediate sign of life.

With his attention only occasionally on the road, he didn't see the pig until it was almost too late. He stamped on the brakes as it dashed from the undergrowth. The SUV came to a rest ten feet from its snout. The animal's beady eyes stared at him, and he stared back, baffled. It was a pig, not a boar. From its size, and the bright red tag on one ear, it wasn't a wild one.

"Where'd you come from?"

It had to be a smallholding or maybe an organic farm, and it had to be nearby. The pig gave a disdainful snort before walking sedately across the road and disappearing into the undergrowth.

A fence must have broken. Or perhaps a dying farmer had released the animals so they could forage and so have a chance at life. It was as likely a story as any other, and the notion pleased him. He decided to believe it was the truth. He reached for the door handle, intending to step outside and see if he could spot the farm. He stopped. There was a reason that animal was running. An obvious threat that it was trying to escape. He put his foot on the gas and continued.

He'd seen few cars – far fewer than during the days before his capture. There were no contrails in the sky, and no voices on the radio. The only humanoid figures he saw were distinctly dead. He'd always considered himself a loner. He'd been happy living alone, dining alone, working alone. Now that there was nowhere to hide from that lie, he saw it for what it was: an excuse for having no one to live, eat, or work with. That was why he'd created Sholto. For that matter, it was why he'd created Tom Clemens. It was why he'd delayed taking revenge for his parents' death when he'd had the chance. He'd been holding onto the idea that he could have a normal life, even when he knew it was impossible. He'd spurned companionship because nothing based on the lie he lived could ever last. But now, above all, he wanted to see a living person, and know he wasn't alone. As such, even if it wasn't for the need to find a Geiger counter, when he saw the sign for the town of Fairview, he decided to stop.

Half a mile from the town, he came to a checkpoint. Five-foot-high corrugated metal sheets stretched across the road, supported at either end by cement-filled oil-drums. It was deserted, at least by the living. Three zombies had been squatting in the road, almost touching the metal barricade. The sound of the engine had woken them from their torpor.

He stopped the vehicle fifty yards away, climbed out and reached for the carbine. He raised it to his shoulder, but hesitated. There was something desolate about the checkpoint and the town beyond. He checked behind and to either side. It did appear that there were only these three zombies in front of him. All wore bright colored fleeces, now covered in a fine coating of mud and dirt. There was nothing unusual in their clothing, yet something felt wrong. He reached for the axe he'd brought from the farm.

One of the zombies had a limp. Tom wondered if the person it had been had sustained an injury, or whether it was something that had occurred since its undeath. It was an idle thought, something to distract his mind from the snapping teeth and clawing hands. He raised the axe, resting it on his shoulder, and walked away from the truck. When he felt he had room enough to swing, he stopped, waiting.

There was a trace of tape around the wrists of the closest zombie. Had that been to keep gloves on, or because the person had been tied up? Had he been tied down after being infected? The zombie was now ten feet away. Tom swung low, a great scything sweep of the axe. The head smashed into the zombie's leg, ripping away a chunk of decaying muscle. The zombie fell, hitting the concrete jaw-first in a spray of teeth and gore. Tom took a step back, shifting his grip, and then took a step forward. He back-swung the axe into the legs of the second zombie. It fell, toppling onto the first. The third was still twenty feet away. Tom swung up, down, up, and down again, swiftly crushing the skulls of the two fallen zombies, before side-stepping them and walking toward the last. An overhead swing, and he crushed its skull.

"Easier than shooting them," he murmured. And almost as quick, but the axe was now covered in brown-black gore, and he had nothing with which to clean it. He dropped it on the road, climbed back in the truck, and drove on to the checkpoint.

The metal sheeting was easily pulled back. There was no one beyond, though the presence of disposable paper cups suggested that there had been.

"Recently, too," he murmured. "I'm no detective, but there's coffee still in that cup." It had been watered down by rain, but the cup was only a quarter full. He stared at it for far longer than was necessary.

"That's right," he said. "You're no detective, and you're not going to leach out any more meaning than that."

He drove the truck through the barricade and stopped again to drag the metal sheets back into place. It wasn't for his own protection, but someone had decided the road needed to be blockaded. Was that to keep the zombies out, or perhaps to keep something in?

The road was quickly bracketed by houses. Some doors and windows were open. Clothing and other possessions littered the driveways, suggesting the inhabitants had fled in haste. He saw no one by the time he reached the square at the center of town. Ringed with benches, it was dominated by the statue of a man in a frockcoat and three-cornered hat. On the far side of the square was a grey-stone and white-paint municipal building signposted as being shared by the police, fire service, and mayor. He pulled the truck to a halt by the public entrance and got out.

He resisted the urge to shout and yell. If there'd been people in the town, they would have heard the engine. So where had they gone?

A bloated crow flapped down from a streetlight and landed on the roof of the SUV. It twisted its head so that one beady eye, then the other, could give him an almost curious examination.

"What have you been eating?" Tom asked, and then wished he hadn't. There were no bodies, at least that he could see. Nor were there bullet holes or other signs that the town had been overrun. He told himself that if the buildings were full of the undead, they would head toward the engine. Even so, he wanted to get out of the town as quickly as possible.

He looked again at the crow. There was another possibility, another method by which all the townsfolk could have died. The presence of the bird was slim comfort against the dread that he'd walked into a hot zone.

"Find the Geiger counter, and get out," he murmured, repeating it to himself as he headed to the firehouse. The shutters were down, and the door near it was locked, but easily broken. Two gleaming fire trucks were inside. Next to the nearest were buckets and rags from where someone had been cleaning it before their abrupt departure.

He found the Geiger counter in a locker on the furthest truck. It looked unused, almost forgotten. The display was digital, suggesting the municipality's concern was for accidental spills rather than thermonuclear war. It worked, and that gave him comfort as he deciphered the reading. It was a little above normal. He waved it over himself, then went back outside, and tried the SUV. The reading didn't change. He aimed the device at the crow. The bird flapped its wings and managed a ponderous few feet of flight before landing heavily on the road. The display stayed the same.

As he relaxed, he realized how tense he'd been. That only left the mystery of where the townsfolk had gone. The desire to leave was still there, but it no longer had the urgency of earlier.

The doors to the police station were unlocked. There was no one at the desk, or inside the small office behind. From the chairs, he doubted the town had more than twenty officers. From the shuttered stores on Main Street, he guessed a population in the low thousands. They hadn't died from radiation, or all been infected. What did that leave? What if there was something else, some chemical weapon that had been used? And why not? Why would any nation, on having made the decision to unleash the zombie virus, and then a nuclear war, not use everything else in their arsenal?

He grabbed at papers on the desk, rifling through them, scattering them on the ground as he searched for some answer, some vague reassurance. There was nothing. He kicked a bin. It skittered across the floor. After it had come to rest, he heard a sound. Something faint. He raised the carbine, turning, looking around the room, but it was empty. The sound was still there, a beating noise that came from behind a door. And was that a voice?

He crossed to the door. Even without the cautionary signs, he would have known it led to the cells. On the nearest desk were a bundle of keys. He checked the door with the Geiger counter before he unlocked it. Carbine held awkwardly in one hand, he swung the five-inch-thick door open. The smell hit him first. Then the heat. Then the voice.

"Mitch, please, let me out. You've got to let me out!" It was desperate, male, young, and beyond terrified.

He propped the door open and retrieved the keys before taking two steps down the corridor. The first three doors were closed and led to sealed rooms. Just beyond, and on opposite sides of the corridor, were two larger, old-fashioned cells with floor-to-ceiling bars. Arms stretched out through one.

"Please, Mitch!"

"Step back from the bars," Tom called.

"I'm not near them. Who are you?"

"Step back."

"I'm not by the bars!"

Tom took another step, and a third. He glanced through the small window of the sealed room, but only long enough to confirm it was empty before he returned his attention to those arms. They were causing the knocking. As he got closer, he saw where the skin had been worn away. On the floor, underneath, was a drying brown-red pool.

"Please. Whoever you are, you have to help me!"

"Stand back!" Tom called, not talking to the young man, but to the other figure. He didn't expect a reply, and as he took another step, and saw her face, knew that she couldn't.

The zombie turned its sightless eyes toward him. The arms moved more frantically. No sound came from its mouth. Its jaw hung loosely from a wrecked face it had beaten raw against the bars. He glanced at the other cell. A young man in sweat-stained clothing cowered in the corner.

"Stay back," Tom said as kindly as he could manage. He fired a single shot into the head of the zombie. The creature collapsed.

"Thank you. Thank you," the man said. "Please. Please let me out."

"Sure," Tom said. He took a closer look at the man as he made a production out of finding the correct key. He was unshaven, unwashed, and around twenty-five, with a once-broken nose, and a star-shaped tattoo on the inside of his wrist. His accent wasn't strong, but nor was it out of place. In his cell were two pallets, one of water, the other of canned food. It was the same in the cell across the corridor. From the abrasions on the bars, and the broken can opener, the man had tried to cut his way out with the kitchen implement.

"What happened to the town?" Tom asked. "Where's everyone else?"

"They took shelter," the man said. "Because of the bombs. To avoid the radiation."

"Where?"

"The old mine."

"A mine?" Addison's guards had said something about a mine, but surely this was too far north. There were plenty of mines in America. "Why didn't you go with them?"

"Because I'm not from around here," he said. "That's all. She was the same. They left us here to die from radiation."

Tom tried a key he knew wouldn't fit. "There's no radiation here." He tapped the Geiger counter.

"Then the bombs didn't fall? They were lying?" the man asked.

"No, they fell. At least two of them," Tom said. He tried another key that was the wrong shape and size. He wasn't sure if he should let the man out. It wasn't the mention of a mine that was making him hesitate. It was the presence of the water and food in the cell. Whoever had locked the man up hadn't wanted him to starve, yet didn't want him to come with them to safety. Equally, they hadn't simply let him go. The only alternative to freeing the man was to find the mine, and the people therein. Assuming they were alive. Assuming they weren't all undead.

"She wasn't a zombie when they locked her up?" Tom asked.

"She turned. Please. Please let me out."

If she was infected, others probably were, too. They had gone into a mine when they heard some warning about the bombs. They had been infected, and that would explain why they hadn't emerged. He might be wrong, but he wasn't about to unleash thousands of undead from some underground tomb. That left him with a decision about whether he should free the young man, but it wasn't really a decision at all. He opened the cell.

"Thank you. Thank you," the man said.

Tom shrugged away his thanks and walked back out into the police station, then out into the street. He wanted to feel the fresh air again.

"Thank you," the man said again, following him outside. "I'm Rufus Greenwald."

"You said you weren't from around here, so where were you heading?" Tom asked.

"North. To Canada," Rufus said.

"I wouldn't," Tom said. "I met some soldiers yesterday. They said they'd seen a mushroom cloud near the border." Although, now he thought about it, they hadn't said where along the border. "Me, I've come from the south. There was at least one bomb dropped somewhere in New York or Pennsylvania."

"Where are you going now?"

"To the coast. So what happened here?" Tom asked.

"I was driving through. I stopped, asking for gas. They locked me up. They said that bombs had fallen on Houston and L.A."

"How did they know?"

"The emergency broadcast system, I guess," Rufus said. "I don't know. Said they were going down to the mines until the radioactivity had passed. Left us locked up."

"Who was the woman?"

"I don't know. She died before she could tell me."

"Where'll you go now?" Tom asked.

"Home, I guess. I mean, I don't know. Pennsylvania, Canada, Texas, California. It's the end of the world, right? I'm going home. If I have to die somewhere, that's where I want to be."

"You might find another Geiger counter in the fire station," Tom said. "Good luck."

"Yeah. And you."

Tom got back in the SUV and drove to the edge of town. There was something about the man that made him regret what he'd done. He couldn't place what, but it was that instinct that he'd developed growing up on the streets, and honed during his years manipulating the paths of power. It was why he'd not told him where he was heading, and why he'd not told the man his name. He reached the edge of town, and another barrier across the road.

On the far side were the undead. He picked up the carbine, climbed onto the roof of the SUV, and picked the zombies off, one by one. When they were lying motionless on the ground, he turned to look back at the town. There was enough death in the world; he'd done the right thing letting Rufus out. He jumped down, opened the gate, and drove through. Pausing only to close it again, he continued east.

Chapter 20 - No Bed, No Breakfast
Crossfields Landing, Maine

Crossfields Landing was on the southern side of a crescent bay. One good road led from the west into Second Street. A far more neglected one ran north to south through Main Street, following the coast. Tom's cottage was off an unpaved, seldom beaten track on the northern edge of the bay. To the north of the bay and south of the village were a pair of decrepit bridges whose repair had been promised for the last eight election cycles. Anyone driving anything larger than a pickup along the coastal road had to divert ten miles inland. This had kept the developers away, but not the tourists. There were a handful of guesthouses and bed-and-breakfasts inside the village and out. During the summer, they'd fill up, but the population of Crossfields Landing was as seasonal as the income. As soon as the leaves began to turn, the tourists would depart, and the majority of the residents went with them. The few that stayed survived on pensions or savings. There was no school, no police station, no nearby industry. It was a place where people scraped by, retired to, or used as a temporary refuge from the rat-race further down the coast.

Tom had fallen in love with the village the moment he'd stumbled across it. When he'd first arrived in America, he'd spent eighteen months drifting from place to place, masquerading as a university student on a year abroad. It wasn't so much that he was searching for a home as that he was seeking a new identity. He tried Los Angeles and Las Vegas, New York and New Orleans, the Floridian delta and the Blue Ridge Mountains, and anywhere else he'd heard mentioned in song or film. He took to hitching and hiking, and by accident had stumbled into Crossfields Landing. Quite literally. Having spent his entire young life in a city, he'd been unaccustomed to reading a map or using a compass. He thought he was heading west, so when he caught sight of the tempestuous Atlantic, he assumed it was the Pacific, and was baffled by how he'd traveled so far so quickly. That had caused some amusement when he'd said as much in the only restaurant that was open during that stormy November afternoon.

He'd booked a room for the night and stayed for a month. He would have stayed longer, but there were too many questions he didn't know how to answer.

It was a decade before he'd returned, this time with an American accent. If anyone remembered the geographically confused student, they didn't connect him with Tom. He'd bought the cottage, and dreamed about being able to live there permanently. His fantasies were always muted by the knowledge that the world would have to be turned upside down before he could ever retire. The world *had* changed, but the idea of retirement had been forever lost along with so much else.

He slowed when he reached the sign marking the village as ten miles ahead. In strident lettering was the familiar admonishment that heavy vehicles wanting the coastal route would have to take a different road at the next intersection. Over that was a new, hand-painted message. He couldn't quite make out what it said because of the zombie standing in front of it. He brought the SUV to a halt. The creature staggered out into the road. It appeared to be alone, but he checked and double-checked before getting out of the vehicle. He grabbed the carbine. The zombie lurched another step, moving more erratically than the undead usually did. As it drew nearer, he saw why. It was wearing cowboy boots, high-heeled with pointed toes. Now he was looking for it, he saw the shirt's rhinestones occasionally glittering amidst a layer of dirt.

"Were you a singer? Or at some fancy dress party? Or do you always dress like that?" Then he silently berated himself for asking questions that could never be answered. He fired. The zombie fell. The shot echoed across the landscape, and he wished he had a quieter weapon.

"A sword would be good. Or something medieval. A pike, that's the —" He stopped, as he saw what was written on the sign. *Warning. Quarantine Zone. Do Not Enter.*

There was something achingly familiar about that sign. Before he could work out what, he heard a shot. It wasn't close, and he couldn't pinpoint its direction. There was another. Then a third. Then silence. Was it a hunter? Or a survivor needing assistance? He climbed onto the roof of the SUV, taking in his surroundings. He saw no one, and no more shots came.

Agitation grew as he got back in the truck, but he'd only driven a hundred yards before he thought he heard more shooting. He stopped. Got out. Listened. His stomach twisted in knots. There was a person, somewhere close. Were they trapped by the undead? He could imagine their fear all too easily, and that blossom of hope when they heard the engine. He could also imagine how that hope would fade as the sound of the truck receded into the distance. He grabbed the carbine and fired a shot into the undergrowth. Five seconds. Ten. Twenty. A minute. No reply came. Reluctantly, he got back in the SUV. More slowly than before, with the window wound down, he drove on.

After a quarter mile, he saw the intersection with the roads that ran north and south for vehicles that had to bypass the broken bridges. On the far side of the junction, two bed-and-breakfasts loomed at one another from opposite sides of the road. One was painted red, the other blue. There was a story about the buildings, how they'd once been owned by two families whose rivalry put the Hatfields and McCoys to shame. His mind wasn't on that, but on the smattering of corpses by the buildings, and the pack of zombies in the road between the two properties. They'd heard the sound of the engine and were drifting toward the road. Someone inside the red-painted house had heard it, too. A bearded man had opened the window and was waving at him.

Tom did a quick calculation and came up with an estimate of between thirty and fifty zombies. They were getting nearer. He stuck the SUV into reverse and drove back thirty yards. Balancing the carbine on the open doorframe, he took aim. He fired one careful shot after another. Not all hit, and not all those that did were fatal. A zombie collapsed, but it was only when it stood up again that he realized the bullet had taken it in the chest. When the magazine was empty, twelve lay unmoving on the road. The rest were heading toward him, the nearest now less than a hundred yards away. He drove back another fifty yards. He reloaded, took aim, and began firing again. He downed five before he had to drive back another four dozen yards. Three of the slower-moving creatures had turned back to the house. He fired. Aimed. Fired. Reversed. Reloaded. Fired. Twelve zombies were left, and they were all heading back to people trapped in the house.

He got back in the SUV and drove forward. He raised his foot over the brake, but, wanting to end the confrontation quickly, slammed it into the gas. The SUV rocked as it drove over the bodies of the twice-dead until he reached the trailing line of zombies drifting back to the house. The bumper slammed into one zombie. He swerved left, dragging another under the tires. Right, and he'd lost too much momentum. The creature was pushed along the road, its arms slapping against the hood. He hit another, and then stopped three feet from the broken white-picket fence. The zombies moved toward him. In the mirror, he saw one of those he'd mowed down slowly stand up. Before he could be surrounded, he put his shoulder to the door, slamming it open and into a snarling face. Not waiting to finish the creature off, he grabbed the carbine and clambered onto the roof.

The SUV rocked as the zombies walked into it. His feet slipped as elbows and arms, knees and legs, faces and palms beat against metal and glass. As those grasping, reaching hands stretched up to him, he tried to aim, but it was as much as he could do to stay on his feet. He fired, missed, and hadn't braced the gun properly. The recoil put him off balance, and as the vehicle rocked sideways, he slipped, falling to his knees. Cursing his stupidity and the ridiculously small target a head made, even at such a close range, he fired at shoulders and arms and any piece of necrotic flesh he could see.

"Go! Go! Go!" a voice bellowed. Out of the corner of his eye, he registered that the door to the house had opened, and people were running out. Three or six, he wasn't sure. He fired again, now trying to keep the creature's attention. When he glanced at the house, he saw a small mob running out the door. A grey-haired man was in the lead. He slashed a bowie knife across the neck of a zombie with such force it neatly decapitated the creature. The others weren't so well armed. With crude wooden clubs, or the butts of their rifles and shotguns, they beat and struck at the zombies. The air filled with the sound of breaking bone and primal screaming that drowned out the low rasp of the undead.

179

With the arrival of this new prey, the zombies turned away from the SUV. It stopped rocking, and he was able to stand, aim, and fire. Aim. Fire. Aim. Fire. And with one last savage slash of the bowie knife, the old man killed the last of the zombies.

"Tom?" a familiar voice called in a tone of sheer disbelief. He turned. He saw Helena.

"It is. It's you!" she said.

He jumped down from the vehicle, his feet landing softly on a road covered with dark brown gore. "Sorry, I'm a bit late."

"Tom?" the grey-haired man asked, walking over to him. "As in Tom Clemens?"

"I am," Tom said. "I remember you. You live in Crossfields Landing." He didn't remember much more than that. The man was about sixty, and six feet tall, with a lined face that spoke of experiences of twice that number of years. The slight paunch he'd been developing the last time Tom had seen him was starting to disappear.

"Jonas Jeffreys," the man said. He didn't extend his hand. Instead he carefully peeled off gloves covered in dark brownish blood. "So this is the guy, is it?" he asked Helena.

"This," she said, "is the guy."

"You're the one who tried to stop the outbreak?" a younger man asked. "He clapped Tom on the shoulder. "Our savior! We ran out of ammo. Would have been in trouble if you hadn't turned up."

"Wouldn't have had any problems at all, Gregor, if you'd kept a proper watch like I told you," Jonas said, running a rag down his monstrous blade with a theatrical flourish.

The young man dropped his head and walked a few steps back to the house. The others, a mixture of men and women of a variety of ages, watched Tom with a mixture of interest and caution.

"What happened, Tom?" Helena asked.

"The short version?" he asked.

"The very, *very* short version," she said. "I've told them all you told me."

"It was Charles Addison," Tom said. "He was behind it. The cabal recruited him at some point during the election campaign. They wanted someone in Max's administration who could be blamed for all that happened. He figured that out and began killing off the conspirators himself. He drugged the president and arranged for the military and other assets to be moved to the countryside where they'd be safe from the undead. He intended to redeploy them once he'd secured his grip on power. He got Max to appoint him to the cabinet and began killing off those in the line of succession. That was his plan. It was never going to work, and in the end, it didn't."

"He was behind the zombies?" Jonas asked.

"No. I don't know who was," Tom said. "Did she tell you about Dr Ayers? Well, the only reason they abducted her was because I had looked up her address on a computer that they found when they were looking for me. Though they got there first, they were actually following me. She didn't know how to stop the zombies, and they wanted me alive because, in part, they thought I did. The other part was to frame me as the one responsible for all this."

"What about the bombs?" Helena asked.

"You heard about those? Russia or China, I guess. There was something Addison said that made me think we retaliated. There was a failsafe plan that devolved command and control to the field, and I'm pretty sure that was put into action. Addison's dead. I shot him myself. A nuclear bomb was dropped within twenty miles of the place they were holding me. Factor in the people Addison killed, and though there might be a few members left, the cabal's effectively been destroyed. But they killed the president, and the first family. That's a story for somewhere else."

"What you're saying is that it's over," Jonas said.

"Yeah. I'd say so. On my way here, I met a few people and learned that bombs fell on Los Angeles and Houston, and somewhere along the Canadian border, probably close to Montreal or Ottawa. There have to be other bombs, but the good news is that I found a Geiger counter, and from the border with Vermont all the way here, the reading has been normal."

"It's over," Jonas said, speaking to the group. "Which means we've only got to worry about food, water, the zombies, the weather, and disease. Get your gear. Get the trucks loaded. We're moving out in twenty minutes. Gregor, keep watch. A proper watch this time. And… yeah, pass out the ammunition. But keep your safeties on, everyone. I don't want a repeat of what happened a couple of nights ago."

"And… and what about Bobbi?" a dark-haired woman asked.

"We'll take her body back with us," Jonas said. "Go on, move."

The survivors hurried back to the house, all except Helena.

"Hey," Tom said.

"Hi," she said. A smile crept over her face. "You're alive."

"So are you. And you're here."

"This is where you said we should go," she said. "After the helicopter landed, I drove the truck. Kaitlin stayed behind with the rifle."

"She did?"

"Of course. She stalked through the woods. She was going to shoot them, but they took you on board before she could get a clean shot. There's a lesson there, Tom."

"And Kaitlin? The children?"

"Fine. All fine. Kaitlin was taking a group south today. She wanted to see whether the bridges could be demolished. The kids are in the village. It's a… it's a nice place. I go to sleep at night inside a house, knowing I'll wake in the morning. I never thought that would be as much as I'd need, but it is."

"The sign by the road, the one warning of a quarantine zone, that was you?" he asked.

"Sort of. I told them what we'd seen near Providence. Everyone was worried about too many refugees coming."

"They didn't come?" he asked.

"A few people arrived after we did, but not many. Not enough. Have you seen many others?"

"Since I escaped, since the bombs fell, there was a farmer who was infected. She died. And there were six soldiers, and one guy in a small town. And now you."

"You two can catch up later. For now you can help," Jonas called from the house.

"Help with what?" Tom asked Helena as they walked up the path.

"Supplies," she said. "We're collecting everything that's not nailed down from everywhere that's nearby. Then we're going to come back for the nails. What we can't make, we need to find, and what we can't find, we'll have to learn to do without. That's what Jimmy says. It's become his mantra."

"Jimmy? The kid who runs the restaurant? He's still here? I thought he'd have gone bankrupt."

"Well, that's something we never have to worry about again," Helena said.

"Here, Tom, give me a hand," Jonas called. He led Tom inside, and to a front room where a dead woman lay on the floor. She looked almost peaceful. It was an odd sight, but it took Tom a moment to work out why. It was that he could see her face. No one had destroyed her brain.

"How did she die?" Tom asked.

"Bled out," Jonas said. The dark-haired woman passed him a sheet. "Thank you, Naomi," he said.

Together, they wrapped the woman up. "Tom, take her legs."

Tom grabbed hold, and together they carried her out to the pickup.

"She didn't turn," Tom said, as they placed her in the back of the vehicle.

"No," Jonas said. "She was bitten as she was trying to get the box of ammo from the van. My fault." He sighed. "We need to conserve ammunition, and this lot, they shoot at shadows. We've Kaitlin and a few veterans, but most people haven't even been on a range. Lost a couple to friendly fire a few nights ago. Literally a couple. They went for a moonlight walk. Didn't tell the sentries."

"Damn."

"Yeah. So I was keeping the ammo in the truck," Jonas said. "I thought that would be safer, get people out of the habit of relying on guns for when the ammo is gone. It was a tragic miscalculation, based on never having seen more than a couple of the undead at a time. Don't know where those zombies came from. I mean, they came from over there." He gestured to the north. "You can see the trail they cut, and they must have heard the sound of the engines, but where they started from, that's the real question. One that's going to give me a lot of sleepless nights." He rested his hands on the tailgate. "You worked for the president. They say you were some kind of secret agent."

"Entirely civilian," Tom said. "I worked for him before he was elected. When Addison realized he was going to take the fall for the conspiracy, he set me up."

"I guess what I'm asking," Jonas said, "is whether you know of... I don't know, a military command or... Is it just us? Is any help going to come?"

"I don't think so."

"Helena said something about Britain being free of the zombies. That they were putting together an evacuation or something. You think they might have survived?"

"Who knows where the bombs have fallen? But I might be able to find out. And there might be other survivors. I saw a few, but I was held prisoner for over a week. Their attempts at torture were crude and brief, but it was far from restful. The bombs saved my life, but since then I've been on the road. Ask me my opinion after I've had some sleep and a decent meal, and I might have a better answer." He looked down again at the corpse. "She didn't turn."

"No. Bled out before she could. I think an artery was cut, though the position of the wound is wrong. I could carry out an autopsy, I guess, but to what end? Dead is dead. That's even more true now than before."

Chapter 21 - The Village At The End Of The World
Crossfields Landing, Maine

Tom drove, following Jonas and the others back to the village. Helena sat in the passenger seat. The rear was filled with half-empty boxes and hastily packed suitcases.

"I can't tell you how good it is to see you," Helena said. "There's been so much bad news of late."

"Getting here was that difficult?"

"It wasn't easy," she said. "I'll tell you about it sometime, but we got here. That's what matters. And they let us in. I wasn't sure they would. Martha swung it. Or the presence of the children did."

"Who's Martha?"

"You'll meet her. We're living with her, me, Kaitlin, and the kids. She and Jonas are running things. Well, not exactly running. It's not as organized as that. They know what to do, or they act like it, and everyone else is happy to follow. More or less."

"Who's 'everyone else'?"

"It's a mix," she said. "Some are locals, if you count anywhere within fifty miles as local. Some are refugees, and there're a few who lived here years ago, moved away for work, but headed back because they couldn't think of anywhere safer. Not everyone stays. That's the weird thing. People sometimes leave. Not in the last couple of days, but there were a few who decided to take their chances elsewhere. They were hunting for a better refuge than we had to offer. And there were three guys who... well, I don't know what happened, but I think Jonas kicked them out. He's a good guy. Most of the people are. Sort of."

"Sort of?"

"I don't know, Tom. It's all too much to take in. Against what standards should their actions be judged? The old ones seem inadequate. Everything works for now, and it will probably work tomorrow. That's as far ahead as I'm willing to guess, particularly after... after the bombings. What's it really like out there?"

"On the road? I'm still processing it." The convoy began to slow. They passed another sign warning of a quarantine zone ahead. Just behind it was a pile of twice-dead zombies.

"Abigail was worried about so many refugees coming that their farm would be overrun," he said.

"Who's Abigail?"

He told her about the old farmer he'd met, reaching the point where she died just as the convoy came to a halt.

"It's the roadblock," Helena said. "They've got to move the razor wire out of the way."

A moment later, the minivan started moving again. As he drove past, Tom saw a great mass of razor wire to the side of the road. Thick wooden boards had been attached to the side so that the wire could be moved, allowing the vehicles to drive through. Once all three vehicles were past, the wire was dragged back into place. Fifteen feet deep, it stretched off to either side of the road, wrapping around trees, occasionally reinforced with concrete and metal.

"Impressive," he murmured.

"It stops the zombies. Not that there are many," she said. "Only a couple a day. Until today."

The barricade beyond the wire was little different to the other hastily built emplacements he'd seen. Metal and wood, reinforced with concrete, set around a movable gate. Behind it was a crude rampart, currently manned by a pair of sentries who looked simultaneously bored and curious as to who this new arrival was.

"Is it really over, Tom?" she asked.

"The conspiracy, yeah, I think so. I think Jonas had the right of it. All we've got now is the zombies, starvation, radiation, the weather, and all the rest to worry about. I guess it really could be worse."

The convoy came to a halt on Main Street.

"We're using the old tackle shop as a storeroom," Helena said, getting out. Tom followed her. A small crowd had gathered, though their attention wasn't on him but on the corpse that Naomi and Jonas were maneuvering out of the truck's bed. Tom stood and watched, not looking at the funereal labor but at the people. Living, breathing people. Some looked upset, others tired, but none looked scared.

"Too many zombies came," Jonas said. He didn't shout, but his voice carried clearly over the small crowd. "About fifty of them, all told. Bobbi died. It's sad. It's very sad, but some of you are meant to be on guard. For everyone else, we'll be burying her in the old cemetery in half an hour."

Tom watched as people went to help carry the dead woman's body. He wanted to help, but it wasn't his place. He hadn't known her, and his presence would only bring questions that would detract from a moment that should be about the life of a woman who'd died.

"The children will want to see you," Helena said.

"Sure. And I'd like to see them," he said.

They were staying in a house off Second Street. Almost big enough to be a hotel, it was a private home, belonging, he guessed to the spry woman who opened the door. Her fiery-red hair would return to grey when the dye ran out, and there was a taut smoothness to the lines around the mouth suggesting a recent lift, but nothing could hide the experience in the eyes or the kindness in her smile.

"This is Tom Clemens," Helena said.

"It is? How wonderful," she said. "I'm Martha Greene. I'm sure we'll have lots to talk about, but for now you can distract the children. I saw the body from the top window. Who was it?"

"Bobbi," Helena said.

"That's sad," Martha said. "Any death would be, but hers, now?" She sighed. "If you can watch the children, I'd like to go to the cemetery."

"You came back!" Luke exclaimed. Only a protest that he needed to wash and change prevented Tom from being mobbed. He was halfway through a cold shower before he realized why the children were so excited. In this new world, when people left, they seldom returned. Washed, and wearing someone else's clothes, he had no excuse not to go downstairs. Luke was waiting in the hall, Soanna in the doorway to the front room.

"You have to tell us what happened," she said. Her tone was accusatory. He let himself be led into the room. Other than an old sofa, older armchair, and very new TV, it was sparsely furnished. The children were rectifying that with an odd assortment of toys, a semi-permanent blanket fort, and almost as many books as had been in the library of the house they'd stayed in the first night he'd met them.

"Well?" Soanna prompted.

"Do you remember the helicopter?" he asked.

"Of course," she said.

After he'd sanitized the events of the past week and a half, the version he told them was almost as brief as the summary he'd given Helena, Jonas, and the others outside of the bed-and-breakfast.

"I see," Soanna said when he'd finished. Before she could pronounce judgment on his tale, the door opened. Kaitlin came in.

"You made it," she said.

"So did you," Tom said.

"You missed the story," Luke said.

"He was telling us what happened," Soanna added.

"Are the children safe?" Kaitlin asked.

"Safer than they would have been," Tom said.

"Good," she said. "That's what matters. I'm glad you're alive, but word's spread that you're here. Everyone wants to know what you saw."

He eased himself out of the chair. Leaving Helena to watch the children, he followed Kaitlin back outside.

The meeting was being held in the restaurant. The old sign had been taken down, but the new one had yet to be put up. He wondered whether Jimmy even had the funds to have had a new sign made. In a place where little ever happened, the arrival of Jimmy and Andy had been talked about so much the previous summer that even Tom, during his one brief visit, had heard of it. The rest of the details had been provided during his last weekend here after the election.

They were two brothers. Andy had been in college, a quarterback on a football scholarship. Jimmy was still in high school when Andy had sustained a head injury during a training session. It resulted in irreparable neurological damage, though Tom wasn't precisely sure how that manifested. Andy and Jimmy's parents, on getting the phone call no parent ever wants, had jumped into their car, sped away from their home, and then died in a five-car pile-up on the freeway five miles from the hospital.

With the insurance claims to both accidents tied up in court, Jimmy had sold their parents' home, and moved himself and his brother to Maine. The building had been a tackle shop and store, and part of their inheritance, though it had been shuttered for years. They'd brought a couple of friends with them and hadn't arrived with empty pockets. Even so, their funds had been seriously drained when they'd opened a restaurant in a place that only had customers for three months of the year. However close they must have been to absolute penury, the cruel twists of fate that had brought them here might just have saved their lives.

Andy still had a footballer's physique, and looked incongruous in apron and rubber gloves standing in the door to the kitchen. Jimmy, half his size and a quarter his width, bustled about and behind, carrying trays of bowls to the tables. A quick headcount told Tom there were around seventy people inside the building, seated at tables that had been pushed together into two long rows. Light came from lanterns hanging on supporting joists, turning quizzical features into sinister expressions.

"Come on, over here," Jonas said, taking Tom's arm and leading him toward a bar from which all the bottles had been removed. "You're going to have to sing for your supper. Or talk, at least. Tell us what's going on in the world."

Tom looked at the faces staring back at him. They all had the same expression of exhausted curiosity.

"It began a long time ago, but I'll start with the election," he said. He talked as food was served, as it was eaten, and for long after the empty bowls were pushed away. He kept to the truth, and almost the entire truth at that. When he finished, their expressions had changed. Some were shocked, some confused, others were angry.

"That's bombs fallen on California, Texas, Pennsylvania or New York, and across the border in Canada," Jonas said in summary. "No help is coming. We're on our own, and we don't know the extent of the devastation. We'll have to talk about this, and what it means, and how it changes what we have to do, but not tonight because it doesn't change what we have to do tomorrow. Thank you for sharing what you know, Tom," he finished. "Jimmy, is there anything left for him to eat?"

The teenager placed a bowl on a table by the kitchen door. Tom was grateful to sit, and kept his eyes down as he ate. It was actually quite good, a fish stew where at least the principal ingredient was fresh. He didn't look up when he heard chairs being pushed under tables and people moving to the door.

"It is a lot to take in," Jimmy said quietly when the restaurant was almost empty.

"Not really," Kaitlin said. "This morning, we woke knowing nuclear bombs had fallen, but we didn't know where. All that's changed is that we know Addison was behind some part of this apocalypse, and that he's dead. That doesn't alter what we have to do tomorrow."

"No," Jonas said. "It doesn't. Find enough supplies to create a stockpile. Always more supplies. Food's a priority, but medicine's a close second. There's a lot of people here running low on their prescriptions."

"And we need more crockery," Jimmy said. "Andy and me'll be up until midnight washing this lot. We'll be up again before dawn, chopping the wood to burn on the stove to heat the water to wash the bowls from breakfast." He said the last as if it was a nursery rhyme, and with a smile as if to emphasize that he didn't mind the labor.

"Chickens," Andy rumbled from the doorway. Tom waited to see if anything more would be added.

"Thanks for reminding me," Jimmy said. "We've been talking about it. Eggs would make a nice change from fish."

"Another thing to look for tomorrow, then," Jonas said, standing up.

"Tomorrow," Tom said. "Can I borrow a flashlight to get back to my cottage?"

"No," Jonas said. "Everyone sleeps in the village."

"Everyone sleeps on Main Street or Second," Helena said. "But you can sleep in the house."

"Sure," Jonas said. "He has to go back there, anyway. Martha will want to know the story, too."

They bid goodnight to Jimmy and Andy, and stepped out into the dark street. The complete absence of electric lights and the lack of engine noise made it impossible to pretend that it was an ordinary night. Whether it was the company of others, the organization of such a large group, or the welcome he'd received despite everything he'd told them, he felt hopeful. The old world was gone, and with it his old life. A new one was beginning. It would never be easy, but for him, if for no one else, it might be a better one.

Chapter 22 - A New Day, A New Life
March 15ᵗʰ, Crossfields Landing, Maine

He was woken by the sound of children running down the wooden stairs. He didn't move. He couldn't remember the last time he'd slept so well. It was the smell of coffee that finally dragged him out of his warm cocoon. He searched for the candle he'd been given the night before, and then for the book of matches. By flickering flame, trying not to think about a past long before he was born, he dressed in borrowed clothes. The only clue as to whom they'd once belonged was that the label in the thick sweater was for a store that had gone bankrupt a decade before.

He found his way along the dark corridor to the bathroom. The sound of the flush was one of the sweetest he'd ever heard, even if the cistern then had to be refilled from a bucket. It was all so close to normal, yet so different. The man who stared at him in the mirror was unrecognizable. Grey poked through hair that had been dyed black a month before. Stubble had grown into a ragged beard that was more salt than pepper, and barely hid the deep lines that cut into sunken cheeks.

"You're alive," he whispered. He repeated the words, but found them hard to believe. They were still raw, but his experiences were becoming memories. He made his way downstairs, pausing by the partially open door to the living room. The children were inside, playing quietly. He listened, telling himself that whatever he might have failed to do, they were alive, too.

The door to the kitchen was open, the room brightly lit compared to the rest of the house. Flames crackled in a stove and flickered from a pair of candles on a kitchen table where Martha and Jonas sat opposite one another.

"It's nice to hear them," Tom said, nodding at the adjoining wall through which the children could be heard. "Reminds you what life's all about."

"You have no children?" Martha asked. "That's a blessing in times like these. There's oatmeal for breakfast. Sit down, I'll fix you some."

"And coffee?" Tom asked.

Jonas leaned back and picked up the old-fashioned pot from the stove. He poured Tom a cup. "Coffee we have a lot of," he said. "And oatmeal. For now, at least."

"For about a month, I think," Martha said. "It depends on how many more people come. We can't turn them away."

"No, I suppose not," Jonas said, in a tone that suggested that was what they'd been discussing before Tom had entered the room.

"That was our big concern," Martha said, "that we'd be swamped by refugees. The stories Helena told us about your time on the road, and what Kaitlin and others said, turned concern into fear, but we've hardly seen anyone."

"Where are Helena and Kaitlin?" Tom asked.

"On guard duty," Jonas said. "They've got the midnight to six a.m. shift on the main road. We need steady hands and calm minds for that watch."

"It's because of the monsters," Soanna said. Tom turned around. The girl stood in the doorway. "They come at night so Kaitlin and Helena watch for them. No one goes out at night. It's not safe."

"That's right, dear," Martha said. "Now go back and watch the others."

Soanna gave a half-shrug as if she wanted to stay in the room, but then thought better of arguing. She left.

"They come all the time," Jonas said. "Never as many as we saw yesterday, at least not in one go. At night you can't see them. You hear them getting caught up in the razor wire. We burned through a lot of ammunition when people got nervous and fired blindly at sounds. Of course, the gunfire woke up the entire village. By the time we got a light on the road, we saw it was just one or two of them. So since then, we've had a new policy. Everyone stays in at night. The guards are to warn us if the zombies make it past the razor wire. That's when we take to the walls. If the monsters stay beyond the razor wire, we deal with them at dawn."

Martha smiled. "Monsters? The children are rubbing off on you."

Jonas gave a noncommittal shake of his head. They knew each other, Tom thought, and for a long time. They weren't a couple, but were clearly comfortable in each other's company.

"How long until the candles are gone?" Tom asked, gesturing at the flickering flame.

"Another week," Jonas said. "And then we'll be using the batteries and the flashlights. We've been keeping them for when we have to patrol. Candles aren't safe for that. But we'll be out of batteries before the days get long enough that we don't need them."

"I can't offer you honey," Martha said, putting a bowl down in front of Tom. "We have to keep that for wounds. We're sorely lacking in medical supplies. And I can't offer you sugar, since we don't want to waste it on sweetening when it can be used in baking and for preserves. We do have peanut butter."

"This is fine, thanks."

"It's the wrong time of year," Jonas said, refilling his cup. "If this had happened in April, the bars and restaurants would have begun stocking up for the summer trade. As it is, we've got what little Jimmy had in his storeroom and what we can find in the unoccupied houses, but most of the seasonal inhabitants emptied their larders when they went home last fall."

"It should get easier," Martha said. "When the zombies stop."

"It's been three weeks since it began. I don't see why they should stop, not ever," Jonas said. He looked at Tom. "Unless I'm wrong?"

"I've no better idea than you," Tom said.

"Then that brings us back to the problem of ammo and food," Jonas said. "But no," he added, "we can't turn anyone away. We'll need people more than we need anything else."

"Not many have arrived here, then?" Tom asked.

"There were a few who followed the coastal road, but most kept going," Jonas said. "But that was only a couple of vehicles a day. I guess anything larger heading along that route detoured inland, and if they'd come this far, saw no reason to stop. We've had a few who came in on foot."

"And by sea?" Tom asked.

"A lot of boats passed us by," Jonas said. "Sailing ships, pleasure cruisers, trawlers, even a few tankers. Where the roads were quiet, the sea was abuzz. We've a shore-to-ship radio, and we broadcast a message saying that we'd been overrun, that we were trapped. Some would talk with us, but Martha was the only person who came ashore to investigate."

"I thought this was your house," Tom said to her.

"Who in their right mind would want to retire to a place like this?" she replied.

Jonas gave a snort. "It's my house. Those are my clothes you're wearing."

"Oh. Right. Thanks. Um... you said you spoke to the people in the ships? Where were they heading?"

"Some were just trying to get as far away as they could. Those with a plan were heading to Canada or Greenland. I'm not sure why, except I guess a rumor started that it was safe, and it spread because people wanted to believe it. We saw people going north. We didn't see anyone come back. We did hear whispers of a naval battle somewhere in the eastern Atlantic. The word mutiny was repeated a few times. Mostly we heard a lot of desperation."

Tom found his bowl was empty. He reached for his cup. "Part of my original plan was to sail to Britain. I was going to make most of the journey on a fishing trawler, but I was going to start with the boat I have by my cottage."

"It's not there anymore," Jonas said. "We moved it down to the jetty. We've got all the boats there. If we get overrun, we'll take to the sea. That's as much of an escape plan as we have. We stripped your cottage as well."

"Did you find the hidden room?"

"No," Jonas said. "The FBI didn't either."

"They came here?"

"At the end of January. Said the guy who owned the place was implicated in a series of bombings. There were only two of them, and they didn't stay long."

"It was Addison who was behind the bombings," Tom said. "And no, I knew no one had found the room before the power was cut. I had an alarm set up that would have sent me an alert if anyone tried to get inside. I couldn't rig the house itself, that would have been too obvious a sign that there was something valuable hidden there. Even so... no, they probably weren't FBI."

"Does that matter?" Martha asked.

Tom weighed it up. "No. But there's some M16s and ammo in there, along with some long-life rations. More importantly, there's a server to which I copied files on the outbreak, the conspiracy, and the collapse. I don't know how much it will help, but it might fill in the details of everything that's happened."

"That's of questionable value right now," Jonas said. He gestured at the window. "Dawn's coming. I need to check the perimeter. You fancy a walk?"

From the tone, it wasn't a question. Tom finished his cup, took a longing look at the pot, and stood.

"You'll need weapons," Jonas said.

"My carbine's in the truck," Tom said, following Jonas out into the front hall.

"It's not. Kaitlin has it. She cleaned it last night and took it out with her. We'll have to get those assault rifles from your cottage later." He took a key from a hook and unlocked a metal cabinet that was completely out of place amidst the faded wallpaper and ancient paint. "I take it those M16s are fully automatic?"

"Yeah."

"You mind telling me why you have them?"

"In case of the end of the world," Tom said. It wasn't true, but now wasn't the time to explain the quest for revenge that had consumed much of his early adult life.

"Huh. A month ago, I'd have called you crazy," Jonas said. "I guess I now have to call you prescient." He opened the cabinet. The first thing Tom noticed was the framed badge and ID.

"You were a cop?"

196

"I was. Ten years as a detective in Florida, ten years in… ah, but what does that matter? Here." He held out a hunting rifle. "We've plenty of .30-06, what we're lacking are people who know how to shoot."

"I thought there would be plenty of hunters around here," Tom said, taking a bag of ammunition.

"You don't hunt cod with lead. In the summer, it'd be different. In the winter, you have people who retired here. Since you do that for the scenery rather than the weather, we've a lot who know how to wield a paintbrush and not much else. Here." He gave Tom a .45 and a bowie knife, already hanging on a belt. "You seen much action?"

"Enough," Tom said, slinging the belt around his waist. "All I'm missing is a ten-gallon hat."

"How things change," Jonas said with no trace of a smile. "How they stay the same." He locked the cabinet, and placed the key back on the hook where it was just out of reach of a child's hands. "Moved the cabinet in from the shop when the children arrived. Stopped hanging the key around my neck last week when the zombies got past the wire. Security versus safety. What a world. Martha, we're leaving!" he called.

The children appeared in the doorway.

"Where are you going?" Luke asked.

"We need to have a word with Kaitlin and Helena," Jonas said. "We'll be back soon. You know the rules?"

"Stay inside," Amber whispered.

"We always stay inside," Soanna said. "But we will, I promise."

"Hot coffee," Martha said, passing Jonas a flask. He put it in a satchel, and gave Martha a nod. Tom gave the children a smile. Only Soanna returned it. The others had anxiety written clear across their faces.

"What a world," he murmured.

Dawn added a soft glow to the dark streets as they walked out onto the road. There was an expectant air to the dark houses as if people were already awake but putting off facing the horrific reality around them.

"You were a detective in Florida," Tom said to fill the silence. "Is that why Martha came all the way up here?"

"There's no short answer to that question," Jonas said. "But I didn't want to exchange pleasantries. Do you know of any reason things might get better than this?"

Tom took in the dark streetlights, the parked cars gathering dust, the wood and metal barrier blocking off an alley between two silent stores. The flickering candle in the window of the restaurant gave him the answer. "I don't see any reason they should get any worse."

"The radiation. That's the reason things will get worse," Jonas said. "Los Angeles and Houston are far away, but the Canadian border isn't. You don't know where that bomb was dropped?"

"No," Tom said. "I should have asked them, but I was so grateful to find people who were alive that most questions slipped my mind."

"What about elsewhere? Other countries?"

"I've no idea," Tom said. "I'm reasonably certain that Addison wanted our missiles to fire, but whether they did, or what targets were hit, I don't know. If Helena's still got my sat-phone and tablet, I might be able to find out."

"What I'm asking is whether there's somewhere out there in the world, somewhere safe. If we get overrun, if the radiation increases, if we have no choice but to take to the sea, where do we go?"

"Britain? They're meant to have a vaccine for this, though I'm suspicious as to whether there's any truth in it."

"Unless I can see it, I won't believe it," Jonas said. "And we didn't see any boats coming back this way. I doubt they found refuge in Canada or Greenland. For those that still had fuel, Britain and Ireland are the only logical destinations. They'll be as overrun as anywhere else. Besides, I doubt we'd make it that far. I don't think we've got the fuel, not for all of us. I thought you might have heard about an aircraft carrier at sea, or a brigade that had disappeared somewhere in the Rockies or... something."

They passed the fire truck. It was more battered than he remembered and somehow seemed smaller.

"No, sorry," Tom said. "I'll try to find out, but while a satellite image might show bomb craters, it won't show much else."

"And the zombies? With what Helena told us about Dr Ayers, I thought you might know something."

"No. Addison didn't either. Whatever Dr Ayers discovered, it wasn't a way to stop them."

"So they might die tomorrow, or still be here next year," Jonas said. "Or out last us all. That's what I thought. Hoped I was wrong. It's this way." He led Tom away from Main Street, onto Second, and toward the barricade built between an antique shop whose stock looked like junk, and a boarded-up frontage whose sign proclaimed art and craft supplies.

"Hear anything in the night?" Jonas asked the pair standing on an oil drum and sheet metal rampart.

"Nothing," the young man said.

"No shooting," the woman clarified. "No screaming."

"Good," Jonas said. "I saw the light in the restaurant. Jimmy and Andy are up, and cooking breakfast. You'll be relieved in half an hour, and there'll be a warm meal waiting for you. Good job."

They climbed over the barricade.

"I'm impressed," Tom said, as they walked down the road.

"We've a barricade on each road in the village, and another a quarter mile out," Jonas said. "That's six in total, with two people always on each. Twelve people who can't go out looking for supplies. Factor in the watch that's sleeping, and whoever's watching the children. Subtract Jimmy and Andy, who barely have time to sleep, let alone leave the kitchen. Then there's old Donna Lenetti whose arthritis makes holding a spoon difficult, and Adam Clitheroe who can barely see his hand in front of his face. All told, we're down to a couple of dozen to do the lion's share of the work. The kids eat breakfast and dinner in the house because it would take too many people to check the streets are safe in the dark. Everyone else eats in the restaurant. The duplication of labor represents only a marginal increase in wastage, but that margin might mean the difference between life and death in the days to come. We're already eating food communally, but we'll be out of everything but fish within a month. Our medical supplies are non-existent, and there's no way of replenishing our ammunition."

"I passed through the First Lady's house in Vermont," Tom said. "There's ammo and fuel there, left by the Secret Service. Some food, too. Probably enough to keep everyone fed for a week."

"Vermont? It'll take us a day to get there and back, and what do we do when the week's up and the food's gone? Sure, that will help. A little here, a little there, it adds up, but it won't be there forever. We need a more permanent solution."

"At least you have fish," Tom said.

"We do. That's the saving grace. We won't starve quickly."

Dawn was spreading fast. The early morning light caught the razor wire strung out across the road and the grass and woodland to either side. He saw the shapes of two people at the sentry post in the middle of the road. One waved, not in greeting, but as a signal that they were human. Jonas raised his arm in return.

"Can't farm," he said. "Can't spare the people to clear the ground. Not that we've anything to plant. There's a few truck-gardens at the back of some houses, but so close to the sea, with so much salt-water in the air, not even the most ardent of hobbyists could get much to grow. You hear it?"

The crashing waves were barely audible. Then he realized that wasn't what Jonas meant. There was another sound. A ripping, tearing, sighing noise coming from ahead.

"Morning," Helena said when they were close enough for her to be heard.

"We brought coffee," Jonas said. "How was the night?"

"Four of them," Kaitlin said, gesturing up the road.

Tom climbed up the crude wooden steps to the left of the moveable gate. The barricade had been built in haste with unseasoned timber and metal not trimmed to size, but it was sturdy. On top were a car battery and a barrage of lights, all now switched off. Beyond was the reason for the soldier's warmth-less welcome. Four zombies were trapped in the razor wire.

The wire stretched across the road, and for fifteen feet deep. The nearest of the creatures had managed to crawl almost along its entire length. The wire had ripped through cloth and torn into skin and muscle, lacerating flesh. A dark stain of tattered clothing and shreds of meat marked the metal over which it had crawled. It tried to raise its arm. The barbs dug in deeper. It didn't stop. There was a visceral rip as the metal sliced into its hand between its ring and second fingers. Tom turned away, trying to block out the rasping sigh. It would have been better if the creature had screamed.

"If we're quiet at night," Jonas said, "they don't move so fast. When dawn comes, when they see us, when they hear us, they rip themselves to shreds trying to get at us."

"Let's finish them," Helena said. She grabbed a long-handled boathook. Tom took another.

"The wire's attached to boards at the side," Jonas said, pushing the gate open. "You drag that back onto the road, as close to the zombies as you can get. You kill them, pull them off the wire, move onto the next." He pulled on a pair of thick, reinforced gloves, and walked to the side of the road, utterly ignoring the four snarling creatures.

Tom raised the boathook and waited. The task at hand was no different to what he'd done a hundred times since the outbreak. If anything, as they were trapped by the razor wire, it was far safer. It was how Jonas, Helena, and Kaitlin were treating it as a chore that got to him. He suspected that was the reason he'd been brought here this morning.

The boathook had a sharpened spike protruding beyond the curved edge. When Jonas had rolled the wire back three feet, Tom was able to step in, stab down, and skewer the zombie's brain.

"Now you have to hook it, and drag it onto the road," Jonas said.

It was harder than he'd thought. The last remnants of the zombie's clothing tore. Its skin ripped, and he lost his grip. He tried to think of it as meat, but it was impossible. Arms, legs, head. It had been a person. By the time he got it onto the asphalt, the next creature had crawled its way close enough that he could skewer it.

"I get your point," Tom said, dragging it clear. "Life's changed."

"That's the message I usually try to imbue," Jonas said. "Today's different."

"This way of living is impossible, Tom," Helena said. "That's what we were talking about last night. We hoped... I don't know what we hoped, but we each had a fantasy of things getting back to normal. Your arrival's just made us accept that it won't happen. Living like this is impossible, but we have to find a way to make it work."

"We've a few ideas how," Kaitlin said, "but we're open to suggestions."

Jonas rolled the wire back. Tom speared the boathook down, piercing the zombie's brain. It sagged onto the wire, motionless. He then stabbed the hook through the shredded flesh. Turning, twisting, and pulling the creature free, he tried to come up with a solution.

When the fourth had been dragged onto the road and then rolled to the side, Kaitlin ran a Geiger counter over them. "Safe," she said.

"It's not that we expect you to have the answers," Jonas said. "It's that everyone has to think about the question." There was a shot in the distance. Everyone looked in that direction.

"Come on," Jonas said, dragging the razor wire back into place. "Better go and see who that is."

The shot had come from the road leading to the north. The barricade had been set up on the far side of the bridge. The razor wire beyond was laid more thickly than on the road that led west. At least forty feet deep, there was a single, motionless zombie caught in the barbs. On duty were two men, one of whom Tom recognized as Gregor, the man who'd been at the bed-and-breakfast the day before.

"Who shot it?" Jonas asked.

"I did," Gregor said.

"You got it in the head. That's a good shot, but there was no need," Jonas said. "It was trapped. You were safe."

"It's one bullet, Jonas," Gregor said.

"And that's a bullet we might need," the old detective said. "Come on, Tom, grab a boathook and make yourself useful."

"That's a crater," Jimmy said.

"Yeah, but where is it?" Tom replied.

"Zoom out," Jimmy said.

"Hang on," Tom said, trying to remember what to type.

"Here," Jimmy almost pushed him away from the keyboard. Tom watched as the young man's fingers danced. The sat-phone and tablet had been in the fire truck, forgotten. Now they were plugged into a laptop which, in turn, was plugged into an extension-socket snaking out from the kitchen. The other end was attached to a generator. Other than the computer, it was powering a barrage of hotplates, currently being tended by Andy. A lot of the food wouldn't keep much longer. Together with fish caught that morning, anything that could be bottled, canned, or preserved was bubbling away in the kitchen. Tom wished it was being done elsewhere. It made the weak stew they'd eaten for lunch seem even more bland.

He'd spent the morning standing guard on the road leading to the north. By way of punishment, Jonas had sentenced Gregor to a double-shift on duty. The man talked a lot but had little to say, and made no attempt to hide the fear in his voice. It was the unknown. Radiation, zombies, refugees; at any second, so many might come that the village would be swamped. In a bid to assuage that fear, when they were relieved Tom went looking for the sat-phone and tablet, and a laptop into which they could be plugged.

"Have you done this before?" he asked as Jimmy's hands flew over the keyboard.

"Of course not, but it isn't difficult. You need to remember that the forces acting on a satellite are different from those acting on a target on the ground. There, that's the coast."

"The coast of where?" Martha asked. She'd been supervising the work in the kitchen when Tom had arrived.

"That's Florida, isn't it?" Tom guessed.

"No, I don't think so," Martha said.

Jimmy tapped at the screen. The image zoomed out.

"The water's on the right, so it's the East Coast," Tom said.

"But the east coast of where?" Martha asked. "I don't think it's America."

"Hang on," Jimmy said. "I think that's the problem. Yeah, it's the orientation. It's not aligned north-south." The image zoomed out again. "Got it. It's Australia." The image rotated, forming a more familiar shape.

There was a shared moment of understanding, replaced by gloom as they realized what it meant.

"They bombed Australia," Martha said. "Why?"

"Mutually assured destruction," Tom said. "Destroy everywhere. I just didn't think anyone would truly go through with it."

"They didn't," Jimmy said. "That's only one crater. It'll take a while, but we can find out how many hit Australia."

"There's no point," Martha said. "Look for something closer. Can you get an image of us?"

"Now I know where the satellite is, sure," Jimmy said. "But not immediately."

"Then start with that, and work your way up and down the coast," Martha said. "Find the places that have been destroyed, and the ones that are still intact."

"Sure, okay," Jimmy said.

"How long will it take?" Tom asked.

"How long's a piece of string?" Jimmy replied. "While you're waiting, there's pans to scrub. There's always pans to scrub."

Tom went into the kitchen. Andy was standing sentry over the rows of hotplates, a wooden spoon in each hand, an intent expression on his face.

"Hi," Tom said.

The huge man gave a vague nod of acknowledgement. Tom turned his attention to the sink. There were a lot of pans. Some were from breakfast, a few were from the previous night. The water was tepid, but the work was easy and as he set to it, he tried to remember the last time he'd cleaned a dish. He'd rinsed a mug or two during his time in hiding between the inauguration and the outbreak. Before then, he'd had a dishwasher for mugs and bowls, and restaurants and takeout menus for everything else.

"Never did much cooking," he said.

Andy gave a grunt.

"Always meant to learn, though," Tom said, speaking to himself. "There was a foodies' market every second Saturday not far from my house in Maryland. I'd sometimes go there and look. I liked the incongruity of what's exotic here is commonplace elsewhere. It's the economics of scarcity, I suppose. Of course that now means something else entirely."

Andy gave another grunt.

"Yeah, I suppose economics of any sort doesn't mean much anymore." He took a wire brush to a caked-on stain that an overnight soaking had failed to dislodge.

After a morning of thinking, of turning the problem this way and that, he saw what Helena, Kaitlin, and Jonas had. The village would survive until it didn't. It was a trite way of putting it, but there were too many external factors to be more precise. If the radiation level rose, they would have to leave. If too many zombies came, they would have to leave. If they exhausted the supplies here, and anywhere within reach, they would have to leave. In fact, the end result of every worst-case scenario had the village being abandoned. That was the reality, but it wasn't a depressing one. There were enough sailing boats in the bay to take people along the coast. At least a third of the village would be able to fit in Martha's schooner. There was no destination as yet, but one could be found. Radiation, starvation, disease, and the undead were problems they would face everywhere. And perhaps there would be no need to leave.

Higher walls could be constructed further down the road. Stockpiles could be built up. Other survivors found. In short, they had to keep on doing what they were doing now. It would work, but if it didn't, there was the sea for escape. The village might not survive, but the community would.

Chapter 23 - Loose Ends
March 16th, Crossfields Landing, Maine

A second night in a comfortable bed was too much. It was two a.m. according to the wristwatch that, like the clothes and everything else, he'd borrowed from Jonas. Closing his eyes didn't bring sleep, just idle trains of thought, like whether the watch had been a retirement gift to the old detective, whether that retirement had been voluntary, and why the detective had moved here. At three, he got up, having resolved to go to his cottage so that he would at least be wearing his own clothes. He walked soft-footed down to the kitchen and set a match to the already laid stove. It took him two minutes of twisting the faucet before he remembered that there was no mains supply. He filled the pot from the bucket, set it to boil, and sat down to wait.

"Heard you get up," Jonas said, walking into the kitchen. Tom hadn't even heard him approach.

"You move quietly," Tom said.

"Old habits. I thought I'd check you weren't going outside."

"I was going to swap with Helena, let her get some sleep," Tom admitted. "Doesn't seem much point in both of us being awake."

"No, you can't do that," Jonas said. "It's too dangerous having people walk around at night. The noise of people calling out to identify themselves would rile the zombies. But without that greeting, the sentries might think you're undead yourself." He walked over to the cupboard and took out a tin. He gave it a shake. "Really need to think about rationing the coffee. Of course, rationing's not going to magically create more of it. You given much thought to what we talked about?"

"About the future of this place? Sure," Tom said. "Build up the walls and build them further from the village, far enough away that the zombies can't hear. Stay inside and keep an eye on the Geiger counter. Keep the other eye on the boats and be ready to leave. I'd send someone up the coast to look for somewhere to which you can retreat."

"In short, keep on doing what we're doing," Jonas said. "Yeah, there's a limit to how much planning we can do until the risk from radiation is known. I must have checked the Geiger counter twenty times yesterday. It's becoming a compulsion. But I figure in a month we'll know, one way or another."

He placed the pot on the table and sat opposite Tom. "It's the waiting that gets me. I always hated it."

"When you were a cop? What was that like?" Tom asked.

"Not as exciting as they make out on TV. A lot more dangerous, more tedious, and more frustrating. It never ends. You lock up a killer, and there's always another that has to be caught."

"Is that why you retired?"

He shrugged and changed the conversation. "What was the president like? I voted for him. I don't think I would've if Sterling wasn't his opponent. I wasn't sure *he* was sure he was up to the job. Carpenter would have been a better choice."

"The general had no political experience," Tom said. "It would have been a hard sell. Maybe you're right, though. I can't help but wonder if I did the right thing."

"You did what you did," Jonas said. "Trust me, better to accept it than live a life of if-onlys. So what was he like as a man?"

"Max? He was honest," Tom said. "Completely and utterly honest, to a fault and beyond." He told Jonas about the first time he'd met Max, about the run for the governor's mansion, about Claire and their children. As he talked, he found he was able to remember his dead friend in happy times.

"Sounds like a nice guy," Jonas said. "But I don't know if nice guys should be politicians." He poured a cup of coffee. "So what are your plans?"

"Today? I'm going to my cottage. I'll get the server and go through the files on it."

"I meant longer term," Jonas said.

"You mean am I going to leave?"

"You're not the only one thinking about it."

"I'm not?" Tom asked.

"If you'd brought any other news with you, or if the zombies stopped, or if there was the faintest hint of a rumor of somewhere with better prospects, half the people here would risk a thousand-mile trek through the unknown. You have to admit, things can't get much worse, and when they're like that, it's easy to imagine that they have to be better anywhere else. Do you think there's going to be anything useful on your computer?"

"If you mean something that will immediately help us, no. It's more about Max, and everyone who died. I had an algorithm that was trawling the internet, picking up files that mentioned zombies and the outbreak. I was trying to track its spread, but it collected a lot more. A lot of videos of people giving their last farewells before they went out to face the undead. They must have known it was unlikely that anyone would ever see them, and that it was unlikely that they would survive. We should watch them. Someone should watch them, and maybe there's a lesson in them that the children can be taught."

"Maybe there's a lesson in there for us as well," Jonas said. "But that's not the whole reason. It's something to do with Britain, right?"

"I forgot you were a detective. No, there's a guy in London who had access to the files. He might have left me a message. It's a slim chance, but I have to check."

"And that's the real reason. That's the thing that's more important than how this all began, right? What are the chances he's still alive?"

Tom shrugged. There was no way of answering that question. He glanced at the window. There were still a few hours until dawn. "Let me tell you about General Carpenter, and the night Max asked him to join the ticket."

"Sure," Jonas said, though Tom saw in his eyes that the conversation wasn't over.

Just before dawn, and just as he heard the sound of children failing to get up quietly, he left the house. The slung rifle, holstered sidearm, and sheathed knife were growing into familiar weights. Once again, the only light came from the window of the restaurant.

He headed north, toward the bridge. He was surprised to see Helena there with Gregor.

"Morning," he whispered.

"You don't need to whisper," Helena said.

Gregor gave a thin smile. "Have you come to relieve us?"

"No, I'm heading up to the cottage. I wanted to get some of my own clothes, see what supplies are there. I'll be back in a couple of hours. Where's Kaitlin?"

"To the south. We're dividing our efforts," Helena said. Which was a polite way of saying that the more collected people were being spread out in the hope that composure was as contagious as the infection. "Sounds like two of them," she added gesturing down the road. There was enough light now to make out a pair of shapes turning and twisting amidst the wire.

"A quiet night, then?" Tom asked.

"I guess so," Helena said. "I think I like this place, Tom. I can see why you bought a house here. There's a tranquility to it."

"Even now?"

"Especially now," she said. "Out on the road, we were refugees. Before that, before the outbreak, I was... I guess I was running from my past, refusing to accept it was a part of me. Now, I feel like I'm home. Don't misunderstand, I'd rather the zombies weren't here, and the world hadn't torn itself apart, but I think this is where I'm meant to be."

"I'm happy for you." And he meant it.

The sun rose. A dark, dripping trail marked the razor wire where the zombies had crawled, shredding themselves on the sharp barbs.

"Hideous," Helena said. Gregor was swallowing, trying not to throw up. It was easy to see why. The creatures' clothes must have been close to rags before they reached the wire. What was left had been destroyed in the first few feet. It had taken them hours to crawl nearly to the barricade, and that had ripped away hair and flesh, exposing muscle and sinew, and patches of white bone under a bubbling, oozing brown-red film. The fingers on the closest zombie flexed a fraction of an inch.

"Look at that," Tom said. "As inhuman as they seem, they have very human frailties. That arm isn't tangled in the wire, but its tendons and sinews have been severed. It can't raise the hand or bend the fingers."

Gregor turned away, gagging. Helena glanced at the creature, then at Tom. She gave a sigh.

"It makes me want to weep," she said. "Not watch."

"I'll finish it," Tom said.

"Wait. The radiation." Helena walked back to the barricade and picked up a Geiger counter. She held it close to the creature. "Nothing," she said. "Lower than the ones we saw yesterday on the road to the west. That's something to think about. Certainly, I'd rather think about that than him." She gestured at the creature.

It was close enough now that Tom could almost reach it. He drew the bowie knife, and barely had to bend to slash the blade down on its skull. The other zombie required the boathook to finish it. Tom hooked the creatures, dragging them off the road and into the ditch. There were five other zombies already there.

"Do you know where the razor wire came from?" he asked. "I was thinking that if there was more of it, running for a mile, the zombies would never get close."

"Until there were too many bodies," Gregor said. "And they were crawling over the dead."

"No," Helena said. "If they come in those kind of numbers, we'll take to the sea and wait until they go. We have to..." She smiled at Tom. "We have to hope for the best. That they won't come in great numbers. That they'll stop. That the winds won't bring the radiation this far. That if we work and strive, we'll survive. Here we stand, right?"

"Only because there's nowhere else," Gregor said.

Helena rolled her eyes.

"I'll see you back at the village," Tom said.

They needed a new way of thinking, or perhaps it was an old-fashioned way of thinking. Or perhaps it was that they simply needed to think less. The world had changed completely over the last month, and that had left a great deal of uncertainty about the months ahead. It wasn't just radiation and the undead, but the more mundane. A coach-load of hungry survivors might arrive, halving how long the supplies might last. Or a grain-carrier might sail past, the living crew looking for a safe landfall, and so subdue hunger for the next year. A fighter jet might appear in the sky, a message be heard on the radio, or a tsunami might wipe them from the face of the Earth.

If he'd learned anything in the last month, it was that the impossible happened, and that every moment should be enjoyed. That was easy to do until he saw the zombie on the track that led to his cottage. Tom slowed his pace, watching the creature, which hadn't seen him. It wore a long, blue coat. Wool, he thought. Warm, but not suited for the outdoors, and too small for the bearded man who'd donned it. He must have been caught outside unprepared, or lost his own gear. Running from the undead, seeking shelter, he'd scavenged the coat as protection against the elements. It had offered none against the zombie that had infected him.

Tom's boot scuffed against gravel. The creature twisted its head. It saw him and gave a hissing gasp as its lurching gait sucked air into dead lungs. Tom picked up his pace, walking briskly toward it, wanting it to be over. The coat's stitches tore around the shoulder as the zombie raised its arms. Tom ducked, swinging low, hacking the blade into its legs. It fell, still reaching those grasping hands toward him. He kicked them out of the way, hacking the blade down onto its head.

"Another one dead." He listened, expecting to hear more. He didn't. Everything was still. There weren't even any birds. Cautiously he walked along the track, eyes open, ears listening for what he knew must be ahead. Just as the roof of the cottage came into view, he saw the creature. A pack was still on its back, hiking poles strapped to either side. The straps were tight around its chest.

He was tempted to draw his gun. It wasn't that he was physically tired, but the presence of the creature, here in his refuge, had sapped his earlier optimism. He stood his ground, waiting for the zombie to move away from the cottage. He sidestepped as it lurched the last few feet toward him. Unbalanced by its heavy bag, it toppled forward as its arms clawed at the empty air. Tom swung the blade down as it hit the ground.

The body, oozing brown-red fluid from its cracked skull, represented another problem. How would they dispose of it? That off-color blood posed another. For how long was it infectious? He wished for someone like Dr Ayers who could give them the answer as an alternative to another interminable wait for an unspeakable death.

Pausing to wipe the bowie knife clean, he walked toward his cottage. In truth, it was too large and ugly a place to be called that. The name had stuck because that was what he'd intended it to be. He'd planned to replace the floors, strip the walls, put in a sundeck, a new kitchen, a luxurious bathroom, and so much more. But that mental image of his ideal home was as close as the reality had come.

Just as it was never really a cottage, nor was it ever his home. It had been a refuge, a place from which to escape the lies he told in the city. From his cottage he'd always had a choice. He could get on board his boat and flee, or return to the existence that was never truly a life. As long as he was there he had the option; when he was on the boat, it had always been only a matter of time before he had to sail back to shore.

He climbed up the three creaking steps that led to the front porch. The paint was peeling around the windows. It was around this time of year that he'd take a scraper to them, sometimes stripping an entire wall before his phone would buzz and a message about some distant crisis would force him to leave. He'd promise himself he'd finish the job, but, as certain as spring turned to summer, by the end of August, he'd never have done more than half the house. Usually, the first weekend after the first autumn rains, he'd slap on a quick overcoat, always with the pledge that the following year, he'd do the job properly.

The door needed work, too, but that wasn't what had caught his attention. There was no FBI notice admonishing against entry, nor crime scene tape. The door was open, but that might have been done when Jonas came to loot the house. He pushed. It swung inward.

Inside, it was almost as he remembered it. The meager provisions he'd forgotten to clear out of the store cupboard were gone, as were a few utensils, blankets, and sheets. The newest of his all-weather jackets was missing, but the more comfortable one remained. As he changed into his own clothes, he thought through what he'd seen. The meaning was obvious. The people who'd come here weren't FBI. They'd worked for Addison. Perhaps they'd even planted some evidence in the house, to be discovered at a later date when it would further incriminate him. He glanced up at the low ceiling. It might be up in the crawlspace. There was no point looking for it, at least not now.

He folded the clothes he'd borrowed from Jonas and went back outside. The hidden room was the only real improvement he'd made to the house. He removed the bench from the back porch and lifted up the decking. The gap beneath was filled with broken planks. On each were a few spots of paint. They formed a pattern that told him no one had taken them up since he'd been here last. At least, if they had, they'd put the planks back in exactly the right place.

Quelling the return of that familiar sense of paranoia, he removed the planks and opened the hatch. Everything was there, just as he'd expected. The rifles, the ammo, the server. Even the alarm looked intact, though without power and with no cell network or internet over which to send a signal, it was utterly useless. He carried the weapons into the house and then went back for the server. He left the planks lying loose on the ground, but put the decking back in place, and the seat on top of that. Not thinking about the future, or the past, he sat down to watch the sea.

He must have drifted off to sleep because he was woken by the roar of the waves. They seemed to be loud, growing louder. It wasn't waves. It was something mechanical. He stood, jogging toward the front of the cottage, expecting to see someone driving up the track. He was at the side of the house when he realized he was wrong, and what the sound was. It grew louder, changing into a world-encompassing buzzing. He looked up in time to see a blue and red helicopter appear from the north. It flew low, not over the cottage, but above the road, and it was heading to the village.

Was it rescue? Had help come? For a moment he believed it, but out of all the places in the world how would anyone know to come to this exact spot? Trying to believe it was only paranoia, he ran back inside and grabbed an M16. Surely he could be wrong. He loaded the gun and pocketed a spare magazine. He knew he wasn't wrong. He knew this time it wasn't paranoia. There were few lights at night, barely any smoke during the day, no radio signals going out, and no reason for anyone to come here. No reason but him. Wishing he had a weapon more powerful than an automatic rifle, he ran back out of the house and along the track.

The distant tone from the helicopter had changed. Had it already landed? He wanted to be wrong. He hoped he was wrong. He knew he wasn't. Powell hadn't been at the industrial site when the bombs had fallen. If Tom had survived, then why couldn't he? There were two zombies on the road, lurching slowly toward the village. He fired two hasty shots before he had the range. Three more shots and they were down. He saw another drifting through the trees four hundred yards to the north. There wasn't time to deal with it. Not now. He ran.

The satellite. It had to be the satellite. Powell had used that to track him before. In the heady joy of having found survivors, of finding Helena alive, of surviving the nuclear blast, he'd forgotten about Powell. And the man's agents had been here, to the cottage. He knew precisely where to come. Tom pumped his arms, sprinting furiously. More than that, he remembered Powell's threat just before he'd captured him. Powell had guessed where the fire truck had been heading.

He saw the barricade ahead. Only Gregor stood behind it.

"Did you see?" Gregor called. "Did you see the helicopter?"

"Help me move the wire!" Tom snapped back, cutting his hands as he dragged the planks across the road.

"It's help. Help's come," Gregor said. "I knew it would!"

Tom had managed to move the plank a few inches, giving him a narrow path down which to walk. Walking heel to toe, the wire snagging on cloth, ripping into skin, he eased himself toward the barricade.

"Where's Helena?"

"She went to see," Gregor said. "But she didn't seem happy."

Tom reached the moveable gate and pushed it across. "There's a zombie down the road. Keep watch for it."

"Wait," Gregor said, but Tom was already sprinting over the bridge and toward the village.

Please let me be wrong, he thought. The sound from the helicopter changed again, getting lower, softer, as the rotors slowed. Please let me be wrong. Ignoring the stinging pain in his legs, he ran until he reached the low crest and the village below him. The helicopter had landed on the patch of asphalt that became an outdoor market during the height of summer. It looked as if everyone had gathered nearby, though all were staying some distance from the helicopter.

He slowed his run to a walk and raised the rifle, trying to catch his breath so the barrel would stop wavering. His finger curled around the trigger, but he held his fire. He needed to get closer. He had to know. The helicopter was a civilian model, but it wasn't the same one that had been at the industrial site. It was slightly larger, and on the side was a gold logo in the shape of a stylized wave. The door opened. A figure wearing a military uniform got out. Even from the distance, Tom saw it was ragged, worn, stained. A couple of people in the crowd stepped forward. A few more stepped back. Tom kept walking, but held his fire. He had to be certain. He could still be wrong.

The soldier had a sidearm at his belt, but his hands were empty. The next uniform to climb out held a rifle one-handed with the barrel pointing down. Tom was a hundred yards away now. The pilot stepped out, followed by a fourth military uniform, this one also wearing a helmet. The pilot raised a hand, waving at the crowd.

The barrel of Tom's rifle lowered an inch. The pilot reached into the helicopter and picked up a rifle as the fourth figure removed his helmet.

"Powell!" Helena's voice echoed above the crowd. A shot was fired, but not from Tom, nor from the guards. It missed. The second one hit the pilot in the chest. The other three took cover. Tom was too close to the crowd now fleeing in every direction and he'd lost the elevation that would have given him a clear shot. He ran forward, rifle raised. There was a third shot, but he couldn't see who fired it. Powell and his men opened fire, shooting indiscriminately into the crowd. Tom didn't have a clear target so he aimed at the helicopter, emptying his magazine into metal and glass. Out of the corner of his eye, he saw people fall. He heard them scream. He heard others yell.

He ejected the magazine and slotted the spare into place. There was nowhere to run. Nowhere to hide. No haven anywhere in America, except this one. It was being destroyed, and it was his fault. He ran, firing burst after burst, and realized that he was almost alone in the open. A helmeted figure rose from behind the helicopter's skids, a pistol in his hand. Tom pulled the trigger. It clicked. The magazine was empty. He dropped it, but before he could reach the holstered .45, the man's head was blown apart by a shot that came from somewhere to Tom's left. Tom drew the pistol. The last guard reared up. Tom fired, emptying the magazine into his chest.

"Powell!" he bellowed as silence descended. The shooting had stopped.

"Powell!" he yelled again, ejecting the magazine and slotting a fresh into place. The only sound was the screaming of the injured and the sobbing of the dead.

He saw the man's legs underneath the helicopter. For a moment, he thought Powell was dead, and then a foot twitched.

"Get out!" Tom barked. He grabbed at the man's ankle, tugging him from under the skids.

"You wouldn't shoot an unarmed man?" Powell asked, cowering.

Tom would, but he held his fire. He glanced around. He saw Kaitlin, a hunting rifle in her hand, walking across the lot toward the bodies. He saw Jonas bending over one. No one was approaching them. He turned back to Powell.

"It's just you and me, Powell. Why did you come here?"

"To end this," Powell said, pushing himself into a sitting position with his legs bent, his hands held across his knees. "You know, I said you should have been killed years ago. Your old family friend did like things done in far too complicated a fashion."

Tom raised the gun, but stilled his rage. There were too many questions that had to have answers. "How did you find me?"

216

"Where else would you go? The satellites confirmed it. That fire truck was like a signpost."

"Where did you come from?" Tom asked.

"You mean is anyone going to come after me? Everyone is dead, Mr Clemens. America is gone. The country is in ruins. It's all your fault, you know. If you'd simply played your part, even now, our nation would be rising from the ashes. Instead, you clipped the phoenix's wings. It will never fly again."

"You betrayed the cabal, didn't you? You and Addison. He schemed to put himself on top, and you planned to kill and usurp him."

"How can you betray a conspiracy?" Powell replied. He placed his palms on the ground and pushed himself to his feet.

"Stay down!" Tom barked.

"Addison was a pawn, just as Farley and Sterling were," Powell said, raising his hands above his head. "Not too dissimilar to what Maxwell was for you. Addison's betrayal didn't matter. It doesn't matter. None of this does. You may have destroyed this country, but you did not destroy us. The cause lives on, eternal."

"What? Hiding out in some bunker? Where?"

"A bunker? Oh, no. The world is a big place, Mr Clemens. So, as I said, I came here to end this. I didn't start the gunfight, nor did I want to. I didn't come here with violence in my heart. But what do you want, Mr Clemens? A trial? An execution? Or would you prefer a prisoner exchange?"

"Your life in exchange for whose?" Tom asked.

"There's someone you need to speak to," Powell said. He turned around and reached into the helicopter.

"Don't!" Tom warned.

"It's a radio, Mr Clemens," Powell said, holding a small black box up by a corner. "Mr Clemens. Mr Sholto. Thaddeus. There is someone who wishes to speak to you."

He held out the box. Tom stared at it. Powell tossed it at him. Tom fumbled the catch, taking an involuntary step back, and caught the glint of something metal in Powell's other hand as the man leaped.

217

Tom managed to grab Powell's wrist, holding the knife back, but the man's momentum pushed them both over. Tom landed hard, Powell on top, and the man had his other hand on Tom's gun hand, holding it down as the knife's gleaming blade inched closer and closer.

"I told you," Powell hissed. "I wanted—"

But before Powell could finish, he was pulled back and off. Tom saw Jonas throw Powell down onto the asphalt. He saw Jonas level his gun and fire three times into the man's chest.

"No judge, no jury," Jonas said. "Just me."

"No." Tom said. "No." He pushed himself up, and over to Powell's body, but the man was dead. He ran to the helicopter. There was no radio beyond the microphones built into the helmets.

"No. No. No," he hissed. He walked back across the cracked lot and picked up the object Powell had thrown at him. It was a small black plastic case. Inside were iodine tablets.

"What?" Jonas asked. "What did he say? What are you looking for?"

"Tom!" Kaitlin yelled. He looked up. She was crouched over a body fifty feet away. He knew who it was long before he reached her. Helena lay unmoving, though her eyes were open. A red stain spread across her chest.

He reached down and took her hand. It was already cold.

"You're going to be okay," he said.

"Tom?"

"I'm here," he said, leaning closer. Her eyes didn't focus.

"I never found Jessica," Helena whispered. "I wish I had." She gave a rasping cough. "I looked for her. That's important. I did what I could, didn't I?"

"You did," Tom said. "You went looking for her, and she knew that. Your sister knew that you wanted to make amends. She knew that, Helena. Helena?"

She was dead.

He wanted to bellow. He wanted to scream. It shouldn't be like this. Not her. Not here. Not now. Kaitlin went to help with the other injured. Tom stayed on his knees, trying to think of something to say, of anything that might give meaning to Helena's death.

"It's over," he finally said. And it should have been. There should have been time to grieve, to repent, to regret, to revel in victory, or dwell on Powell's last words. There wasn't time. Instead, there was a shot. Then another. They came from the north.

"Zombies." He was running before he realized, and halfway to the bridge before he remembered he was unarmed save for the bowie knife at his belt. He didn't turn back.

Gregor stood on the barricade, hunting rifle in hand, firing shot after shot down the road. With the sheet-metal gate closed, Tom couldn't see what lay beyond, but he could hear it. Even the crack of the rifle couldn't drown out the sound of hundreds of feet, of hundreds of sighing, gasping dead mouths. He ran to the barricade, and up the steps. Standing next to Gregor, he realized he was wrong. There had to be thousands of them. A long thin column that stretched as far the eye could see, and probably a lot further.

He grabbed the rifle from Gregor's shaking hands. "Go back to the village. Get more people. More ammo. More guns. Go."

He took aim. There was no shortage of targets. He fired, reached for a cartridge, and properly took in the horde. In truth, there was no way of knowing how many there were. The long column stretched to where the road bent out of sight, but the creatures weren't sticking to the path. A low wall ran from the bridge to fifty yards beyond the edge of the razor wire. Beyond that was a metal crash-barrier. The zombies spilled around and over those low impediments. He fired, hastily reloaded, and fired again. The razor wire was thick on the road, but stretched thin across the ground to either side. He fired. Reloaded. Fired, barely aiming. He had to get them to head toward him, toward the barricade, toward the razor wire that might slow their progress. He aimed. Reloaded. Fired. An undead woman in a red coat reached the razor wire. Tom fired at a zombie behind. The red-coated creature's legs caught in the wire. It fell, face first, into the mass of razor-sharp blades. He fired, not looking where he hit. Another creature reached the wire. This one tripped on the squirming, living corpse. He fired. Hats, bare heads, coated and bare-armed, freshly dead and others with skin ripped away; their features blurred into one as

219

he aimed and fired, aimed and fired. He ignored the zombies, focusing instead on the growing pain in his shoulder as the rifle bucked with each shot.

There was a roar of sound to his left, and again to his right. Jonas, Kaitlin, and the dark-haired woman he'd met at the bed-and-breakfast were there, firing into the seething mass. He aimed, fired, and tried to remember her name.

"Do we aim at the ones on the razor wire, or the ones behind?" the woman called out.

"Just shoot them," Jonas yelled back. The zombies fell as bullets hit. Some were dead, but some rose back up. Tom reached for another round. The box was nearly empty.

"We need more ammo," he said, but his voice was drowned out by the tramping feet and snapping mouths, ripping cloth and tearing flesh, and hammer's hitting percussion caps at far too infrequent a rate. "Ammo!" he yelled. "We need ammo!"

"Naomi," Jonas said, grabbing the woman's arm. "Go back to the village. Tell Martha to get the children onto the boats. I want a couple of people on the other barricades to the west and south, but everyone else is to come here. Bring all the ammo. Go. Run!"

Tom fired, picked up the last cartridge from the box, reloaded, and aimed just below the brim of a red baseball cap. He fired. The cap flew off as the zombie collapsed.

"I'm out. We're out."

"One magazine left," Kaitlin said, firing a round. She ejected the magazine and inserted her last.

"Can we blow the bridge?" Tom asked.

"That wouldn't slow them for long," Jonas said. "Not nearly long enough. We need to hold them here until Martha's had time to load the boats."

"Here we stand," Tom said, grabbing a boathook and jumping down onto the far side of the barricade.

"You have to stand somewhere," Jonas said, following him down. Above and behind them, Kaitlin fired one measured shot after another.

The razor wire was slowing the zombies. Tom raised the boathook, but there was no close target. Despite their furious thrashing of limbs and snapping of mouths, they still didn't move quickly.

"Here we stand," he murmured again. "This is not what I thought when we came up with that slogan."

The zombies tripped on the wire and fell. The creatures following lost their footing as they tried to walk over an undulating sea of corpses. On hands and knees, they crawled forward until the mass of death behind pushed them down onto the wire where they, too, became ensnared.

Jonas raised his .45, braced his left hand on the butt, took careful aim, and fired. Tom waited, feeling worse than useless. This was a fate that he had brought on the village. Albeit unwittingly, he was nonetheless responsible.

The nearest creature was caught in the wire fifteen feet from them. Funneled by the barrier and the low brick wall, the rest were getting closer. The front rank of that column fell, but there were always more behind. A wall of snapping, snarling, hissing death, a twisted mockery of the people they'd once been. Jonas fired, slowly emptying his gun.

"I'm out," he called, holstering it and drawing his bowie knife. "That was Powell, was it?"

"Powell? Yeah."

"He was the guy who came looking for you in January," Jonas said. "Said he was FBI. Had brown hair, and didn't have the scar, but I recognized him."

"The zombies followed him here, and he followed me. I'm sorry," Tom yelled back.

"If you want to apologize for something, it's for buying a house here in the village. But if it wasn't here, you'd have bought one somewhere else, and that doesn't mean you wouldn't be here now. Even if you weren't, who's to say Powell wouldn't have turned up. Where does it begin? Where does it end? Someone once told me that a life well lived is a life full of regrets." He said something else, but Tom didn't hear it over the noise of the undead. They were getting closer, a great heaving mass of death that the two of them stood no chance of stopping. Tom raised the boathook.

The firing had stopped. Kaitlin must be out of ammo. He didn't turn to look. He wasn't sure if he wanted to see her there, or see that she'd gone back to the village to help the children escape.

The nearest zombie was less than five feet away, crawling over the wire on wrecked legs and shredded hands. As it looked up, opening its mouth in a snarl, Tom stabbed the boathook forward, spearing the point neatly through its eye. With a tug, it came free. The zombie collapsed, but there was another behind it, and one on either side. He stabbed forward again and again at the heaving carpet of death. The zombies were four feet from him now. Three feet, and being pushed from behind more than pulling themselves along. He stabbed down again.

"Go," Tom yelled at Jonas. "Get out of here."

"Yep. Any second now," Jonas said, raising his knife.

It was stupid. Futile. Once the zombies were past the wire, he and Jonas would be killed in seconds.

"Go!" Tom yelled. "Get out of here. Go and—"

And his words were drowned out by gunfire. One shot, then a dozen, then a fusillade. Jonas grabbed his arm, dragging him back to the barricade. There were ten people standing on the low rampart, firing shot after shot into the undead ahead and those to either side.

A zombie reached the end of the wire. It pulled itself forward onto the asphalt. Its legs shredded to the bone, it was unable to stand. Tom darted forward, stabbed down, then moved back to the barricade. The fusillade continued. Another zombie reached the end of the wire. Jonas ran forward, slashing his knife at its skull. Tom went to meet the next, and a pattern was established. They dealt with the creatures that reached the barricade while the shooters aimed at those further away. For the first ten minutes, Tom was sure they would be victorious. After half an hour, as his strength ebbed, so did his confidence. The boathook broke. He drew the bowie knife. He slashed. He hacked. After another hour, he was exhausted. One more zombie, he decided, and then someone else would have to take over. He cleaved the knife down on a scabbed scalp absent of hair. One more zombie. After the next he'd take a rest, but the next came, and he hacked down and stood his ground.

The firing slackened. It didn't stop, but the aim had shifted toward the left and right. He blinked, focusing on the road beyond the immediate few feet in front. It was littered with bodies. Some were still, but others moved, twitched, and thrashed. The wire trapped some. Others were immobile due to broken limbs and shredded muscles. At the end of the wire, the zombie in the red coat, now torn and tattered and stained a far darker crimson than the dye, staggered to its feet. A shot rang out. It collapsed.

"Is it over?" Naomi called out from behind the barricade.

"Not yet," Jonas said. "Not today. But someday, maybe."

"There's more coming," Kaitlin called. "I count eight. No, ten."

Tom wiped his hands on his coat. He had stood his ground, waiting for them to come once before, at the motel. If he survived the day, he doubted that this time would be the last.

Epilogue - Departure
March 18th, Crossfields Landing, Maine

"Tell me about her," Kaitlin said.

They stood by Helena's grave. Tom made a final adjustment to the pieces of wood that he'd tied together. He'd burned her name onto them, but it seemed a pitiful marker, especially since there was no chance of anything more formal ever being erected.

"She was a teacher," Tom said.

"I know that. I meant something else."

Tom thought of their escape from New York, and their journey through Pennsylvania. There hadn't been many happy moments. Not that he hadn't been glad for Helena's company, but their time together had been spent fighting for their lives. "She wanted to help other people," he said.

"That's a good epitaph," Kaitlin said. "A better one than most people get."

It was a little over forty-eight hours since the helicopter had landed and Helena had died. After the initial wave of zombies had been killed, the undead kept coming, just not in such great numbers. It was fifty in the first hour, twenty in the next, and then a handful every hour for the rest of the day and through the night. They'd used lights rigged to car batteries to illuminate the road, and killed the last zombie just before dawn. Of course, they'd not known that at the time, and no one had felt confident saying it until an entire day and night had gone by, and another sunrise arrived, with no more shambling creatures appearing on the road to the north.

When they'd counted the undead, they'd discovered fewer than three hundred had been in that first wave. Tom still couldn't believe it was so few. He was sure he'd killed at least that number himself.

"I think he lured them here," Tom said.

"Who lured what?" Kaitlin asked.

"Powell and the zombies," Tom said. "He did it before, at the motel, the first time he nearly caught us. Nearly caught me. Helena saved me, then."

"I don't want to talk about him here," Kaitlin said. "To be honest, I don't want to talk about him at all. He's dead, and from what he told you, no one else is going to come."

"No. Not here, at least," Tom said.

"Then I don't want to talk about him, I don't want to think about him. Not here. Not now. I just want a few moments to remember a friend before the work of the day truly begins."

Tom stood in silence by the grave, looking at the dirt he'd helped shovel over Helena's wrapped body. Hers wasn't the only new addition to the old cemetery. Eight other markers had joined the moss-covered stones of the graveyard, all victims of the brief gunfight that had followed Powell's arrival. There was a ninth grave, this one in the far corner. It had been dug a little deeper, and it would never be marked. There had been a fiery debate about what to do regarding the bodies of Powell and his cronies. Burying them was more efficient than burning them, and less problematic than dumping the corpses with those of the undead. Nevertheless, their presence in the cemetery was a source of resentment for those who'd lost someone when Powell's men had opened fire. And that resentment was focused on Tom. He didn't care.

Yesterday, after an hour had gone by with no more zombies seen on the road, he'd gone to collect the remaining M16s and ammunition from his cottage. They were sorely needed. The defense of the village had depleted their stores of ammo. He'd found eight zombies lingering along the track between the road and the cottage. He'd killed them, hacking them to pieces with the bowie knife. When they were dead, he stalked the perimeter of the house, looking for more. Finding none, he'd started walking north. It was five miles before he'd found one.

The zombie was crawling along the road on broken legs, managing less than a hundred yards an hour. He'd stood twenty feet away, watching its mouth gape open, its teeth snap against each other, its hand curl and flex, and then he'd shot it. He'd stood there as its blood congealed, uncertain whether he wanted another horde to appear. It wasn't that he wished for death, not exactly. He wanted an end to his quest, but Powell's last words had robbed him of that. The man might have been speaking simply to distract Tom, but there might have been some truth hidden in the words. In which case the new life he'd thought he might have in Crossfields Landing would have to wait, as his old one wasn't yet done with him. He'd walked back to the cottage he would never call home, more weary than before.

He'd taken the rifles and ammo back to the village, and then returned for the server. Not wanting to face the grim messages of farewell in the videos, he'd given it to Jimmy to do with as he would.

Kaitlin turned away from the grave. Tom followed her out of the cemetery.

"I'm going to Jimmy's," Kaitlin said. "And then I've got to check on the sentries. What about you?"

"I'm still not sure," Tom said, though he was answering a very different question than the one she'd asked. He followed her to the restaurant.

In one corner, the tables had been pushed aside. The server sat atop one, a trio of computers were plugged into it. Jimmy stared at the screens, headphones balanced over one ear, a strangely serene expression on his face. He glanced up as they entered.

"There's some good ideas here," he said. Each of the three displays showed different people in different videos, though there was a commonality to their resolute expressions. "Homemade napalm, for one."

"We tried setting fire to the zombies at the motel," Tom said. "I'm not sure whether it harmed them, but the building burned down."

"No, I meant for destroying the bodies," Jimmy said. "We'll have to take care of those before we can think of farming."

"Right. Sure," Tom muttered. Kaitlin headed into the kitchen. He walked over to the table and picked up the tablet he'd found in Powell's pocket. It hadn't been damaged, but it was locked.

"Any luck with the code?" he asked.

"There's a password," Jimmy said, glancing briefly up before returning his attention to the screens. "Not just a number, but an actual word. Any ideas what it could be?"

"Not a clue," Tom said.

"Then no, there's no way of getting it open," Jimmy said. "So forget about it. It won't help, but this might. This is the third video I've found where someone says they were bitten but haven't turned."

"Does she show you the bite marks?" Tom asked. "Does she say how long ago she was infected?"

"No."

"Then don't believe it," Tom said. "You don't want to bet your life on someone else's desperate hopes." He walked over to the window from where he could see the bay. His own boat was down there, but Martha's large schooner was gone. She'd taken it north, scouting for a location to which they could flee should more zombies come. She'd asked if he wanted to go with her. He wished he'd said yes, but he had a decision to make. He could easily see himself taking on one task and then another, putting it off until so much time had passed that the decision was made by default.

"If you're not busy, you should make yourself useful," Jimmy said.

"Sure. Of course. How can I help?"

"There's always the washing up," Jimmy said.

He went into the kitchen and began attacking the pans, but soon stopped with one only half scrubbed. He stared at the water, trying to discern some clue as to which path he should now take.

"I've found it!" Jimmy yelled.

"He found it," Andy said, carefully placing the pot he'd been drying on the shelf. Tom followed the hulking young man out into the restaurant.

"Found what?" Tom asked.

"How it began," Jimmy said, excited. "The zombies! The outbreak!"

"Let me see," Tom said.

Jimmy pressed play. Tom watched. He froze. He understood. "Play it again." But he didn't need to watch it all. "There. Stop it."

"You said there was a woman with Addison when you were captured," Jimmy said. "Is that her?"

"No. No, it's not," Tom said. "I don't know her, but I know that man. Where did you find this video?"

"It was in an email. Here." He showed Tom.

"That was sent to Farley on the day of the outbreak. I completely forgot about it," Tom said. "It came from an NSA account. It doesn't say who sent it."

"It has to be whoever went into the room and found the camera," Jimmy said. "Who's the man?"

Tom didn't reply. He went back through the files, looking at one, then the next, then moving onto others that he'd found, copied, and stolen long ago. Everything made sense now.

"What's going on?" Kaitlin asked, coming back into the restaurant.

"I've found how it began," Jimmy said. "There's a video."

"Show me," Kaitlin said.

"Yeah. Sure. It's here." Tom set it to play. "Jimmy, those satellite images you were playing around with, I need to see them. I need to see if a place still exists."

"Why? Where?"

"Just get the thing set up."

It took three hours during which the restaurant filled up as people came in to watch, and then stayed to watch the video again and again.

"There," Jimmy said. "That's it."

"Are you sure?" Tom asked.

"Yeah, those are the co-ordinates you gave me. It looks like an airfield. What's there?"

"I think, no, I'm sure, I'm absolutely certain that is the facility where the virus was created," Tom said.

"You are? How do you know?"

"There's another file. Another video. Not a recent one. In it there's a scientist. The guy who created it."

"You sure?"

"Positive." Tom walked over to the laptop where the footage of patient zero was being replayed for the sixtieth time. When he reached over to press pause, there was an instant uproar. He backed away. It didn't matter. He knew what was on that video. He knew it was the same man, the same scientist in both. He left the restaurant. He wasn't walking anywhere in particular, but found himself heading toward the barricade. Jonas and Naomi were on sentry duty.

"What's wrong?" Jonas asked.

"There's a video," Tom said. "From my server. It shows how it began. Literally. The first zombie. Patient zero. Everything. The people who were there and why. Go and see."

"No, I'll stay. Naomi, you go and have a look if you want. Tom can take over your shift on guard. And pass the word around. I guess everyone should see it."

"I think they already have," Tom said. "Everyone's in the restaurant watching."

Naomi headed toward the village, leaving Tom and the detective alone.

"It explains it?" Jonas asked. "The outbreak?"

"I think so," Tom said. "If you take it with a few other files I've got on there, it forms a pretty complete picture. A few of the fine details are missing, but it gives enough of the broad strokes that I can work out the rest."

"And does it say how we can stop it?" Jonas asked.

"No. I don't think it can be stopped. Not now."

"Pity. So what's wrong? You look like death warmed up."

"It's the person who's behind it," Tom said. "He's not dead. Powell said something. I thought he was stalling, speaking just to keep me off guard, but Addison said something similar. It was a threat. At the time, I thought I was about to die, so gave little thought to his meaning. Then there was the mushroom cloud and I forgot but... but it's not over. Not yet. Not for me. It isn't just that video of the first zombie. There are other files, ones I collected a long time ago. In that video of patient zero, there's a scientist. That same man appears in another. He's in the lab, giving a

229

tour of it. It's the lab where the virus was created. It's still there. I have to go to the lab. I have to destroy it."

"Why?"

"Because Helena's dead," Tom said. "Max is dead. Claire is dead. Their children are dead. Murdered. It's not just them, but everyone in the entire country and across the world. Everyone who died because of the outbreak, and everyone who died trying to stop it. Someone has to make sure that every vial is destroyed and every scrap of paper that details how it was made is burned. Who else is left but me? No. I have to leave. I have to do this."

"You sure it's still there?" Jonas asked.

"I am."

Jonas sighed. "I'd like you to stay. I know that there's a lot of anger directed toward you at the moment, but we could do with your help."

"This is important," Tom said.

"Important to you, maybe. To anyone else? I don't know. But go if you have to, if that's where you feel your destiny lies."

It did. The people here in Crossfields Landing were safe. They had a place to stand and the ability to retreat if they had to make that stand elsewhere. He would make sure that scientist who created it was dead and that the facility where it was made was destroyed. But first, there was something else he would do, somewhere else he would go. It was the words Helena had spoken before she died. There was a chance for him to make amends for the greatest regret of his life. So he would cross the ocean, go to the lab, and then, if he didn't die along the way, he would return.

"If I can, when it's all done, and I'm certain that this world is as safe as it ever can be now that the dead walk the Earth, I'll come back," he said.

"Don't make a promise you may never be able to keep," Jonas said. "Up the road. Do you see it?"

A zombie in a torn green coat limped around the bend.

"First one we've seen for almost a day," Tom said. "I'll take care of it, but then I'll go."

"You'll leave today?"

"I have a long way to go," Tom said. He picked up an axe before stepping out into the road. It *was* a long way, and he might not make it, but he had to try. He owed all those who had died at least that much, but if he could, he'd return, and finally turn that cottage into a place he could truly call home.

The end...

Made in the USA
Middletown, DE
16 June 2017